D0269156

THE PARIS ENIGMA

PABLO DE SANTIS

The Paris Enigma

Translated from the Spanish
by Mara Lethem

HarperCollins*Publishers*

This novel is entirely a work of fiction. The names, characters and incidents portrayed in it are the work of the author's imagination. Any resemblance to actual persons, events or localities is entirely coincidental.

HarperCollins*Publishers*
77–85 Fulham Palace Road, London W6 8JB

www.harpercollins.co.uk

Published by HarperCollins*Publishers* 2009
1

Originally published as *El enigma de París* by Planeta in Spain in 2007

A catalogue record for this book is available from the British Library

ISBN 978-0-00-726900-6 (hardback)
ISBN 978-0-00-726901-3 (trade paperback)

Set in Sabon by Palimpsest Book Production Limited, Grangemouth, Stirlingshire

Printed and bound in Great Britain by Clays Limited, St Ives plc

For Ivana

CONTENTS

PART ONE

Detective Craig's Final Case

ONE

My name is Sigmundo Salvatrio. My father came to Buenos Aires from a town north of Genoa and made his living as a cobbler. When he married my mother, he already owned a shoe-repair shop specializing in men's footwear (he never felt comfortable fixing women's shoes). As a child, I often helped him with this work. Today, people in my profession view my method for classifying fingerprints (the Salvatrio method) with high regard – I owe that crime-solving innovation to the many hours I spent among the lasts and soles that filled our shop. I came to realize that detectives and shoemakers see the world from beneath, both focusing more on the footsteps that have strayed away from their intended path than the path itself.

My father was no spendthrift. Every time my mother asked for a little extra money, Renzo Salvatrio would say that wanton spending would eventually force us to subsist on boiled boot soles like Napoleon's soldiers had done during their Russian campaign. But despite his frugality, once a year he allowed himself an extravagance: on my birthday he would buy me a jigsaw puzzle.

He began the tradition with a hundred-piece puzzle, and each year the puzzles got more and more complex, until finally they had fifteen hundred pieces. They were made in Trieste and came in wooden boxes. Once they were complete you'd discover a watercolour of the Dome of Milan, or the Parthenon, or an old map with monsters lying in wait at the ends of the earth. It always took me many days to finish them. My father believed that jigsaw puzzles were rigorous training for mental and visual acuity. He helped me enthusiastically but generally wasn't very good because he paid more attention to the colour of the pieces than to their shape. I let him do it his way, and then I fixed them when he wasn't looking.

'An investigation and a jigsaw puzzle have nothing in common,' swore Renato Craig, who would later become my mentor. But nevertheless it was this hobby that, in February 1888, led me to answer the advertisement Craig published in the newspaper. Renato Craig, the famous detective, the only one in Buenos Aires, wanted to share his knowledge, for the first time, with a group of young people. Over the course of a year, the chosen students would learn the art of investigation, preparing them to assist even the best of detectives. I still have the newspaper clipping; the ad was on the same page as a story about the arrival of Kalidán, a Hindu magician touring the country.

The detective's ad excited me, not only because of what it heralded, but also because it meant that Craig, Craig the loner, was finally willing to allow other human beings to learn his methods. Craig was a founding member of the Twelve Detectives, a group of the most elite detectives in the world. It was Craig himself who had introduced the term 'acolyte' to the Twelve Detectives as a way to refer to their assistants. During one of the group's first meetings, in 1872, he explained this designation with a definition from a dictionary of Latinisms: *ACOLYTE: said of one that follows another as if he were his shadow.*

Every member of the club had his acolyte, except for Craig. In the magazine, the *Key to Crime*, Craig had often defended his position by saying that acolytes weren't necessary to a detective, and that the nature of the profession called for solitude. Another member of the group, Viktor Arzaky, who was Craig's good friend, had always been critical of this assessment. The fact that Craig was now willing to train assistants was a direct contradiction of his previous philosophy.

TWO

In order to be considered for the Academy, I had to send a letter in my own hand that explained why I was applying. There was one rule: 'Don't mention your background; nothing that you've done up until this point has any value to me.' I asked my father for a few of the pages that he used for his business correspondence, with letterhead that read *Salvatrio's Cobbler Shop* above a drawing of a patent leather boot. I cut off the top of each page: I didn't want Craig to know I was the son of a cobbler.

In my first draft of the letter, I wrote that I wanted to learn the art of investigation because I had always been interested in the big crime cases that I read about in the newspaper. But I tore up that page and decided to start over. I really wasn't interested in gory crimes but in the other kind: the perfect enigmas, the ones that, at first glance, were inexplicable. I liked to see how –

in a disorganized but predictable world – an organized but totally unpredictable way of reasoning emerged. I had no hope of becoming a detective; just being an assistant was a goal worthy of my concerted efforts. But at night, alone in my room, I imagined myself aloof, ironic, and pure, making my way, like Craig, through a world of façades, discovering the truth buried beneath the false leads, beyond the distractions and the blind gaze of habit.

I don't know how many nervous, hopeful people sent letters to Detective Craig's house at 171 De La Merced Street, but it must have been a lot, because months later, when I was already one of the Academy's top students, I found a heap of dusty envelopes. Many of them had never been opened, as if one glance at the handwriting had been enough for Craig to know if an applicant was unsuitable. Craig maintained that graphology was an exact science. Among those letters I found the one I had sent; it was also still sealed, which left me baffled. When Craig ordered me to burn them, I did so with a sense of relief.

On 15th March 1888, at ten o'clock in the morning, I arrived at the door of his building on De La Merced Street. I had chosen to walk instead of taking the tram, but I soon regretted that decision because a freezing rain, a sign that autumn was on its way, fell the whole way there. When I got to the door I found about twenty other young men, all as nervous as I was. At first I thought they were aristocrats, and that I was the only one who had arrived without status, family name, or fortune. To cover their unease they tried to inscribe their faces with the contemptuous expression Craig wore when his picture appeared on the front pages of newspapers or the yellow cover of the *Key to Crime*, a biweekly serial that sold for 25 cents. It was the local version of *Traces*, the official journal of the Twelve Detectives, published by Adrien Grimas in Paris. But the *Key to Crime* was an inexpensive publication of only thirty-six pages, while *Traces* had the format of an academic journal. Two or three cases filled the pages of the *Key to Crime*. The cover was yellow, with an ink drawing that showed either an illustration of one of the detectives, or the most horrific image from the account of one of the cases. On the last page there was a column titled 'In Hushed Tones' where brief notices of the detectives' lives appeared. I sometimes complained about the rather frivolous nature of this section (it informed readers that Detective Castelvetia was keen on snuff, that Rojo spent quite a bit of time investigating the brothels of a certain Madrid neighbourhood, or that Caleb Lawson had finally broken off his engagement) but I very much enjoyed reading it.

Surprisingly, Craig himself answered the door. We were expecting some sort of butler who served as a buffer between the detective and the world. We were so disconcerted that, instead of going in, we each made way for the others to enter first. The comedy routine would have continued for hours if Craig hadn't grabbed hold of the first arm he found and pulled it inside.

Immediately, we all followed in a line, as if tied together by rope.

I had read about that house in the *Key to Crime*. Having no assistant, Craig wrote about his adventures himself; in these stories his vanity transformed the house into a temple of knowledge. While the other detectives maintained a dialogue with their adherents, who served as the voice of the common man, Craig had these conversations with himself, asking the questions and providing the answers, giving the impression that he was quite insane. He depicted himself in the solitude of his study, admiring his collection of Flemish watercolours or cleaning his numerous weapons: daggers hidden in fans, pistols in bibles, and swords in umbrellas. His favourite secret weapon, of course, was his cane, which appeared in many of his stories: its lion-shaped handle had cracked open more than one head, its retractable stiletto had rested, threateningly, on the carotid artery of numerous suspects, and its resounding shot had cut through many a night. One hardly needed to carry anything else. Inside, we went through the rooms searching the high walls, furniture, and mantelpieces for those weapons and instruments, which to us were like the Holy Grail, Excalibur, or the Mambrino's helmet of detective work.

For me, going into that house was like visiting a sacred site. When you actually encounter that which you've always dreamed of, the details aren't as important as the fact that it's real, that it is dense and limited, without that intangible tendency to shape shift that dreams have. It is delightful when the fantasy becomes real, but disappointing that it means the fantasy must come to an end.

Craig lived with his wife, Margarita Rivera de Craig, but their residence had that damp coldness of empty houses, a feeling that was enhanced by the unfurnished rooms and bare walls. Fifteen years earlier they had lost a child, only a few months old, and it seemed as though they had abandoned most of the house. The Craigs' bedrooms were on the third floor and his study was on the first. It was carpeted, and had a huge desk that held a Hammond typewriter, which at that time was a novelty. Other than that, there were just empty halls and vacant rooms. For a moment I had the impression that Craig had decided to set up the Academy just to vanquish the lonely dampness of that house; it was too big for the servants they had: Angela, a Spanish woman from Galicia that took care of the kitchen, and a maid. Angela barely spoke to Craig, but twice a week she made rice pudding with cinnamon, his favourite dessert, and she always eagerly awaited Craig's approval.

'Not even in the Progress Club do they make rice pudding this good. I don't know what I'd do without you,' said the detective. And that was the only time he ever addressed her.

The cook had abrupt mood swings, as if the power the house held over her was sporadic. Sometimes she would sing old Spanish songs at the top of her lungs as she dusted, so loudly that Mrs Craig would scold her. Angela either didn't hear the reprimands or she just pretended that she couldn't. Other times, she took on a resigned, defeated attitude. When she opened the door for me in the mornings I would remark on the weather, and no matter what it was, she took it as a bad omen.

'It's awfully hot. That's not a good sign.'

Or, if it was cold, she'd say, 'Too cold. That can't be good.'

And if it was neither hot nor cold: 'On a day like this a person doesn't know what to wear. Bad omen.'

Drizzle, rain, lack of rain, storms, long periods without any storms, any climatic condition would get the exact same condemnation from Angela.

'Up until yesterday, we were having a drought. Now comes a flood.'

That first day, one of the happiest of my life, Craig spoke to us about his method. But his talk seemed designed to discourage us: he listed obstacles, described failures, probably to weed out those of us who weren't truly dedicated to that occupation which required endless patience. But none of us could hear the language of defeat, because no matter what happened during our training period, even the bad things, this was all an adventure that we yearned to have. He could really only scare us by threatening us with a normal life – practising law, responsible parenthood, going to bed early. All twenty-one of us that showed up that first day came back the next, and the next. The big, empty house began to fill up. Craig ordered new things that arrived constantly. He seemed to have the irrational idea that the accumulation of things was meant to contribute to the cult of reason. From the very beginning Craig's teachings were destined to alert me to that ambiguity: it is in the moment when we are thinking most clearly that we are closest to madness.

THREE

Only Angela, the cook, dared to confront Craig; reproaching him for the baskets overflowing with filth and all the horrible things that were filling the house. The cook challenged him:

'I'm expecting a letter from my cousins in Lugo. When it comes, I'm leaving. And goodbye rice pudding.'

But he paid her no mind.

Craig gave classes in the morning. At that time of day his voice was filled with a self-confidence that was tempered over the course of the day. Sometimes he preferred to take us out on a field trip, always at night, to some place of ill repute where a woman's throat had been slit, or the hotel room of the latest suicide.

'Suicide is the great mystery, even more than murder,' Craig told us. 'Every city has a stable suicide rate. It doesn't vary according to economic circumstances or historic events; it's a disease of the city itself, not of individuals. No one commits suicide in the countryside; it's our buildings that transmit the horrible infection and irresponsible poets that celebrate it.'

The first time we went into the room where a suicide had taken place we hung back, letting Craig and the corpse take over the scene. The dead man was dressed in his Sunday best and had tidied up the room before drinking the liquid from a small blue glass bottle.

From the middle of the room, Craig invited us to take a closer look.

'Look at this man's expression, notice how he carefully neatened his room, how he packed his suitcase before taking the poison. Hotel rooms, guesthouses – never has loneliness been so complete. Suicides are drawn to one another; if there is a suicide in a hotel it leaves a mark on that building, and there'll be another at that location the next month. Soon there'll be hotels devoted solely to these impatient travellers.'

We learned that the key to solving a crime wasn't in the larger picture but in the symmetry of blood droplets, the hairs stuck to the floorboards, the crushed cigarette butts, or under the fingernails of the dead. We went over everything with a magnifying glass. Tiny objects became enormous, distorting all of life.

Sometimes Craig's old friends also taught us. Among them was Aquiles Greco, the great phrenologist, a tiny doctor with nervous tics, whose hands trembled as if they had a life of their own. They were like small animals, anxious to leap on to your face in order to feel your cheekbones or your superciliary arches, or to estimate, just by touch, the circumference of your skull. He always reminisced about the years he had worked at the University of Paris with Prospère Despines, the illustrious but forgotten mentor of Cesare Lombroso. Greco had us pass skulls from one hand to the other, palpating the protuberances and noting the murderers' frontal sinuosity, their prognathism, their prominent jawbones and flattened foreheads. With our eyes closed and our fingers moving we had to answer the question: 'Thief, murderer, or con man?'

I once shouted out 'Murderer!' and Greco responded, 'Even worse. That's the skull of a Jesuit.'

The visits to the morgue weren't as pleasant. Dr Reverter, who was tall and had the parsimonious and melancholic character of those born under the sign of Saturn, would cut open the cranial lid and show us the encephalic mass, teaching us to recognize the many calluses and marks on murderers' brains.

'Their future crimes are written here, from the moment of their birth. If we had some apparatus that allowed us to see people's brains, we could arrest those who bear these marks before they committed their crimes, and murder would disappear.'

At that time physiology was a main focus of criminology, and doctors and policemen dreamed of a science that could separate the innocent from the reprobate. Today it has lost all of its scientific value, and even mentioning Lombroso's name in an auditorium – and I have often done so – is enough to set off derisive laughter. Today's dismissive mockery is just as irresponsible as the blind faith of the past. After more than twenty years of tracking down murderers, my experience has shown me that Fate's signs do show on our faces: the problem is that there is no single system for interpreting them. Lombroso didn't err when choosing his field of study; his error was in believing that all those clues hidden in faces and hands were subject to only one interpretation.

Did Craig believe in physiognomy or any other variant of criminal physiology? That was hard to say, the murders that interested him most were the ones that left traces only at the crime scene.

'Those easily identifiable criminals – the ones with prominent ears and protruding eye sockets and enormous hands, for them there's the police. The invisible murderer, the murderer that could be any one of us, that's the one for me.'

FOUR

Sometimes when Craig mentioned one of the Twelve Detectives in passing, we found the courage to ask him questions about how the association was founded, about its unwritten rules, and about the few occasions when some of the members had gotten together. Craig answered the questions vaguely and with annoyance; we attempted to fill in the blanks later, among ourselves. We repeated the names as if we were memorizing them, as if we were studying a particularly difficult lesson. The most famous detectives – the *Key to Crime* always published stories of their adventures – were Magrelli, also known as the Eye of Rome; the Englishman Caleb Lawson; and the German, Tobias Hatter, a native of Nuremberg. The magazine often reported the frequent conflicts between the two men who both wanted the title of Detective of Paris: the veteran Louis Darbon, who considered himself the heir to Vidocq, and Viktor

Arzaky, a Pole and Craig's good friend, who had settled in France. Even though his cases weren't published very often, the Athenian detective, Madorakis, was one of my favourites. The way he solved crimes made it seem that he wasn't just accusing one particular criminal but the entire human race.

Buenos Aires' Spanish community closely followed the exploits of Fermín Rojo, a detective from Toledo, who had such extraordinarily entertaining mishaps that the murders themselves were beside the point. Zagala, a Portuguese detective, was always by the sea: interrogating the fierce crew members of boats lost in the fog, searching the beach for remains of inexplicable shipwrecks, solving 'locked-cabin' cases.

Novarius, Castelvetia and Sakawa rounded out the Twelve Detectives. In our imagination we associated Jack Novarius, the American detective, with legendary cowboys and gunmen. The meticulous Anders Castelvetia, who was Dutch, crawled into dusty corners without ever dirtying his white suit. We didn't know a thing about Sakawa, the inscrutable detective from Tokyo.

We repeated those names behind Craig's back. The nebulous subject of the Twelve Detectives was not on his syllabus. He preferred that we learn law, taught by Dr Ansaldi, a former classmate of Craig's at the Colegio San Carlos. Ansaldi explained that law was a narrative practice. Lawyers tried to compose a story – one of innocence or of guilt – and make it seem the only possibility, taking advantage of the conventions of the genre and of human nature, which was so eager to confirm its prejudices. Our fellow students Clausen and Miranda, both sons of lawyers, were the only ones who didn't sleep through the law classes; in fact, they eventually became lawyers. The rest of us didn't care for that stagnant world, filled with unreadable books, lived behind a desk. To us it was diametrically opposed to the danger and intellectual excitement promised by detective work. Even Craig hated law.

'We detectives are artists, and lawyers and judges are our critics,' he would say.

Trivak, the only student that I became friends with, had read De Quincey in his father's *Edinburgh Gazette* collection, and dared to correct him.

'The murderers are the artists, and the detectives their critics.'

Craig was silent, preferring to save his response for later. Trivak was the boldest of the group, and when Craig hid clues around the house – one of his endless exercises – Trivak got closer to solving the mystery than anyone else. It was rumoured that in one painstaking pursuit he hadn't even stopped at Mrs Craig's bedroom, but had gone in and searched through her clothes. Trivak didn't confirm the rumour, but he didn't deny it either, saying, 'There should be no limits to one's investigation.'

I suspected that Trivak had started that rumour himself, along with another, more persistent one, that the Academy was just a means for Craig to groom an assistant. The newspapers often criticized him for lacking a second pair of eyes to lend credence to his adventures.

Craig, along with Arzaky and Magrelli, was one of the most adept and prudent of the Twelve Detectives, yet, without an acolyte, he was considered to be somewhat inferior to his colleagues. The Portuguese, Zagala, had Benito, a remarkably agile Brazilian; Caleb Lawson, a knight of the Queen and Scotland Yard's most famous collaborator, had Dandavi, the Hindu, who followed him everywhere, sometimes putting false leads and real dangers in his path just to create a more exciting tale to tell. Arzaky, who competed with Louis Darbon for the title of Parisian Detective, had old Tanner as his helper. Tanner's health had been compromised by so many rigorous adventures that now, stooped over, consumptive, and with his days numbered, he spent most of his time in his tulip garden and only assisted Arzaky by post.

The idea that Craig had set up an entire academy just to find himself an acolyte didn't seem preposterous, and it filled us with an enthusiasm that we didn't dare admit to one another. By then, several students had quit, terrified by the unknown world that detective work had revealed. Visiting prisons to meet famous murderers and attending the execution, by firing squad, of the anarchist Carpatti, who, even when riddled with bullets, continued to spit insults at his executioners, had disheartened those who thought that investigation was an intellectual game, a spiritual puzzle. Of course, none of those who abandoned the Academy ever admitted to being afraid or disenchanted. They all pretended that their change of course was due to a recent, sobering maturity; a realization that they wanted to be family men, to follow in the footsteps of their fathers, who were businessmen, doctors, and lawyers. As our numbers dwindled, our hopes grew that we would be the chosen one.

Deep down, we knew that if Craig really had set all of this up in order to find an assistant, he had already made his choice. As much as Trivak tried to dampen his sarcasm and impress his teacher, it was Alarcón who was the favourite. Gabriel Alarcón, whose skin was so pale that you could see his veins. Gabriel Alarcón, whose beauty was more befitting a girl than a man. Craig was happy when he proved to be shrewder than us, when he could accuse us of missing the logic in an exercise of reason and then demonstrate his absolute superiority. Craig was eager to beat us, but he was even more eager to be defeated by Alarcón, and when from his disciple's feminine mouth came the words that bested him, then he smiled twice as proudly.

We hated Alarcón for that. We also hated him because his family was richer than any of ours, their fortune built on the construction of ships. He could aspire to be an ambassador or devote his life to travelling and women, and yet he had chosen to compete amongst us. And he was outdoing us. Trivak and I loathed him most: I was a shoemaker's son and Trivak's father was one of the few Jewish lawyers in the city at that time. But even as we hated him, we recognized his merits (which, far from assuaging our hatred, increased it).

Alarcón always followed an unexpected and solitary

path. He never asked for permission, but moved through the world as if all doors were open to him. His familiarity with the Craigs was unnerving. He had tea with Mrs Margarita Craig every afternoon. When the detective was out of town, she spent hours in his company. He became a substitute – of course, only at teatime – for her husband.

When Craig revealed the solution to the case of the locked room – one that had obsessed the detectives – Alarcón responded, 'Calling a murder a "locked-room crime" is the wrong approach to the investigation, because it assumes that locks are infallible. There are no truly locked rooms. Calling it that presupposes an impossibility. In order to solve a problem, it has to be correctly posited. We mustn't let semantics cloud our logic.'

We hated him. We competed among ourselves, not with him. We were fighting over second place, in a race where only first place mattered.

On the days when Craig was travelling for a case, things were more relaxed and we went home earlier than usual. Trivak would stare, perplexed, from the doorway at Alarcón, who, instead of leaving, would go upstairs, with those slow, almost weightless, steps of his, to accept Mrs Craig's excessive hospitality.

FIVE

In the Academy, on the first floor, there was a meeting room that was never used. An oval table with chairs around it stood in the middle. Both the chairs and the table were heavy, impossible to move, as if the wood had petrified. We called it the Green Room, because there were branches and vines painted on the ceiling by an artist who had begun his work with patience and diligence and had obviously tired of botany by the end. The exacting calligraphy of stems and veins became a confused mass of branches whipped by a storm. The walls were covered in dark wood, hung with swords, harquebusiers and coats of arms; it all had a somewhat pretentious air, like the houses of antique dealers. The room looked like the remains of some abandoned project: the headquarters of a Masonic enclave, or a dining room that Mrs Craig had envisaged for illustrious visitors that had never arrived. Called one day to convene there, we sat around the table, which was completely empty except for the dust, and Craig spoke.

'Gentlemen, in the last few months you have learned everything there is to know about crime. At least everything that can be taught in a classroom. Life is a perennial teacher, especially when the subject is death. Theoretical knowledge has its limits. Beyond those limits lies intuition, which is not something supernatural, as our friend Trivak, future member of the spiritualist brotherhood, insists. Rather it is the sudden relationship that we establish with other hidden, less dominant realms of knowledge. To intuit is to retrieve subconscious memories, which is why experience is the mother of intuition. It is nothing more than a specialized type of memory. Its goal is to find a pattern, connect the dots of this chaotic life.'

Distracted, I let my finger trace my name in the thick layer of dust that covered the table.

'For a while now I've been waiting for a suitable practice case to present itself, and now I have it.'

Craig spread a newspaper page across the table. We were looking for some big headline about an honest tailor shot to death, or a woman found floating in the river, but there was only an advertisement for the performances of the magician Kalidán, the same magician who had commenced his tour of the city when Craig announced the launch of his academy. At that time great magicians often came through our city, though now it's not so common. Various types of phantasmagoria were popular in Europe and the public filled the theatres to see skeleton battles, luminous ghosts, decapitated bodies that spoke, and other marvels created with smoke and mirrors.

'For some time now I have noticed that this magician's tours seem to coincide with murders and disappearances. The victims are always women: in New York a chorus girl disappeared, in Budapest a flower seller, in Montevideo a cigarette girl was found exsanguinated. The Berlin police questioned him in the death of a nurse, but they couldn't prove anything. The few corpses that have been found (because our killer always tries to either hide or destroy the bodies) revealed that he drained the victims' blood and then washed them with bleach. He always performs this purification ritual.'

Craig explained the case detachedly; six of us cracked our knuckles, angered by the murders. Only Alarcón responded to the tale with equal indifference. They both approached the challenge without emotion.

'Kalidán will be in the city for fifteen more days. Then he continues on to Brazil and we won't have anything to investigate. I'll continue explaining the case, I'll stress the importance of distinguishing coincidence from inevitability, but those of you who are any good will leave me here talking to myself, you'll leave Detective Craig raving alone in this dusty room.'

All six of us rushed to the door, but by that time Alarcón had already disappeared.

SIX

We bought tickets for the performance and settled into the dilapidated seats of the Victoria Theatre. We wanted to find some connection between the illusions with swords and guillotines in the magician's show and real murders. But far from the gravity that we, in our inexperience, expected from a murderer, he joked as he did his tricks. Instead of exaggerating the mysterious air lent by his name and his sleight of hand, Kalidán poked fun at his fake exoticism.

After that first sighting, we each came up with our own strategy. Trivak pretended to be a journalist from *The Nation* and went to interview the magician in his dressing room. Miranda seduced an usherette and was able to go through his Chinese screens, boxes with holes for housing swords, and even the trunk with Edgar Allan Poe's severed hand, which on stage tirelessly wrote the refrain of *The Raven*. Federico Lemos Paz had his uncle, who owned the Ancona Hotel where the magician was staying, employ him as a bellhop so he could search for clues in his room.

At dusk we met in a corner café near the theatre to exchange accounts of our progress, which wasn't much. The only one who didn't come to our meetings was Alarcón. Jealous and tormented, we imagined that Craig had sent him on a more important mission while he distracted us with the magician's games. Since we didn't trust each other, we kept the information we thought most essential to ourselves while, with an air of secrecy and revelation, we reported irrelevant details. It was my job to search Craig's archive.

The more progress we made, the more convinced we were that the fake Hindu, who was actually Belgian, was guilty, and that he hadn't been caught because he always chose inconsequential victims: the daughters of immigrants, lonely girls whose bodies no one claimed.

After a week had passed, we met in the Green Room to present our findings. Our fingerprints were still there on the dusty table, a reminder of the last meeting. We listed the facts we had been able to prove, and we bragged about our various ruses to get into the magician's life and spy on his past. Craig, bored, pretended to listen. Occasionally he would congratulate someone on his inventiveness (he approved of Lemos Paz passing himself off as a bellboy, he recognized that my archive search had been methodical and responsible), but his congratulations were so insipid, so apathetic, that we would have preferred that he spat out a reprimand or some sign of contempt.

Only when he started to speak did he seem to emerge from his melancholy state. He heard the sound he liked best: his own voice.

'Detective work is an act of thinking, the last corner in which the philosopher seeks refuge. We are logic's last hope. Which is why I ask that you accord the clues their true place, without exaggerating their importance. The correct interpretation of a flower petal can be more valuable than the discovery of a blood-covered knife.'

As he spoke, baffling us, Craig looked towards the door. He was expecting Alarcón, waiting for his prize student to make an entrance that would relieve him of having to hear more, and relieve us of our awkward attempts to impress him. He was waiting for Alarcón to come in and deliver definitive proof.

It was late and we began to leave; finally Trivak, Craig and I were left there alone. To lighten the atmosphere, Trivak said that surely Craig had sent Alarcón on one of the good cases, a 'locked-room' crime (which at the time was considered the non plus ultra of criminal investigation), while keeping us distracted with the fake Hindu magician. Without taking his gaze off the door, Craig responded, 'Every murder is a "locked-room" case. The locked room is the criminal's mind.'

SEVEN

After a tour through the cities of Tucumán and Córdoba, Kalidán the magician returned to the Victoria Theatre for four farewell performances. We were there, and we saw that the magician's assistant – a tall and extraordinarily thin girl, who had appeared to be another artful trick of catoptrical magic – had been replaced by a young man who wore the blue uniform of an imaginary army. The new assistant was none other than Alarcón; he operated the machinery, moved the screens, offered himself as a human target for the dagger trick, and allowed his skull to be hooked up to some cables that led to a strange machine. That machine supposedly projected the assistant's thoughts on to a white screen: we saw some fish, some coins that dropped and were lost, the naked silhouette of a woman who seemed to me to be the exact replica – though I didn't dare mention it to anyone – of Mrs Craig. Alarcón had got further than anyone; he was working with the magician. It made our clumsy attempts to get information seem like child's play.

We continued meeting in the Academy's rooms, but we were disheartened. We expected Craig to finally release us from the course, from the obligation, from our hopes. Craig had his acolyte and there was no reason to go on. But the detective still taught us, and he never mentioned any need for an assistant.

In the following days, Alarcón still hadn't returned to the Academy and Craig asked us if we knew anything of his whereabouts. His question surprised us, because we thought that it was Craig, not us, who was in contact with Alarcón. The performances at the Victoria Theatre had by now ended and the newspapers announced that the magician was travelling to Montevideo.

One afternoon, after class, Craig handed me a wad of banknotes and told me to go to Montevideo that same night.

'No one has heard from Alarcón, and his family is beginning to worry,' he said to me in a hushed voice.

'I'm sure he's found something and wants to surprise you.'

'If there's one thing I've learned, it's to hate surprises.'

That night, I crossed the river on a steamship; the boat's movement kept me awake. In the morning, I bought an orchestra seat for that day's show at the Marconi Theatre. First a pianist played a piano that sounded like brass, and then there was some sort of duel between two actors dressed as gauchos, each representing one side of the River Plate. That was when I fell asleep. When I woke up, Kalidán's show was about to end. I only saw a little of it, but enough to know that Gabriel Alarcón had been replaced by a black girl whose skin was slathered with some kind of oil that made her look like a statue.

I telegraphed Craig to tell him the news. He came to the city the next day and got a room at the Regency Hotel, which had a few pool tables at the back: in those days the game was new and was played according to the Italian rules. Craig listened in silence to the account of my inquiries while he drank one brandy after another.

After the performance we went to the magician's dressing room. Kalidán received us wrapped in a golden robe and smoking an Egyptian cigarette. Craig entered timidly and indecisively; I couldn't tell if it was a brilliant act or if the detective actually felt intimidated by the magician.

'I'm a private detective; I've been sent by the Alarcón family.'

'I know very well who you are. You are one of the founding members of the Twelve Detectives. I'll never forget the Case of the Severed Hand, and how, based on a drop of wine left in a glass –'

Craig didn't let him continue. 'The family's youngest son, Gabriel Alarcón, whom you hired as an assistant, has disappeared.'

Kalidán didn't seem to be alarmed by our presence, although he still hadn't taken off his makeup, as if he didn't want to show us his true face. He spoke with the affable common sense that is so universal among killers, at least according to the pages of the *Key to Crime*.

'I hired a young man for five performances, but he wasn't named Alarcón. He said his name was Natalio Girac. I don't ask a lot of questions. In show business, everybody has a fake name. My real name, as you can imagine, is not Kalidán, and I'm not actually from India. I'm used to doing my act with a woman, but the assistant I had got sick and Girac replaced her very well. I gave him a good tip. I would have liked to bring him with me, but Sayana, the woman you saw, was waiting for me here in Montevideo. We have worked together before. The audience comes to see her, more than me, and I couldn't disappoint them.'

For years I had read accounts of Craig's cases in which he bombarded suspects with seemingly simple questions until the distracted murderer made a fatal mistake. On the printed pages of the *Key to Crime*, Craig was always the absolute master of the situation. But here, in front of the magician, he seemed more like an awkward, frightened policeman who fell for the first lie he heard. He didn't ask any more questions, he just apologized and then we left the dressing room. I wanted to lay in wait for the magician so we could see his real face, but Craig refused. We left Montevideo at dawn. Leaning on the steamship's railing, we were silent for a long time, until finally Craig spoke.

'Did you notice anything odd about the name that Alarcón used? Natalio Girac.'

'What about it?'

'Girac is an anagram of Craig. And Natalio is the name of our only son, who died as an infant.'

Over the next few days Craig continued to do nothing, in spite of the pressure from Alarcón's family. If he had a secret plan for finding out the truth, he didn't mention it. There were many stories in which the detective feigned indolence, or left town, or acted crazy for a while, and then later it would be revealed that what had seemed like apathy or delirium had actually been the patient application of a genius plan. But in this case Craig's revelation was slow in coming.

Gabriel Alarcón was born into a family of boat manufacturers. The Alarcón shipyards supplied the merchant marines of several countries. It was a powerful family and all sorts of emissaries visited Craig in the days following our return, demanding that he find the boy. Craig received them all, and he asked them all for more time to work. The police beat him to the punch and Kalidán the magician was arrested as soon as he got off the steamship that had brought him from Montevideo.

The magician's capture appeared on the front page of the papers. He had travelled disguised as a Hindu, in his turban and yellow tunic, with shoe polish on his face. Craig gave all the reports we had gathered to the police, but there was no indication of the boy's whereabouts in them, nor any proof of Kalidán's crimes. The police interrogated him for fifteen days and fifteen nights. Kalidán, in spite of being driven mad with the beatings, the cold and the lack of sleep, didn't say a word. When it was clear that they couldn't make a case against the magician, the police released him with certain restrictions: he couldn't leave the country, and every four days he had to report, in person, at the police station.

Gabriel Alarcón's disappearance marked the end of the Academy. The newspapers, who had so celebrated the detective's achievements in the past, now attacked him mercilessly: he had sent a novice, an innocent, to an uncertain fate. The other students, pressured by their families, stopped coming. Trivak and I decided to stay in the empty building as a show of confidence in Craig. We helped classify the pieces from the forensic museum, we cleaned and oiled the microscopes, and we waited in vain for the classes to start up again. Finally Trivak left as well.

'Your family?' I asked him.

'No. Boredom.'

I had a good excuse to stay: the organization of the archive, which Craig had assigned to me months earlier. I would arrive early, and go to the kitchen: Angela served me yerba maté tea and French toast she made with day-old bread. Once in a while I had tea with Mrs Craig, and we continued the conversations she had begun with Alarcón. I tried to cheer her up, but each time I saw her she seemed paler, dulled by Alarcón's disappearance and her husband's fall from grace.

EIGHT

Tired of the journalists' attacks, Craig swore he would find Alarcón. He called it 'My Final Case', which seemed to be an admission that something had gone terribly wrong, that he couldn't continue. He thought it had a dramatic effect (and he was right). 'My Final Case,' he would say, sometimes even in the third person, 'Detective Craig's Final Case . . .' and then he would pause reverently. His detractors were now silenced, not because Craig commanded respect, but because endings commanded respect.

During the day he stayed at the Academy, afraid the journalists, the snoops, and those sent by Alarcón's parents would follow him. There was no way to talk to him, he stayed shut up inside his study, writing in notebooks with black covers. His handwriting was a trail of ants that didn't know where they were marching.

I thought, at that point, that Craig was beaten; but

he never stopped proclaiming to the journalists, who were increasingly less interested, to his wife, who had stopped leaving the house, and to me, the only one who listened to him, that he was very close to solving the case. One night he took me away from my work – as I classified his old papers, my admiration for his past and my compassion for his present continued to grow – and asked me to accompany him to the Green Room.

Without any particular emphasis, as if he were telling me of a decision made by someone else, or by simple inertia, he told me that I would be his acolyte.

'But you said that you would never take an assistant.'

'The word "never" shouldn't exist; that way we would be less inclined to make promises we can't keep. This designation, in spite of our situation, will be handled with due formality and announced to the Twelve Detectives.'

In that moment, mentioning the Twelve Detectives seemed incongruent, yet at the same time it gave me hope. It was as if Craig had once again invoked his power to invent and amaze, reviving all that I believed in. For a few seconds I saw the image of my name in the 'In Hushed Tones' section of the *Key to Crime*.

The detective rubbed his eyes as if he was waking up from a sleep that had lasted days, and continued, 'You do know this position won't last long. This is my final case.'

My body tensed involuntarily, and my firm voice complemented my martial stance.

'I hope it won't be your final case; I hope it'll be a

new start. But, if it is, if the day when all the city's murderers can sleep easy has arrived, then there can be no greater honour than having a small role in your farewell.'

Craig nodded distractedly at my words.

That day I started to work. The magician had already violated his obligation to appear at the police station and had fled the city. I visited all the hotels where he might have stayed. Once in a while Craig came with me. I was expecting the classic dialogue between acolyte and detective to develop between us. The Hindu, Dandavi, who worked for Caleb Lawson, pretended not to understand anything because he was foreign, which forced Lawson to explain everything to him in great detail; the Alsatian Tanner spoke in almost a whisper, and only raised his voice when Arzaky surprised him with a brilliant revelation; Fritz Linker, assistant to Tobias Hatter, the detective from Nuremberg, asked such obvious questions that he could easily be taken for an idiot. All the other detectives talked to their assistants, but we proceeded in silence. I rehearsed silly phrases, I was taken in by obvious ideas, by the lustre of appearances, and I always had a cliché on the tip of my tongue, leaving room for Craig to dazzle me with the secret logic of his thinking. But the detective never spoke, and we walked through the night as if there was nothing more to be said.

The owner of the Victoria Theatre, a tremendously fat man who had been a tenor in his youth, allowed us to poke around, afraid that the criminal notoriety of the magician would bring him problems with the law. The theatre was a labyrinth that not even he knew very well; the basement levels and the wings stored sets from old shows. In the half-light we banged up against Venetian bridges, plaster storks and Chinese palaces. Whispers could be heard at the back of the endless basement, as if not only sets were stored there but the entire casts of forgotten plays as well.

Renato Craig went about looking for clues, but it was clear that his despondency was preventing him from carrying out an in-depth investigation. It was no secret that Craig hated theatres; his abhorrence was well known to all the students at the Academy, and even to any reader of the *Key to Crime*.

Although he is remembered as the first detective in Buenos Aires, Renato Craig was in fact the second. The first was named Jacinto Vieytes, and he was a tracker that came here to live after some resounding triumphs in his detective work. Vieytes managed to apply trail guide methods to urban crime. And while his skills, when employed in hotel rooms, society halls, and railway stations, didn't yield such spectacular results as when he was studying hoof prints, trails in the grass, or bonfire remains, the police often called him to study crime scenes. He liked to have people around so he could dazzle them with his deductive reasoning, which was half logic and half old country proverbs. An Italian theatre impresario, realizing that he could use the fact that the tracker was such a character to his advantage, organized a performance for him at the Argentine

Theatre. Vieytes shared a billing with Frank Brown, the clown. The theatrical representation of his skills cost him all credibility; the audience thought he had always been nothing more than an actor.

Although he knew that Vieytes had real talent as a detective, Craig felt that his performance diminished the art of investigation. The detective hated theatres because they reminded him of his predecessor's show, as well as the danger of turning the lonely act of reasoning into an empty spectacle. When he worked as a detective, Vieytes never had an acolyte, but when he entered show business he decided to have an actor play the part of the common man who expressed his foolish opinions as a lead-in to the detective's brilliant conclusions.

So the heavy work was left to me. With my magnifying glass I traced the floorboards of the dressing room in search of a letter, some scrap of paper, or even a hair. Beneath a trunk of such enormous dimensions that it couldn't have fit through the door, I found a receipt for the purchase of a boat passage. I showed it to Craig.

'He's left the country, sir. Here's the receipt for a ticket on the *Goliardo*, which left port a week ago.'

Craig held up the receipt and studied it under the magnifying glass.

'It seems to be genuine, but I'm afraid Kalidán bought the passage just to throw us off track. I'm sure that if we pay a visit to the shipping company they'll tell us that cabin berth remained empty.'

Craig turned the paper over. He studied the footprint on the edge.

‘Kalidán pushed the paper under the trunk with his foot. Here is the mark. You’re a shoemaker –’

I was surprised Craig knew that about me. I had never told him.

‘The son of a shoemaker.’

‘But you can tell me what type of shoe it is.’

It didn’t take me more than a few seconds to come up with a response.

‘It’s the print from a sailor’s shoe.’

‘Are you positive?’

I pointed to the pale lines on the paper. I was happy to be able to show Craig something, although I wasn’t convinced that it was something he didn’t already know.

‘It is a shoe with wide lasts, and grooves to grip the deck’s slippery surface. I think he disguised himself as a sailor so he could blend in with the crew and not be discovered.’ I didn’t really believe that was true, but it seemed an appropriate comment for an assistant to make.

Craig accepted my effort and then said, victoriously, ‘That’s not it at all. He dressed up as a sailor so he could find lodgings at the port and wait until things calmed down before leaving the city. He could easily support himself with his skill at cards.’

Craig’s face was well known in the city, and he didn’t like disguises, so it was up to me to scour the disreputable bars in the port area. In these places with stagnant air and weak light, sailors tried to escape the tedium of their travels with the tedium of terra firma; they pretended to listen to accordion players that played too slowly, or pianists who played too fast; they pretended to talk to women whose faces, in the light of day or a moment of clarity, would have terrified them. In tiny rooms they trafficked in trinkets, foreign money, ambiguous words, opium and infectious diseases.

I went into the bars trying to see without being seen. I was searching for Kalidán's face using an exercise of the imagination: I had to strip him of his Hindu complexion and the bright aura he used to attract attention on stage, and add instead a beard and hats and cloaks and the furtive expression of someone who wishes he could make himself invisible. I tried to strike up conversation with the men that seemed most harmless, but it was hard to trust anyone. A Portuguese man that kept talking about his poor mother stabbed some unlucky fellow who had dared to correct him when he mispronounced the name of a ship; a shy, calm dwarf with a scar across his forehead ripped into the stomach of a drunk who made fun of his condition. No one punished these crimes. I continued to see the Portuguese fellow, and the dwarf too, which made me think that they all must have a few murders under their belts, but since they were in some sort of international territory, no one cared.

I had trouble getting away from the sailors' unintelligible conversations, the greedy women who went through my pockets, and the police spies who looked at me suspiciously. But two weeks later, when I had grown accustomed to getting drunk every night, I heard a rumour about a French captain who was winning a fortune at cards.

He played in a gambling den above a grocery warehouse. Through the dirty windows movement could be seen, but there was no way I could get in; two formidable ruffians guarded the entrance. I waited in the drizzle for the fake French captain to finish gathering his winnings and head home. Finally he came out, sunken into his cloak and beardless. What distinguished him from Kalidán the magician wasn't his disguise but some sort of inner confidence that he couldn't be seen, as if all he had to do was concentrate and he would become invisible. I followed at a distance, carefully, imitating drunken zigzags. He didn't turn to look at me; he walked with sure steps, immune to the effects of alcohol or fear. He was only stopped by a black cat, which he didn't want to cross his path. Then he went into a dilapidated house that looked as if it was about to collapse.

In the morning, so early that my father wouldn't have even been in his workshop, I went to visit Craig. It didn't matter what time I stopped by, he was always awake. I told him of my discovery and described the building's dilapidated condition; I warned him that, in the world of the port, nothing lasted long.

'You've done a good job. But now it's my turn. I sent one boy to his death and I don't want to send another.'

Before the door closed completely, I thought I saw Craig smile for the first time in weeks.

NINE

Five days later Craig brought the journalists who had defamed him together in the Green Room. There was a reporter from *The Nation*, pale and freckled, who was never without a pad and pencil, as if at any moment the perfect sentence was going to jump out and surprise him. The journalist from the *Tribune* was about thirty years old, indigenous looking, and affected gentlemanly manners though it was said that, whenever he got some good information, he sold it to the highest bidder. Another journalist, so tall that he spent his life bent like a question mark, worked for a newspaper in Montevideo, where the case had been followed with interest. There were also three people I had never seen before; I imagined they'd been sent by the Alarcón family.

'As I promised, the case has been solved. It is as we feared: Gabriel Alarcón is dead. His corpse was found in the basement of the Victoria Theatre. The police are taking it away as we speak. The body was covered in lime to hasten the decomposition process.'

'How did you find it?'

'I cannot explain methods that would forewarn criminals and teach them how to proceed in the future so as not to leave clues. But I can tell you that Kalidán, as you know him, or Jean Baptiste Cral, his real name, was an epileptoid criminal who suffered morbid attacks, with a pathological fear of growing old. He believed that drinking human blood would keep him young forever. He was so sure that his crimes would go unpunished that he kept a trophy from each one of his victims.'

Craig opened a large, square box, of the kind women use to store hats.

'Alarcón was prepared to stop his crimes and, against my advice, became his assistant. He took advantage of his proximity to search for evidence about the murders; he found the collection of souvenirs from Kalidán's victims. Unfortunately, he allowed himself to be dazzled by the magician's skills.'

Craig pulled a dull medallion, a scapulary, a bit of lace, and a lock of hair tied with a yellow ribbon out of the box. 'These macabre treasures gave Alarcón the illusion that he had solved the case; but the magician discovered what he was doing and killed him. He drank his blood, just as he had the women's. Then he made the body disappear.'

The journalists took notes as fast as they could; Craig

had shrewdly called this meeting at the end of the day so they wouldn't have time to ask too many questions, since they were already due back at their editorial offices. The moment they left, the detective seemed to lose all his strength and he collapsed into a chair with his head in his hands.

It seemed best to leave him in peace, but I had a thousand questions. Didn't I, his assistant, deserve an explanation of the method that had enabled him to reconstruct the story? When he didn't respond to my questions, I put my hand on his shoulder. Physical contact was something that Craig couldn't stand, but I was experiencing a maddening curiosity, the satiation of which would make even Alarcón's gruesome murder seem like a gift.

'It's true,' he said, sitting up with a piqued expression on his face. 'The method. The perspective. Following clues. Salvatrio, my friend, I am going to give you a lesson on the method that none of the Twelve Detectives can match.'

Overcome by the dark energy that now held sway over him, he dragged me out of the house. We walked at top speed: Craig, the insomniac, went first with a lit lantern. After an hour of walking in silence I wished we had called a carriage. I made some vague remark and he responded by saying, 'Rented carriages can't take us to where we're going.'

I was unfamiliar with those dark, disintegrating corners of the city. We passed a fallen tree and then a dead horse whose bones shone in the moonlight. Later that same night I saw something worse, but nightmares are capricious, and it was the horse's empty eye sockets that haunted me for nights afterward. Further on there was a shed, which was where we were headed. Craig opened the large door, which had no key or lock. Up high there were some broken windows that let in the moon's white light. I thought I heard a whisper, but it was the buzzing of flies.

In the middle of the shed a man's corpse hung upside down. His feet were tied to a beam with rope. Craig raised his lantern so I could see. The man was naked and covered in clots of blood. His inert, open arms seemed to retain something of the gesture he had used, night after night, in distant theatres, to elicit amazement. Beneath the body, there was a lake of blood that the dirt floor was struggling to swallow up.

'He was slow in telling me where Alarcón's body was. Up until the very last minute he seemed to trust that some trick would save him.'

'What are you going to do with . . . that?'

'As soon as the sun comes up I'll go to the police station. I've already thought of how I'll explain it; I'll tell them I came here following the clues I got from the card players. The police are familiar with the harsh ways they punish cheaters. And thus ends Detective Craig's Final Case.'

As I left the shed I had the feeling I was being followed by blue flies. I couldn't go back alone in the middle of the night, so I had to wait for Craig. I didn't want to walk by his side.

Thirty paces ahead, Craig, his lantern raised, showed me the way. Even that light, for the mere fact that it had shone on the macabre sight of the magician, seemed to glow with the incandescence of corruption.

TEN

I went back to my father's workshop and applied myself to the cutting of soles, which was my specialty. I don't know if I mentioned it already, but Salvatrio's Cobbler Shop only made men's shoes. My father refused to touch women's feet. He noticed I was gloomy and he tried to get me to talk about it. I implied that it was a romantic problem, just to reassure my father. He smiled with relief. 'Once you touch a woman's feet, all is lost.'

In the days that followed, my mother insisted I eat well. She prepared stews with long noodles, courgettes and beef. I couldn't touch the meat.

One afternoon a short boy of about twelve years old, wearing a blue hat that was too large for his head, entered the shoe shop. He asked for Mr Sigmundo Salvatrio and it took me a while to answer, because no one had ever called me 'mister' before. He handed me a note written in a woman's round, careful hand.

My husband is in the hospital, suffering from an unknown illness. I need to send you on one last assignment. I'll be home all afternoon.

There was no heading or signature, as if Mrs Craig feared the paper could fall into strange, enemy hands.

I polished my shoes with the black cream my own father made – and which, it was said, also worked as an ointment for burns and wounds – and left the workshop.

The maid opened the door and, as I went upstairs, I looked into the sitting room where papers and dust were piling up. On the top floor Mrs Craig, seated in a white chair, was waiting for me. The table on which she had her tea was like some sort of garden in winter; all the plants that surrounded it were dark and filled with thorns, the flowers fleshy and enormous. The maid rushed to bring tea and a sugar bowl. When I opened it and saw that it was empty, I feared that Mrs Craig was suffering hardships due to her husband's illness.

'Please, help yourself,' she told me, and I pretended to serve myself. Two or three white grains fell into the hot tea.

'How is your husband?'

'The doctors can't find anything. He is sick in spirit.'

'Can I visit him?'

'Not yet. But you can do something for him. The past few days he has talked of nothing else. Are you listening?'

'Of course, ma'am.'

'In Paris, this May, the World's Fair opens. I imagine you've seen pictures in the newspapers of the pavilions, and of the iron tower being constructed. The Twelve Detectives have been asked to participate.'

'All of them?'

'All of them, together for the first time.'

My hand shook and I almost dropped my cup of tea. The Argentine newspapers had followed the preparations for this new World's Fair in detail, as if it were something that somehow belonged to us. I had read that the Argentine pavilion was larger and more magnificent than any of the other South American ones. Passage reservations had long since sold out. But news that the detectives were getting together was more important to me than all the treasures of all the countries, than the works hanging in the Palace of Fine Arts, and the inventions in the Galerie des Machines. I thought that what excited me should be exciting for everyone, and even the tower itself paled in comparison to the detectives' meeting.

'Will they have their own pavilion?' I asked. For a minute I could even imagine the Twelve displayed in glass cases and on platforms, like wax figures.

'No, they are going to have their meetings in the Numancia Hotel and there, in a parlour, they'll display the tools of their trade. Up until now, only a few of them have gathered together at one time; at most six. But this time they'll be twelve. Well, eleven, since my husband can't go.'

What was I hearing? Craig would miss the first meeting in history of the Twelve Detectives?

'He has to go, even if he's sick. You could go with him. You and a nurse.'

'My husband was the driving force behind this meeting, with Viktor Arzaky. They both wanted the art of investigation to be represented among so many other trades. With your youthful enthusiasm, my dear Salvatrio, nothing is impossible, but I know that my husband can't take the long boat trip. Which is why you must go in his place.'

'I couldn't take his place. I'm an inexperienced acolyte.'

'Arzaky – the Pole, as my husband calls him – has been left without an assistant. Old Tanner is sick; he plays chess, he grows tulips, and he sends letters. And Arzaky has to prepare the exhibition of the detectives' instruments. My husband thought that you could go and help him in that undertaking.'

'I have no money.'

'It will all be paid for. The Fair's Organizing Committee will take care of the expenses. What's more, my husband won't take no for an answer.'

I had never travelled anywhere. The invitation both excited and intimidated me. I paused and then said, in a faint voice, 'I know your husband would have preferred to send Alarcón. Today is his memorial service. Are you going to go, Mrs Craig?'

'No, Salvatrio. I am not going to go.'

I took a sip of bitter tea.

'I have something to confess to you. We envied him.'

'Alarcón? Why?'

Mrs Craig sat up in her chair. Some sort of vague flush gave life to her face. I didn't give her the answer she was expecting.

'Because he was your husband's favourite. Because he considered him more competent than us.'

Mrs Craig stood up. It was time to leave.

'You are alive and he is dead. Don't ever envy anyone, Mr Salvatrio.'

PART TWO

The Symposium

ONE

The committee assigned to write the complete catalogue of the 1889 World's Fair continued working in spite of the war. It originally had three members: Deambrés, Arnaud and Pontoriero; Arnaud died three years after the Fair ended, but Pontoriero and Deambrés are still at it. The original idea was to have the catalogue ready before the Fair, then during, and finally after; but the catalogue, over a quarter of a century later, still isn't ready; something that not even the most sombre pessimists nor the most passionate optimists could have imagined. I mention the optimists as well, for the task didn't become an interminable one due to the catalogue compilers' inefficiency but because of the grandeur of the Fair.

So many years later, Pontoriero and Deambrés still continue to receive correspondence from distant countries; sometimes it's idle, solicitous civil servants, but mostly it's spontaneous collaborators who want to correct slight mistakes. They are mostly older gentlemen, already retired, whose favourite hobby, besides correcting the catalogue, is writing indignant letters to newspapers. The main problem is how to combine different classification methods: should it be done by country, alphabetically, making a distinction between everyday objects and extraordinary ones, or by headings (naval, medical, culinary instruments, etc.). Deambrés and Pontoriero published partial catalogues every two or three years, advances on the final version, perhaps with the intention of showing that they were still working on it and at the same time discrediting the fakes that were made for purely commercial ends. One of those partial catalogues, the one devoted to toys, was the basis for the *Great Toy Encyclopaedia*, the first of its kind, produced by the Scarletti publishing house in 1903.

'All of our work consists of avoiding the one word that would free us from all these obligations,' Pontoriero told a journalist in 1895.

'And what word is that?'

'Etcetera.'

It is true that the innovations of 1889 that so dazzled us and promised to turn our cities into dizzyingly vertical landscapes are now old hat. Most of the inventions gathered in the Galerie des Machines (Vaupatrin's submarine; Grolid's excavator; the artificial heart invented by Dr Sprague, who turned out to be a fraud; Mendes's robot for organizing archives) must be stored in a warehouse somewhere, if they haven't already been dismantled. Meanwhile, the war has shown itself to be the true world's fair of all human technology, and Somme and Verdún's trenches the true venues for technology to demonstrate its material and philosophical reach.

None of these considerations have disheartened Pontoriero and Deambrés, who continue their task on the third floor of a building occupied by the Ministry of Foreign Affairs. They have promised to carry on even after their official retirement.

In the second of the partial catalogues, devoted to dual-function objects or, better put, objects that have an obvious use and a secret one, I was pleased to find a mention of Renato Craig's cane, made of cherry wood with a handle shaped like a lion's head. It could become a spyglass, a magnifying glass, and a sword was hidden inside. In addition, it featured compartments for fingerprint powder and small glass boxes to hold evidence found at crime scenes; it could also be used as a firearm, although only on exceptional occasions and at a very short distance, because the bullet came out any which way. Because of its wide range of weaponry, one had to be very careful when using it as a cane; one slip could have fatal consequences.

I was given the task of bringing the detective's cane to the parlour of the Numancia Hotel. After meeting Mrs Craig and accepting her request, I was allowed to visit my mentor in the hospital. I remember the smell of bleach and the chequered floors, recently mopped and extremely slippery. His room was quite dark because one of the symptoms of Craig's illness was aversion to light. It was summer and very hot; Craig had a damp cloth over his face.

He moved the cloth from over his mouth to speak, but kept his eyes veiled.

'When you see Detective Arzaky, remember that he and I are old friends, like brothers; we've managed the Twelve Detectives between the two of us all these years. The others believe that they have always exercised their right to vote, but it never was a democracy. It was a monarchy, shared by the Pole and I. We made the decisions we had to make, because none of the others thought as much as we did about this profession; sometimes we did these things with heavy hearts, still other times we had to buoy up each other's courage, to restore one another's faith in the method. Arzaky is in charge of the exhibition of our craft, in the parlour of the Numancia Hotel, but the discussions between the detectives are going to be more important than the exhibition. And even more important than that will be the words whispered in the hallways, the secret laughter, the gestures between one detective and another, and between detectives and their assistants. Each will bring with him an object representing his concept of investigative work: some will bring complex machines and others a simple magnifying glass. I will send along my cane. Open the closet, take it out.'

I opened a white metal wardrobe and carefully removed Craig's cane. It was incredibly heavy. The detective's clothes were also hung up inside the wardrobe, and seeing these garments empty, without a body inhabiting them, I felt a deep sadness, as if Craig's illness were there, in the wardrobe, in the way he failed to wear his clothes.

'That cane was given to me by a furniture and weapons salesman who had a shop near Victoria Plaza. Actually he didn't give it to me: I bought it for one coin. I had done a favour for the man; I had recovered an old Bible that was stolen from him. I didn't want to accept any payment so he brought me this cane and told me: 'There is a sword hidden inside. I want you to have it, but I can't give it to you. If one gives a blade as a gift, the fate of the former owner is passed on to the recipient. And who wants someone else's fate? Give me the smallest coin you have.' And I gave him a ten-cent coin. Since then, this cane and I have been constant companions.'

I carefully leaned the heavy stick against a chair.

'You will be responsible for bringing Arzaky something else as well. I want you to tell him about My Final Case. Only him.'

'The Case of the Cobra Bite?'

On that occasion, Craig had proved that the cobra was completely innocent: a woman had killed her husband with a distillation of curare, and then pretended that he had been bitten by one of the snakes that he kept.

'Don't be an idiot. My Final Case. The case that has no other name but that one: the final case. Give him all the details. The real version. He'll be able to understand it.'

I thought about Kalidán's body, naked, hanging by his feet. It had been motionless, covered in a cloud of flies, but in my imagination it swayed slightly.

'I can't tell that story. Ask me for anything but that.'

'Do you want me to go to church and confess? Do you think detectives stoop to talking to priests? Repentance doesn't exist for us, nor does reconciliation or forgiveness. We are philosophers of action, and we only judge ourselves by our actions. Do as I tell you. Tell the Pole the whole truth. That is my message for Viktor Arzaky.'

TWO

It was the first time I had ever left my country, the first time I had been on a boat. And yet the real voyage had begun the moment I entered the Academy and left behind my world (my house, my father's shoe shop). From then on everything was foreign to me. Paris was just a continuation of Craig's house, and more than once I awoke in the hotel room with the feeling that I had fallen asleep in one of the Academy's freezing cold rooms.

Following my mentor's instructions, I took a room at the Nécart Hotel. I knew that was where the other assistants would be staying. While Mrs Nécart wrote my name into a thick accounting register, I tried to guess which of the gentlemen smoking in the reception room were my colleagues. They must be the ones who were the most discreet, most observant, and capable of collaborating on an investigation without getting in the way. Shadows.

I was accustomed to the large rooms and open spaces of Buenos Aires, so the Parisian salon seemed to belong in a dollhouse. It was one of those rooms that we visit in dreams, where several different places from our waking life converge in a single dream-space: the faux Persian rug, the paintings with mythological motifs, the shaky end table, the fake Chinese desk; everything was incongruent, theatrical. On the stage one must create the impression of life with a motley conglomeration of furniture, saturated with details, but in the real world empty spaces are needed to allow a little breathing room.

I had barely started unpacking when there was a knock at my door. When I opened it I saw a Neapolitan with an exaggerated moustache who brought his heels together with a military click.

'I'm Mario Baldone, assistant to Magrelli, the Eye of Rome.'

I offered him my hand, which he shook vigorously.

'I know every single case your detective has solved. I particularly remember the one that began with a nun floating in the river. She had a letter fastened to her cap with a gold pin.'

'The Case of the Tarot Cards. I had the great honour of assisting Magrelli with that. It was one of his loveliest cases. There was so much symmetry, such balance in those crimes . . . They were clear, elegant, without so much as one surplus drop of blood. The killer was Dr Benardi, the director of San Giorgio Hospital; every so often he still writes to Magrelli from prison.'

'Would you like to come in?'

'No, I just wanted to invite you to the meeting tonight. A few of us have already arrived.'

'Are we meeting here in the hotel?'

'In the drawing room, at seven.'

I continued to unpack with the feeling that I was taking apart my old life, and that those elements – the brand-new clothes my mother had insisted I buy, Craig's cane, my notebook, with every page blank – were the pieces with which I would construct a new reality.

I laid down for a nap but, because of my exhaustion from the trip – I was never able to sleep through a whole night on board the ship – I didn't wake up until seven thirty. I went downstairs with my head still cloudy from sleep. Seven of the assistants were gathered in the drawing room. Baldone didn't seem at all perturbed by my lateness and introduced me to everyone. The first was Fritz Linker, assistant to Tobias Hatter, the detective from Nuremberg, who offered me an enormous soft hand: he was a dull-looking giant and his lederhosen only accentuated the impression of stupidity coming from his watery eyes. However, I knew very well that his obvious questions, his insistence on discussing the weather, and his idiotic jokes (which drove Hatter crazy) were merely a charade.

Benito, the only black assistant, worked for Zagala, the Portuguese detective, famous for solving mysteries on the high seas. His most celebrated case was the disappearance of the entire crew of the *Colossus*. The case had dominated newspapers for months. Benito's skill with locks was renowned and it was said that he not only used his talents in search of the truth but also to earn some extra money, since Zagala had a reputation for being cheap.

Seated in one of the four green armchairs, not talking to anyone, was a Red Indian who seemed to be concentrating intensely on the spider web stretching over one corner of the room. It was Tamayak, whose ancestors were Sioux; he was assistant to Jack Novarius, an American who, in his youth, had worked for the Pinkerton Agency before founding his own office. Tamayak wore a fringed suede jacket; his long black hair was pulled back tightly. The jacket was eye-catching, but I was surprised he wasn't wearing a feathered headdress, or carrying a tomahawk or a peace pipe or any of the other accoutrements Indians usually have in magazine illustrations. The other detectives often criticized Novarius because he preferred to use fists over reason, but among his many triumphs he had caught the so-called 'Baltimore Strangler', who had killed seven women between 1882 and 1885. Tamayak had been essential to solving that case, although his account of it, filled with metaphors that only Sioux-speakers could understand, had spoiled the story.

'This is Manuel Araujo, from Seville,' said Baldone, as a short man with a toothy smile came towards us.

'Failed matador, and assistant to the detective from Toledo, Fermín Rojo, whose exploits far surpass those of the other eleven detectives,' said Araujo, and immediately launched into an account of those exploits, only to be interrupted by the Neapolitan.

'Surely the Argentine is familiar with the case,' said Baldone. And it was true; I also knew that Araujo exaggerated the detective's adventures to the point that he had damaged his reputation, casting doubt even on proven facts. The accounts of some of his adventures, which I had read in the *Key to Crime*, were suspicious, to say the least. In the Case of the Golden Hen, Rojo had gone inside a volcano; in the Ash Circle he had fought a giant octopus in the Saragossa aquarium. But most aficionados of the Spanish detective said that Rojo allowed his assistant to embellish the tales of his investigations beyond the credible in order to keep the true stories secret.

Sunk into an armchair and looking as if he was about to fall asleep was Garganus, the assistant to the Greek detective Madorakis, who stuck out a weary hand to me. I knew that Madorakis had come up against Arzaky on some theoretical aspects of their profession. Craig had told me a bit about their rivalry:

'Every detective is either Platonic or Aristotelian. But we're not always what we believe ourselves to be. Madorakis thinks he's Platonic, but he's Aristotelian; Arzaky thinks he's Aristotelian, but he's a hopeless Platonic.'

At the time I hadn't understood my teacher's words. I knew that Arzaky's other rival – his true rival, because his competition with the Greek didn't go beyond intellectual folly – was Louis Darbon, with whom he vied for supremacy over Paris. Darbon had always considered Arzaky a foreigner who had no right to practise the trade in his city.

Arthur Neska, Darbon's assistant, was dressed entirely in black and stood in a corner, looking as if he was about to leave. As the days passed I came to understand that he was always like that: in doorways, on staircases, never seated or settled or absorbed in conversation. He was slim and had a youthful air about him, and thin, feminine lips that seemed to convey displeasure towards everything and everyone. When I approached him in greeting he didn't move to shake my hand until the very last second.

Since childhood I had followed the adventures of these men in the *Key to Crime*, as well as in other magazines like the *Red Mark* and *Suspicion,* and now I was actually shaking their hands. Even though they were assistants and not detectives, to me they were legendary characters that lived in another world, another time; and yet here we were, in the same room, surrounded by the same cloud of cigarette smoke.

Mario Baldone raised his voice so he could be heard above the murmuring.

'Dear sirs, I would like to welcome Sigmundo Salvatrio, from the Argentine Republic, who has come on behalf of the founder of the Twelve Detectives: Renato Craig.'

Everyone applauded when they heard Craig's name, and it was gratifying for me to see how respected my mentor was. Stammering in French, I explained that I was inexperienced, and that only a series of unfortunate coincidences had brought me there. My modesty made a good impression among those around me: in that moment I saw a tall Japanese man at the back of the room, who wore some sort of blue silk shirt with bright yellow details: it was Okano, the assistant to Sakawa, the detective from Tokyo. Okano looked to be one of the youngest – he must have been about thirty years old – but it has always been hard for me to guess the age of people from the Orient. They always seem younger or older than they actually are, as if even their features speak an exotic foreign tongue.

Problems always bring us round and keep us alert, but when everything's going well, as it was that night, we forget about possible dangers. They served me cognac, and since I'm not used to drinking, I overdid it somewhat. Modesty began to seem insipid and I thought it was time to highlight a few of my virtues. I left out the fact that I was a cobbler's son, but I did mention my skill with footprints.

'Those are qualities of a detective, not an assistant,' said Linker. I looked at his too-pale eyes, and I recognized, luckily not aloud, that his imitation of a dullard was perfect.

But he wasn't the only one who was bothered by what I had said.

'Where did you learn these skills?' asked Arthur Neska, Louis Darbon's assistant, from a doorway, as always.

I should have kept my mouth shut, but alcohol loosens the tongue and firmly ties up the mind.

'In the Academy,' I said. 'Detective Craig taught us all types of investigative methods, including the principles of anthropological physiognomy.'

'But is it an academy for assistants, or for detectives?' asked the German.

'I don't know, Craig never said. Perhaps he was hoping to train such good assistants that they could become detectives themselves some day.'

I had never in my life heard such a deep silence as the one that followed my words; the effect of the alcohol wore off abruptly, as if their reaction was a splash of cold water. How could I explain to them that it was the cognac, not me? How could I tell them that I was from Argentina and geographically doomed to talk more than I should? The Japanese assistant, who up until that moment had been watching everything as if he couldn't understand a word, left the room looking so distressed that I thought he had gone to find his sword so he could stab me, or stab himself – I wasn't sure.

Linker looked me in the eyes and said, 'You're new and so we'll forgive your lack of information, but remember this as surely as you remember that fire burns: no acolyte has ever become a detective.'

I wasn't going to open my mouth, not even to apologize, for fear that even my apology would be inadequate. But Benito, the black Brazilian, recalled, 'Yet they always said that Magrelli, the Eye of Rome, started out as an assistant . . .'

It was clear that he had brought up an old matter that was familiar to everyone – familiar but unmentionable – because as soon as Benito opened his mouth, Baldone went straight for his neck, as if the Brazilian had insulted his mentor. He took out a sailor's knife with a curved blade and brandished it in the air, searching for the black man's neck. The German and the Spaniard managed to hold him back.

Baldone had given up on French – the detectives' international language – and was swearing in a Neapolitan dialect. Benito backed up slowly towards the exit without turning his back on the Italian, afraid that he'd escape the others' hold and attack him again. When he was out of sight, Baldone calmed down.

'*Maledetto Benedetto*.'

Linker, the German, said, almost into my ear, 'That is an old, unfounded rumour. There are rumours about all the detectives, but we never repeat them.'

Baldone regained his momentum, asserting, 'Of course we shouldn't repeat them! There have always been rumours, but we've never believed them! I've heard gossip about every one of the detectives: that this one is a morphine addict, that one learned everything he knows in prison, the other one isn't the least interested in women! But I would cut out my own tongue before spreading them!'

Some of the arrows had hit their mark because now Neska and Araujo and even Garganus leapt on the Italian as if they were going to rip off his moustache. Baldone was brandishing his knife again, moving it from one side to the other in such an exaggerated way that for a moment I feared he was going to end up hurting himself. A statue of the goddess Minerva that decorated a corner of the room received an unintentional thrust of his blade. Everyone was worked up, except for Tamayak.

Just then a calming voice was heard. It was deep and wise, but at the same time a bit slow. It could just as easily make you fall asleep as get your attention. It was Dandavi, Caleb Lawson's Hindu assistant. In the midst of the argument we hadn't noticed his arrival, in spite of the fact that his clothes were hard to miss. He wore a yellow shirt and turban, with a gold chain around his neck. He looked at all of us as though he could read what was written in our hearts. He spoke for a long time, his words sketching vast generalizations. I only remember the last thing he said:

'There is nothing wrong with a detective having been an assistant. We are all assistants. And who among us has never dreamed of becoming a detective?'

Those words sank the men into a state of confused melancholy. Baldone, seeing that the others had abandoned their bellicose stances, put away his knife. The tips of his moustache, usually smoothly waxed, now drooped towards the floor. Some men went back to their armchairs, to their drinks, to the conversation they had abandoned; others decided to head off to bed. I was glad to know that they weren't so different from me: we all dreamt of the same things.

THREE

The tower looked finished, but there was still movement up at the top. The machinists, organized into groups of four, continued to replace the provisional rivets – cold-fitted– for the definitive ones, which were heated to red-hot and fitted by whacks from a drop hammer. Over the two years of the construction there had been plenty of problems: some were minor, like the flaws in the protective railing, which was being replaced; but others were more serious, like the trade union disputes that threatened to halt the project, or the problems getting the lifts to go up along the diagonal. In his statements to the press, Eiffel seemed more confident about dealing with the engineering problems than with his enemies: the tower had been attacked by politicians, intellectuals, artists and members of esoteric sects. But one thing was certain: the taller it grew, the more the problems faded into the distance. Now that it was almost completed, the voices that opposed it resounded not with the fury that leads to action but with nostalgia for a lost world. The same thing had happened with the unions. It was more difficult to work a thousand feet up than a hundred and fifty or three hundred, because of the vertigo and the freezing winds. But the labourers, so unruly close to the ground, became more obedient the higher they climbed, as if they considered the tower a personal challenge and had reached a place of proud solitude that no longer tolerated the complaints of the herd. Like a good engineer, Eiffel knew that sometimes difficulties made things run more smoothly.

In spite of the fact that the tower was almost finished, there was one enemy that had not given up harassing the builders with anonymous letters and minor attacks. Along with Turin and Prague, Paris was one of the points on the Hermetic triangle, and it was swarming with esoteric sects. All their members hated the tower. The Organizing Committee for the World's Fair had been forced to hire Louis Darbon to look into the anonymous letters. Eiffel, the engineer, wasn't in favour of this investigation. When one of his collaborators made fun of the fanatics, Eiffel defended them: 'They, with their feverish minds, are the only ones who have understood us. We are in a war of symbolism.'

The tower was the entrance to the Fair: once you passed through the tall door made of iron and empty space, you saw frenetic activity devoid of any hierarchy or central focus. That chaos made you understand the dictionary compiler's desire to impose alphabetical order on the world's infinite variety. Everything was being built at once: temples, pagodas, cathedrals. In the streets, carts dragged enormous wooden boxes embellished with shipping and customs stamps from which emerged the tops of African trees or the arms of disproportionately large statues. Displaced natives from Africa and the Americas were ordered to build their indigenous dwellings in the middle of the splendour of European pavilions and palaces. But it wasn't easy to maintain these islands of virgin nature in the midst of all the hustle and bustle, not to mention the machines: when there wasn't a hut on fire there was an igloo melting.

The Fair strove to recreate the world in a finite space, in Paris, but this activity had provoked a strange reaction, and the Fair expanded throughout the city, infecting theatres and hotels, where glass cases were mounted and treasures unearthed from basements that no one had set foot in for years. Even the cemeteries were restored, and the now shiny tombs had an air of artifice, as if the old gravestones had been transformed into facsimiles of themselves. I was surrounded by a world without secrets; there was nothing left that could remain hidden. Up until now we had tolerated the dim imprecision of gaslight, heir to candles and the yellow moon, not the sun. From the tower and from the Fair itself, electric light now exposed a world without subtlety, without yellows, without shadows. It had the transparency of truth.

In that motley city, I walked towards the Numancia Hotel. After convincing the concierge to let me in, I went down the stairs to the subterranean parlour, a former meeting place of conspirators and reprobates. It looked at once like a museum and a theatre; there were glass-covered cabinets on the walls and chairs arranged in a semicircle. At the round table sat Arzaky, looking older than the photographs I had seen of him. He rested his head on the table, as if he had fallen asleep. His pillow was a pile of yellowing scraps of paper filled with his tiny handwriting. He was surrounded by the glazed shelves that would soon showcase the detectives' instruments, but now displayed only an odd newspaper page, dead insects, and some wilted flowers.

The floor, assailed by the basement's dampness, crunched beneath my feet, and Arzaky stood up with a start. His alarm was such that I feared for my life, as if the sleeping detective was prepared for a killer's visit. He was so tall that he appeared to unfold, like a fireman's ladder. Seeing that I was harmless, he abandoned all attempts at self-defence,.

'Who are you? A messenger?'

'It would be an honour for you to regard me as such. I was sent by Renato Craig.'

'And you come empty-handed?'

'I've brought you this cane.'

'A piece of wood with a lion's head.'

'It's full of surprises.'

'It's been a long time since anything has surprised me. Once you reach thirty, everything's a repetition. And I'm over fifty.'

He held the cane in his hands without trying to discover any of its hidden mechanisms.

'He also asked me to tell you about his final case. He didn't want to write it down; he asked me to tell it to you in person. And not to let anyone else hear.'

That seemed to wake Arzaky completely.

'A story! Do they think I can fill up these cases with stories? I need objects, but they won't give them up. They cling to their investigative methods, their artefacts, their secret weapons. They all want to see what everyone else brings; they want the others to show their cards first. The editors of the catalogue have already asked me several times to give them something, but I'm forced to send them off with excuses. It's easier to put together a meeting of sopranos than of the Twelve Detectives. Don't look so distraught, it's not your fault. Let's hear what old Craig has to say.'

I was about to start speaking, but Arzaky silenced me with a gesture.

'Not here. Let's go to the dining hall. This dampness is ruining my lungs.'

I hurried to keep pace with Arzaky's giant strides. The dining hall was still empty. Hesitant afternoon light came in from the street; they had already begun to light the gas lamps. There were some private rooms in the hall, with wooden tables. Arzaky chose one by the window. The waiter approached and I ordered a glass of wine, but all Arzaky had to do was make a sign that meant 'the usual'.

'Don't start yet: wait until I finish my drink. I have a feeling that I'm not going to like what you're about to tell me. Good news arrives in the post; these days, if there's a messenger, that means it's bad news.'

The waiter brought my wine and a conical glass filled halfway with green liquid for Arzaky. The detective put a slotted spoon with a lump of sugar over the glass, and then poured a bit of ice-cold water on it. The liquid turned a milky colour.

He needed to screw up his courage to listen, as did I to tell that tale. I drank half the wine, trying to show a familiarity with alcohol that I didn't really have. I started to tell the story. My bad French motivated me to get it all over with quickly, but at the same time I wanted to put off the ending, which I felt I couldn't possibly tell, so I padded the story with details and tangents. Arzaky showed neither interest nor impatience, and I began to feel as if I were talking to myself.

I was interrupted by the detective's yawn.

'Am I boring you? Should I make it shorter?'

'Don't worry. Both fables of just a few lines and newspaper serials that continue for months reach their end at some point.'

The end was near. I described the scene in the shed; I described the magician's lacerated body, and Craig's indifference to his own crime. I lacked the words to express the horror I had felt that night. Every once in a while, Arzaky corrected my French in a voice devoid of emotion.

'Craig sent me to tell you this. I can't explain why. I don't understand it myself.'

Arzaky finished his third absinthe. His eyes shone with the liquor's green radiance.

'Now can I tell you a story? It's a story told by a Danish

philosopher – philosophy, as you know, is the secret vice of detectives. A great vizier sent his son to quell a rebellion in a distant province. When the son arrived there he didn't know what to do, since he was very young and it was a confusing situation. So he asked his father for advice through a messenger. The vizier hesitated, not wanting to answer directly for fear the messenger might fall into rebel hands and be tortured into revealing the information. So this is what he did: he took the messenger to the garden, he showed him a group of tall tulips and he cut them with his cane, in one fell swoop. He asked the messenger to relate exactly what he had seen. The messenger managed to reach that distant region without being captured by the enemy. When he told the vizier's son what he had seen in the garden, the son understood right away and had all the lords of the city executed. The rebellion was put down.'

Arzaky got up suddenly, as if he had remembered something urgent.

'We'll talk tonight in the parlour. Today's topic will be the enigma. The detectives and assistants will all be there, although of course the assistants are not allowed to speak. I know how you Argentines are, so I feel obliged to offer you some advice: practise keeping silent.'

FOUR

I spent the morning writing letters to my parents and to Mrs Craig. I preferred not to write to the detective himself out of fear that my letter would be left, unopened and unread, on some desk of the now abandoned Academy. I took several long walks during the day, fighting off the feeling that I was in the wrong place. Craig had sent me to help Arzaky, but the Pole didn't seem to want any help. I waited, anxiously, for the hours to pass so it would be time to go to the hotel and meet the Twelve Detectives, who were actually eleven, and who would soon be ten.

I went out dressed in a brand-new suit, a wide-brimmed hat and a vicuna poncho that my mother had insisted I bring. Wearing the hat made me very happy: I had owned it for a while already, but in Buenos Aires I couldn't use it, because just wearing a hat like that on your head was enough to be taken for a knave and challenged to a knife duel. Since I had taken some fencing classes, it didn't seem right for me to accept such challenges, and I avoided wearing it so as not to be lead into temptation. In Paris the hat had no meaning whatsoever.

As I entered the Numancia Hotel, where the detectives were staying, a tall black man in a blue uniform blocked my way. But all I had to do was say Arzaky's name and he stepped to one side, almost reverently. I thought that there was no greater glory in life than making your own name a secret password capable of changing minds and opening doors. I went down to the parlour with the pleasure that conspirators must feel with the thought of every secret and symbol that proves they are involved in something beyond the trivial.

The detectives were seated in the centre of the subterranean parlour. Around them were the assistants, some in chairs, others standing. They nodded their heads in greeting, and I responded with the typical nervousness of someone who bursts into a meeting and worries that they're too early, or late, or inappropriately dressed.

Arzaky stood up and said, 'Before we begin, gentlemen, I would like to remind you that my cases are still empty and awaiting your artefacts. This Fair is a celebration of your intelligence, not your indifference.'

'We'll send our brains in formaldehyde,' said a detective whose hands were covered in bright rings with coloured stones. From his accent, I guessed that it was Magrelli, the Eye of Rome.

'In my case, I'll send the brain of my assistant Dandavi, who increasingly does my thinking for me,' said Caleb

Lawson. Tall, with a big nose, he looked at the world through the smoke of his meerschaum pipe, which was shaped like a question mark. He was identical to the illustrations that accompanied his adventures.

'What could we display?' asked Zagala, the Portuguese detective. 'A magnifying glass? Our work is abstraction, logic. We are the only profession with nothing to show, because our most precious instruments are invisible.'

There was a murmur of agreement, until Arzaky's voice rose above it.

'I didn't know I was in a meeting of purists. Magrelli, you have the largest archive of criminal anthropology in Italy, supervised by Cesare Lombroso himself. And that's not to mention the delicate instruments that you use to measure ears, skulls and noses. Are they invisible, as Zagala says? And you, Dr Lawson, you never leave London without your portable microscope. If you only had one, I wouldn't ask you to lend it, but I know that you collect them. You even have microscopes that can only be seen with a microscope! And you've been acquiring those optical instruments that let you work in the fog for years.' Arzaky pointed to a tall man, who was winding his watch. 'Tobias Hatter, a native of Nuremberg, has given our trade at least forty-seven toys, rumours of which provoke dread in even the worst German criminals. When the killer Maccarius threatened you with a butcher's knife, didn't you let an innocent toy soldier open fire? Wasn't it you who designed a music box whose melody tormented murderers' sleepless nights and forced them to confess? And Sakawa, where is my invisible friend Sakawa . . .?'

The Japanese detective appeared out of nowhere. He was white-haired, much shorter than his assistant Okano and so thin he couldn't have weighed more than a boy.

'Don't you usually contemplate the stones in your Sand Garden, and the Screen of Twelve Figures, to help you think? Aren't your thoughts led by the demons painted on the screen?'

The Japanese detective bowed his head as an apology and said, 'I like the empty cases: they say more about us than all the instruments we could fill them with. But I know that won't sit well with the curious souls who come to visit our little exhibition. I devoted many hours of thought to what I should put in the space allotted to me, but I still haven't decided. I don't want to come across as eccentric. I'd prefer to show something more . . .'

'I know. You, from the East, want to show something Western; Lawson, who works with science, would be satisfied with something stripped of all scientific rigour; Tobias Hatter doesn't want to be taken for a toy maker and instead gives me nothing. You're all hiding your secrets, and I'm stuck with empty cases.'

I edged close to Baldone and, whispering, asked him to identify the detectives. Many I knew from the magazines I read in Buenos Aires, which compiled their exploits with hagiographic devotion. But seeing them in person wasn't the same as looking at the ink drawings that illustrated the *Key to Crime* and *Suspicion*.

The artists usually emphasized one feature or expression, yet, in the parlour, each face said many things at once.

Up until now they had all been speaking in a playful, slightly exaggerated tone, but suddenly a serious, impatient voice was heard.

'Sirs, you may be on vacation, but this is my city and I still have to work just like any other day.'

The man who had spoken was about sixty years old, with white hair and beard. While all the others had some exotic touch to their attire, as if they wanted to be recognized as exceptional beings, this veteran detective was indistinguishable from any other Parisian gentleman.

'That's Louis Darbon,' said Baldone into my ear. 'Arzaky and Darbon have both claimed the title Detective of Paris. But since Arzaky is Polish, he faces a lot of resistance. Some time ago, Arzaky proposed they each take one side of the Seine, but Darbon refused.'

'We understand your situation, and your shock at our appetite for leisure, and we'll forgive your early departure, Monsieur Darbon,' said Arzaky with a smile.

Darbon approached Arzaky defiantly. They were almost the same height.

'Before leaving I want to express my displeasure at the way things are being handled. What are all these meetings that you insist on having? Should we bow down before methodology? Are we priests of a new cult? A sect? No, we are detectives, and we have to show results.'

'Results aren't everything, Monsieur Darbon. There is a beauty in the enigma that sometimes makes us forget the result . . . Also we need a bit of leisure, after-dinner chats. We are professionals, but there is no detective that isn't also a bit of a dilettante. We are travellers, driven by the winds of coincidence and distraction to the locked room that hides the crime.'

'Travellers? I'm no traveller, no foreigner, God help me. But I am in a hurry, and I am not going to argue with you, of all people, Arzaky, over principles or countries of origin.'

Louis Darbon made a general gesture of farewell. Arthur Neska, his assistant, moved to follow him, but Darbon made a spirited gesture that told him to stay.

'Darbon is leaving, but he wants to find out every word Arzaky says,' said Baldone into my ear.

A gentleman dressed in a white suit with bright blue detailing, more appropriate to a theatrical costume than to a detective's work attire, came forward. He clapped with reprehensible affectation; behind me I heard the acolytes' stifled laughter. I gestured to Baldone, silently asking him who it was.

'That's Anders Castelvetia.'

'The Dutchman?'

'Yes, Magrelli tried to block his acceptance as a full member, but it didn't work.'

Arzaky gave Castelvetia the floor.

'If you'll allow me, gentlemen, I'll be the first to talk about enigmas. And I will do so, if you'll forgive me, with a metaphor.'

'Go ahead,' said Arzaky. 'Free us from our obsession with invisible clues, cigarette butts and train schedules. And don't be embarrassed: during the day we worship syllogisms, but the night belongs to the metaphor.'

FIVE

Thus spoke Castelvetia:

'There is an oft-used image that best defines our work: the jigsaw puzzle. It's a cliché, but what is more akin to our investigations than the patient search for a hidden picture? We put the pieces together one by one, searching for the images or shapes that remind us of other images and shapes. Just when it seems that we are lost, we find the right piece, giving us a fleeting glimpse of the complete image. Who didn't do jigsaw puzzles as a child? Who doesn't feel now, while searching in alleys, beneath the moonlight or the green halo of the street-lights, that we are continuing our childhood games? With a board that has grown more complicated, and has expanded to fill entire cities.

'I remember the murder of Lucía Railor, a dancer with the National Theatre of Amsterdam: she was hanged in her dressing room with a prop rope. Prop revolvers don't fire, but prop ropes hang someone just as well as the real thing. It was one of the few locked-room cases that we've had in Amsterdam. The dressing room was locked from inside, the key was in the door. The dancer was found with the rope around her neck and her body was blocking the door. Since no one else could have entered the room, the police supposed that Lucía had hanged herself using the hook where she usually hung her coat; the weight of the body had eventually undone the rope. It was an unusual suicide, but in that period just forming a hypothesis, as mistaken as it might be, was a big step forward for the Amsterdam police. I asked myself the same question as always: if she was killed, how could the murderer have escaped? For days I scoured the room, as if it were an island and I the only inhabitant. I crawled along the floor . . .'

'In that white suit?' asked a snide voice I wasn't able to identify.

Castelvetia ignored the comment and continued.

'First I attended to the small things, then to the imperceptible ones, and finally to those that couldn't even be found with a magnifying glass. I put the pieces together like a jigsaw puzzle: remnants of tulips on the soles of the shoes Lucía wore during the performance, bits of thin glass, loose threads from a cotton rope, a book of poems, in French, by Victor Hugo that Lucía kept in a drawer. And the position of her body, by the door . . .'

Castelvetia paused, allowing the room to fall silent. I'm sure that each one of the detectives already had a hypothesis about the case, but they chose to keep quiet out of courtesy. The only sound was the scratching pencil of a man who looked as if he had slept in his clothes. He was overdressed, not only for the room's temperature but for the entire city's.

'Who's that man taking notes?' I asked Baldone. 'Castelvetia's acolyte?'

'No, that's Grimas, the editor-in-chief of *Traces*. He's going to publish a synopsis of our talks in his magazine. At least, until the fighting starts.'

At Craig's house I had seen an old copy of *Traces*. It was a lushly produced publication, printed on heavy paper, but I still preferred the *Key to Crime*, with its yellowing pages, crowded typography, and the ink drawings that had made such an impression on me as a child. I still remember the staring eyes of a hanged man, a trunk with a hand coming out of it, a woman's head in a hatbox . . .

'And how did the final picture emerge?' asked Caleb Lawson.

'I'll be brief, and go piece by piece. The bouquet of tulips: the killer, who was her ex-lover, the actor Roddelbach, used to bring her flowers. The trampled tulips showed that Lucía had decided to break up with him. The little pieces of glass: Roddelbach knocked the dancer out with ether, but the bottle broke and he wasn't able to pick up all the pieces. The threads of cord: after rendering her unconscious, Roddelbach put a rope around her neck and passed the other end of the rope over the door. The thin cord allowed the door to close easily. Once he was out of the room, he pulled on the cord, hanging the actress. The friction against the door and the frame made some threads come off. Roddelbach had used a very small dose of ether so that the woman would wake up when she felt the pain of the noose tightening around her neck. And that's how he did it.'

'I don't see what the French book had to do with it.'

'The book led me to investigate the dancer's true nationality. Lucía had passed herself off as Dutch to get the job, but she was French, and Roddelbach knew it. He reckoned that in her state of confusion she would try to open the door, as she would have in her home country: counterclockwise. But the old locks still used in Holland have a reverse mechanism. In trying to open the door, Lucía closed it. It was her final act. Roddelbach was so convinced of his plot's success that he didn't even bother to make up an alibi. It was almost as if he wanted to be caught. He thought, as so many murderers do, that the effectiveness of his plan guaranteed that his crime would go unpunished. Yet I have observed that it is often the impulsive crimes, committed in the heat of the moment, that are the most difficult to solve. Roddlebach's arrogance was the final piece of the puzzle.'

Castelvetia bowed his head like an actor after a performance and returned to his seat.

'A statement can be true or false, but a metaphor isn't subject to such verdicts. Which is why I will say that your metaphor is, if not false, at least inadequate,' said

Arzaky. 'In a jigsaw puzzle the image appears slowly: when the last piece is in place, we've already known for a while what the picture is. You give the impression of a gradual method, when actually the truth often comes to detectives like a revelation.'

'Speaking of revelations, I had forgotten you're a Catholic,' answered Castelvetia.

'I'm Polish, and everything that goes along with it.' Arzaky pointed at Magrelli, who raised his hand to speak, like a schoolboy.

'I agree with Arzaky: the revelation of an enigma is not a slow progression, although the path to it requires patience. I hate Milan and the Milanese, but there is a painter from that city named Arcimboldo, an underappreciated genius, whose paintings haunt me. Arcimboldo would paint a disorganized mound of different fruits, or monstrous flowers, or sea creatures. And within those decaying fruits, poisonous, carnivorous flowers, or fish, octopi, and crabs, we discover a human face. For a moment we see the objects, and then suddenly the face emerging: the nose, the eyes, the gaze; and then, in the next moment we see only flowers or fruit. His paintings hang in Prague in the emperor's cabinet of wonders. I had to look into it because of a murder I'd rather not remember. They look like the work of a magician interested in optical illusions and in the fine line between magnetism and repulsion. That is how the enigma is for us; not a progressive journey, but a leap, a complete change of perspective. We gather details until we see that they trace a hidden figure.'

Magrelli stood up. Baldone, proud of his detective, nudged me with his elbow, as if to say, *Here comes the good part.*

'Eight years ago, a series of painting thefts shocked Venice. The important families kept very valuable paintings in their homes, but the thief had consistently chosen minor works that hung in peripheral rooms, rarely used hallways, or servants' bedrooms, works that were easy to steal. When the thefts continued unabated, I was called in. The owners of the paintings were not as upset about the value of the stolen works as they were about the thief's persistence. I consider myself an expert in fine art, but nevertheless, no matter how many times I read the list of stolen works, I couldn't understand the thief's motives. A seascape by an unknown British painter; St Mark's Basilica painted by some duke's uncle, whose intentions were better than his results; the portrait of a bishop that no one remembered any more; some goats grazing at dusk (it's always dusk in bad paintings). I tried to imagine those works and discover something in them, but I wasn't making any progress. I couldn't solve the case until the paintings became invisible to me.'

'They already were invisible – they'd been stolen,' interjected Caleb Lawson.

Magrelli looked at him with annoyance.

'But I had filled my head with descriptions of them and they were hanging in the gallery of my mind. So just as I was able to make myself see them, I stopped seeing them. Renato Craig called this the detective's blindness, the ability to stop seeing the obvious in order to discover what lies behind it. I stopped paying attention to the descriptions of the paintings and I focused on the frames. Again and again they were ornate mouldings, the gold worked with bitumen to make it look aged. All of the paintings had been framed by Egidio Vicci, whose work hardly varied. I'll spare you the details: I soon discovered that Vicci was none other than Cornelio Valgrave, famous forger and art thief. Valgrave had stolen the Tabbia collection ten years earlier: a fatal flaw led the police to suspect him. Since he knew that sooner or later they would find him, Valgrave decided to place the stolen pieces behind the bad paintings that arrived in his workshop. Behind the bishop's face, or the goats, or the Venetian basilica, there was a Giorgione, a Veronese and a Titian. When the police had him cornered, the thief turned himself in without revealing where the paintings were hidden. The police searched his house and his friends' and family's houses: they never found anything. When Valgrave got out of prison he hired a band of thieves to recover the booty. I would never have discovered it if I hadn't reversed my perspective. We always have to do this in order to solve an enigma, remembering Arcimboldo's repulsive paintings.'

There was a low murmuring; I don't know if it was approval or confusion. By this point, the assistants that surrounded me were bored, and anxiously awaiting the moment they could go back to their hotel. In my mind I tried to match the assistants with their detectives: Anders Castelvetia's wasn't there, and never had been;

Benito had taken advantage of a moment's distraction to disappear; the German, Linker, stood his ground; Baldone, in spite of the devotion that he had shown for his mentor, had chosen an isolated armchair in which to fall asleep.

SIX

Madorakis, the Athenian detective, stood up to speak.

'I'd like to thank our good Arzaky for the idea of this symposium,' he said, 'but according to the rules, we must have wine. The ancient Greeks would never have dared converse with their throats dry.'

Arzaky gestured and a waiter, who was standing in the doorway, went to get drinks. Madorakis continued, 'I have heard people talk about jigsaw puzzles many times, but I have never understood what they had to do with our trade, except in terms of patience, something we strive for but often lack. With regard to the paintings of that Milanese artist, I'm not familiar with them. My knowledge of art is limited. But perhaps you will allow me to add an element to our conversation, a venerable image that still has something to tell us: the sphinx.

'Oedipus was our predecessor: he investigated a crime

that, unbeknownst to him, he himself was guilty of. That is something we shouldn't forget: we have an eye for that which is foreign to us, but are blind to the familiar. Let's leave the crime and the crossroads for a moment and focus on the following scene: Oedipus wants to enter the plague-besieged city to find the sphinx, who offers each of her visitors a riddle, an enigma. What is the creature that walks on four legs in the morning, on two at noon, and on three legs in the evening? Oedipus shrewdly answered, 'man', and in doing so finished off that sphinx. That one, and all of the others, because we haven't heard anything from a sphinx since. We can say that, as a man, he was the answer, and would also be the answer to the second enigma, the crime at the crossroads. But let me say something more: the sphinx poses questions, but at the same time she herself is a riddle. We ask questions of enigmas and vice versa. Gentlemen, though we want to live in glass bubbles, to use pure reason, to interrogate witnesses without ever being interrogated, we are always surrounded by questions, and we answer them – subconsciously, through our actions. Through our investigative methods, we show who we are. It is us and not the poets who aspire to live in ivory towers, but time and time again we come down to earth, and we reveal, without realizing it, our worst secrets.

'Sometime around 1868 a rich merchant was killed in an Athens hotel. He was found in his bed, with a knife from the hotel kitchen in his heart. He had been murdered in the middle of the night, and since no one had entered the hotel at that time, it was assumed that the guilty party was one of the guests. Nothing had been stolen, in spite of the fact that the dead man was quite rich and there were plenty of valuables in his suite. The merchant's widow immediately contacted me for help. I went round to the hotel, where the Athens police were detaining all of the guests. Anyone could have easily got into the dead man's room; the spare key was kept in a drawer in the office. There was no danger that the night watchman would wake up; he slept very soundly and only opened his eyes when a bronze bell was rung. Although any of the hotel guests could have been the killer, none of them had a motive.

'I gave the widow a list of everyone staying in the hotel, to see if she recognized any of the names. A glance was enough for her to tell me that only one of the names was familiar to her: Basilio Hilarion, but she couldn't remember how she knew him. This Basilio Hilarion had stayed alone in a room on the third floor. I went to see him. He received me kindly and gave brief, but complete, answers to all my questions. He had been born in Athens, but lived in Thessaloniki; he was an importer of South American tobacco, and his commercial interests didn't compete with the victim's. They didn't live near each other either, so rivalry over a woman was unlikely. He said he'd never met the merchant.

'I went to see the widow and tell her about my interview with Hilarion. She still hadn't been able to work out who he was. She showed me a trunk that had been locked for years and held the dead man's entire past:

medals he had won in his youth, family keepsakes, school notebooks, wrinkled letters. It was in an old letter that I found Hilarion's name.

'They had been classmates. Only a few days after meeting they became inseparable friends. But, when he was thirteen years old, the dead man had seriously offended Hilarion, who had sent him a letter in which he seemed, at once, angry about the friendship ending and truly hurt by it. Shortly after, Hilarion had changed schools and they never saw each other again. I mentioned the incident to the widow and she agreed with me that Hilarion was almost certainly innocent. Who would kill someone over a comment that was made when they were thirteen years old? I left her house empty handed.

'You all know the sibyl's message: Know thyself. I walked back to my house, it was a melancholy walk: those old letters, locked up in a trunk, had filled me with sadness. One day we will all be just a bundle of letters stowed away. I suddenly remembered an episode from my life that I hadn't thought of in years and which surely, had it not been for this unique case, would never have crossed my mind again. When I was thirty years old, I took the steamship that goes from Pireo to Brindisi. I was obsessed with a romantic problem and, in spite of the cold rain, wanted to be alone at the deck rail, far from the crowd inside. Then, standing about ten feet away from me, I saw another young man who was as alone as I was. He had been a schoolmate of mine, and had christened me with a nickname that I won't reveal. It tormented me for years. In time, however, I managed to forget everything: the teasing I suspected my classmates of, the boy who invented the nickname, even the nickname itself. The ancient Greeks spoke of the art of memory, but I believe that there is only one true art: forgetting. I had erased it from my mind, but when I saw my former schoolmate just those few feet away, the hatred rushed back to me, intact. He still hadn't seen me; at that moment I resolved to kill him. Those crimes that are decided in a split second, "crimes of passion", are, in many ways, the most premeditated of them all: they take a lifetime to foment.

'My former chum was a scrawny man, and I, as you can see, while short, am quite strong. I could easily throw him over the rail and no one would notice. No one would hear his screams amidst the sea's crashing waves. I was almost upon him when a young girl came running over, calling out to him. My old enemy, who was obviously the girl's father, answered her call and started towards her. Only then did I realize what I had been considering. My enemy disappeared from my sight and my life for ever.

'The hotel guests, held against their will, were finally allowed to leave. Hilarion was packing his suitcase when I went to see him. I told him the story of my trip to Brindisi. He listened patiently, without interrupting. When I finished, he made a gesture of acceptance, not defeat, and revealed the truth to me.

'Basilio Hilarion was having dinner, alone, in the hotel's dining hall when he noticed that a man near the window was his old childhood friend. Throughout the dinner he watched the man eat and drink voraciously. He, on the other hand, couldn't choke down anything. Hilarion couldn't take his eyes off him. He was not as fascinated by this man that devoured everything in sight as he was by the discovery, in his own heart, of a fury that was as alive on that day as it had been forty years ago. And now, Hilarion knew that his entire life (the constant travelling that allowed him to escape his marriage, his interest in astronomy, a lover who had begun to bore him) had been nothing more than an accumulation of unreal things, compared to the clarity of that hatred. In that fury there was something pure and true that was more real than his everyday life. That hate was him.

'For many years, the fabric merchant's offence (Hilarion never said what it was) had given him chronic insomnia. In time he had learned to sleep well, but that night his insomnia returned. He realized that, almost as if it were a game, he had to plan the crime: he stole a sharp knife from the dining room and followed the victim to his room, but did nothing. This is all a joke, he told himself when he returned to his own room, I'm no killer. He tried in vain to sleep; all night long he just tossed and turned. His usual cures were useless: eating an apple, drinking a glass of milk, taking a hot bath, taking a few drops of an amber-coloured opiate he always carried with him. All useless. At four in the morning, he slipped past the sleeping night watchman, stole the key, then went up to room 36 and murdered his old friend with a single thrust of the blade. He felt guilty about only one thing: he should have told him why he was killing him. It seemed fair that the victim ought to know that his execution was a consequence of his prior actions. When he returned to his room, Hilarion took off his bloody clothes, which he got rid of the next morning, and slept soundly.'

'We appreciate the gift of Madorakis's story,' said Arzaky. 'The next time I travel to Warsaw and come across my old classmates, I'll make sure not to turn my back on them. Who will we hear from next?'

SEVEN

Tobias Hatter, the detective from Nuremberg, came forward and placed a child's small cardboard drawing slate on the table. Then he scribbled on it with a wooden stick. Next, as if it were a magic trick, he removed the sheet of cardboard from its frame, and returned it to the table. The scribble had disappeared.

'Last year a manufacturer of notebooks and paper from Nuremberg brought these boards on to the market. They called them Aladdin's blackboard: as you can see, one can write on them without ink and everything erases immediately. The trick isn't in the little stick but in the board itself: it is a sheet that is put in contact with another black sheet behind it: at the points where the two sheets touch, a drawing appears on the surface. Now, if we take this device apart (don't be alarmed, it only costs a few cents) we see the black acetate sheet. All the marks disappear, but the deepest ones leave a trace on this black page. Some of the erased drawings leave a mark, and those marks together form a secret drawing. Thus, gentlemen, is the relationship between enigmas and their revelation. On the surface, we incessantly gather facts, clues, and words. Who among us can say they've never felt apprehension over the vast amount of trivia that crowds our sight? In the theatre, detectives always say, "Good heavens, the killer has left no clues," but in real life that's not what happens: we are nearly driven crazy by the quantity of clues and the task of sifting through them. And we, slaves to method and intuition, sometimes scratch the surface filled with inconsequential marks – those marks the police earn their salary on – in order to discover the hidden truth.

'I learned the rudiments of my trade in Nuremberg. There is a street in the old quarter where the bulk of the second-hand book trade is concentrated. One of those shops is called Rasmussen's; I was twenty-two when the owner, Ernst Rasmussen, was shot and killed. His son had been a comrade of mine in the army; we served in the same unit. I had never solved a case, I foresaw a military future for myself, but I was very fond of riddles – which I made up and solved easily – perhaps that was why my friend called me to help him find out who had murdered his father.

'Old Rasmussen had died of a bullet to the chest. The killer had surprised him after midnight during a raging thunderstorm. The bookseller didn't usually work so late, but he had said that he would stay to examine a batch of religious books he had bought from the widow of a Lutheran pastor. Fatally wounded, Rasmussen had grabbed a book with both hands, as if he wanted to take some reading material along on his trip. I asked his son Hans about this gesture, and he responded, "My father dealt in all kinds of old books, but his favourites were the children's stories. He was very fond of the Brothers Grimm, the second volume of the 1815 edition. In spite of his violent death, I like to think that my father was showing a final gesture of his love for books."

'His son didn't share that love; he had always preferred less cerebral activities. It was clear that he was destined to follow in the footsteps of so many adventurous types who end up ruining their lives over a woman, or the gambling table in Baden-Baden. The kind that happily receive the news that war has been declared, because in those distant skirmishes they believe they have found some sort of order, a destiny that they are incapable of creating with their own actions. So Hans knew little about his father's business, and he couldn't tell me if anything important was missing. I searched for clues: there was nothing out of the ordinary, except for the muddy footprints left by the killer, the bookseller himself, and the police. I sat in a chair facing the table where the bookseller had been killed and I began to flip through the book by the Brothers Grimm.

'I know the Grimms' work well. Nowadays we think of the brothers as inseparable, like a bust of Janus, but during their lifetime they were quite different. Jacob was a philologist, he faithfully recorded popular folk stories and sought to publish them just as he had heard them, without worrying that some made no sense. Wilhelm, on the other hand, wanted the stories to be edited, expanded upon, and improved. He didn't care so much about being faithful to the anonymous voices as he did to the integrity of storytelling itself. And he kept making changes, in the successive editions, each time taking the stories further and further from their whispered origins.

'I held the book in my palm, and felt tempted on one hand to be like Wilhelm, and let the story end tidily with the bookseller, fatally wounded and unable to call anyone or to write a note, making his last gesture a declaration of his love for books. But on the other hand I felt inclined to follow Jacob's example, and remain faithful to what I had found, the footprints. In that spirit I began to leaf through the volume.

'Books always contain secrets. We leave things between their pages and forget about them: lottery tickets, newspaper clippings, a postcard we've just received. But there are also flowers, leaves that attracted us with their shape, or insects trapped in a paragraph's snare. This edition had all of those things, each marking a different page. Remember the example of Aladdin's blackboard: the surface is filled with marks, but one has to discover the deeper marks, those underneath.

'And I soon found such a mark. It was a page's folded corner. In another book or another situation, that wouldn't have surprised me, but I guessed that a bookseller like Rasmussen would never have folded over the page of a first edition of the Brothers Grimm without a very good reason. So I studied it with particular interest.

'The Brothers Grimm had included some riddles that were taken out of later editions, perhaps because they weren't exactly stories. One told of three women who had all been turned into flowers by a witch. One of them, however, was able to recover her human form at night in order to sleep at home with her husband. Once, as dawn approached, she told him, "If you go to the field to see the three flowers and you can tell which one is me, pull me up and I will be freed from the spell." And the next day her husband went to the field, recognized his wife and saved her. How did he do it, when the three flowers were identical? There was a blank space, to allow the reader time to come up with his own answer. The story ended with this explanation: since the woman spent the night at home instead of in the field, no dew fell on her, and that was how her husband knew her.

'Because of that story I was able to find the killer. The police had identified a suspect named Numau, a man who went from town to town buying up rare books cheaply and then reselling them to the bibliophiles of Berlin. But no one had seen Numau leave the hotel that night. And the police had searched through his clothes without finding anything damp. If any of his clothes had got wet in the storm, Numau had disposed of them, along with the murder weapon.

'The captain in charge of the case let me accompany him on a visit to Numau. Nothing there was damp: no boots or any articles of clothing. But when I searched through his books, Numau went pale: I came across a bible, printed in a monastery in Subiaco by Gutenberg's disciples. Numau's pockets weren't big enough to protect the book, and it was swollen and wrinkled with moisture. He confessed: Rasmussen had refused to sell that edition; he already had a good buyer for it. So he decided to steal the book during the night. Rasmussen, who was working late, surprised him. Numau got frightened and shot him.

'"How did you find me?" the killer asked before he was taken away by the police. I showed him the volume of the Brothers Grimm. "This book showed me that one has to learn to tell the wet from the dry." "As a child, this was my favourite," said Numau. "If any book had to bring me down, I'm glad it was this one."'

Arzaky took Tobias Hatter's toy and amused himself for a few seconds, making drawings and then erasing them.

'This is like my memory. I erase everything in seconds.'

'But something remains on the black sheet, Detective Arzaky,' said Hatter.

'I hope so.'

Sakawa came forward and handed Arzaky what appeared to be an urgent message. It was a blank page.

'What's this? Invisible ink?'

'An enigma. This is what the enigma always is for us: a blank page.'

'What do you mean?' asked Rojo, the Spanish detective. 'That we don't actually do any investigating? That we make it all up? Why, they've even gone so far as to accuse me of inventing my fight with the giant octopus!'

'No, of course not. But the mystery isn't hidden at some unattainable depth; it's right on the surface. We are the ones that make it what it is. We slowly construct the facts; they become a riddle. We are the people who say that one mysterious death is more important than a thousand men lying dead on a battlefield. This shows us the Zen of the enigma: there is no mystery, there is only a void and we make the mystery. Our desire for this, not the movements of killers in the night, guides our footsteps. Perhaps we should set aside crimes for a moment, forget about guilty suspects. Haven't we realized that we all see different things in the same mystery? Perhaps, in the end, there is nothing to see. And even more so in my case than in each of yours. As you all know, my speciality is finding something more ephemeral than the enactor of poisonings, gunshot wounds or stabbings; I search for what we call grasshopper hunters.'

'Grasshopper hunters?' asked Rojo. 'Are you sure that's what you meant to say?'

'I didn't misspeak. Grasshopper hunters are what we call those who incite others to take their own lives. They are the subtlest type of killers. I'll explain the origin of the name a little later.'

As he spoke, Sakawa slowly, and almost casually, moved towards the centre of the room.

'Grasshopper hunters kill without weapons. Sometimes they do it with a few lines published in a newspaper; other times it's an insidious comment or a gesture made with a fan. There are those who have murdered with a poem. And I have devoted my life to the subtle hunt for those who leave grasshoppers. But sometimes I ask myself: What if I've been mistaken about all this from the very beginning? Perhaps I should let men commit suicide, and not try to alter the course of things. Was I finding a puzzle to solve in behaviour that wasn't mysterious in the least, in people who were fated from birth to their unique deaths? I don't have nightmares about crime; I dream about the blank page, I dream that I am the one who draws the ideograms where there was nothing, where there should always be nothing. And that is what I want to ask you all: Should we be not only the solvers of mysteries, but also the custodians of the enigma? Our Greek colleague gave Oedipus and the sphinx as an example. I say we are both Oedipus and the sphinx. The world is becoming an open book. We must be the defenders of evidence, the exterminators of doubt, but also the last guardians of mystery.'

Sakawa's words left the detectives perplexed. If he had been a Westerner, they would have argued with him.

'Tell us about a case,' said Arzaky. 'Maybe that way we can understand what you mean.'

'A boastful display of my skill is unworthy of this forum. I will tell of a case that is not mine, and that way you will know why we call them grasshopper hunters.'

While Sakawa spoke, his assistant, Okano, bowed his head as a sign of respect.

'Mr Huraki was the manager of a bank in the city of S. I won't say the name of the city. In the spring it's overrun with grasshoppers, but the inhabitants of the region refuse to kill them, believing they are good luck. A large sum of money disappeared from the bank; Mr Huraki was not accused of stealing it. When the police showed up at his office they found no evidence that incriminated him, and the only thing that drew their attention to him was that Huraki was extremely nervous and accidentally stepped on a grasshopper that had come in through the window. Huraki's accountant, Mr Ramasuka, whose reputation was spotless up until that point, was put in prison. He confessed to nothing, nor did he accuse anyone else; he spent the years he was locked up reading the old masters.

'Time passed. Ramasuka finished his sentence. By then Huraki was the director of a bank in Tokyo. Ramasuka was determined to take his revenge, but he couldn't imagine himself brandishing a sword or taking up a firearm. All that reading, all that thinking he had done wasn't to fill his head with ideas, but rather to clear his mind of trivial ideas and meaningless prejudices. He had learned to see what others overlook. Taking advantage of an open window, he entered Huraki's house one night: he didn't touch a thing; he just left a grasshopper in the middle of the room, on top of the tatami. Before dawn, the grasshopper's singing awoke Huraki. The banker instantly remembered a verse by a poet from his city (this memory was part of Ramasuka's plan):

The grasshopper you killed in your dream
Sings again in the morning.

'Huraki knew that he had been discovered. He killed himself that very night, by drinking poison.'

The waiter, who had served wine to the detectives and water to the assistants, as dictated by the Twelve Detectives' protocol, offered a glass of wine to the old detective, who refused it.

'Thus Ramasuka established the tradition of the grasshopper hunters: men and women capable of killing with insinuations, signs, invisible traces. But these warriors need a symmetrical oppositional force. I am part of that force. We don't send them to prison, of course, because no judge legislates on grasshoppers and butterflies and poems with secret meanings. But we write and publish our verdicts, and we often drive those responsible to disgrace, exile, silence, sometimes death. But I wonder: what if the enemy is completely imaginary? What if I perceive this enemy – these men and women that conspire in a tradition of subtle murderers – only in my mind? What if I become the murderer by exposing them?'

With small steps Sakawa moved out of the centre of the room. Magrelli pointed mockingly at Arzaky, who was seated in an armchair and seemed to be either concentrating very intensely or sleeping.

'Well, Arzaky, you are the one who organized all this. Now you've got some objects for your glass cases. Which one will you choose to represent our profession?

Incomplete jigsaw puzzles, paintings that fuse fruit and faces, a Greek monster and an inquisitive sphinx, Aladdin's blackboard, a blank page – which one will it be?'

Arzaky suppressed a yawn.

'He who speaks last always has an advantage: the sound of his voice still echoes. But apart from that, I choose Sakawa. I also fear that all investigation is a blank page.'

EIGHT

In spite of my exhaustion, it took me a while to fall asleep. I was surrounded by unfamiliar things, and my mind tried in vain to adapt to the continuous introduction of new ideas, people, and settings. Sleep refused to come, because there were too many things to dream about. I thought about what was said at the meeting: the detectives' statements, the assistants' covert remarks. Time and time again I imagined myself escaping the outer circle of the satellites, and walking with sure steps towards centre stage. I was immensely lucky to be an acolyte, to have been given the chance to meet the Twelve Detectives, and that was enough for me during the day. But at night I wanted more.

I finally slept for several hours, although I had the feeling that I had barely shut my eyes. I was awoken by noises outside the room: people running, and then doors slamming and voices. I washed up, shaved off my shadow of a beard, and dressed. I went out into the hallway still adjusting the knot in my tie. Linker, Tobias Hatter's assistant, bumped into me and kept running without saying a word, as if he had collided with one of those room service trolleys. Benito came charging up behind him.

'They've killed Louis Darbon,' gasped Benito as he passed me.

I thought I must still be dreaming; nobody could have killed one of the detectives. Weren't they immortal? Weren't they immune to silent swords, to ice darts shot through locks and perfect roses with poisoned thorns?

I followed them down the stairs and then into the street. The morning was cool. I had taken the precaution of bringing my vicuna poncho. I secretly regretted having missed breakfast; it's the only thing I like about staying in hotels. The assistants had all left Madame Nécart's hotel at almost the same time and were running towards the entrance to the Fair. We would bunch up together, looking like a group of long-distance runners, and then we would spread out again, separated by the obstacles posed by the future World's Fair: carts that carried materials to the tower, an iron cage that held a rhinoceros, fifty Chinese soldiers as still as statues awaiting the orders of an absent captain.

It took us a full twenty minutes to reach the foot of the wrought-iron tower. Journalists and photographers pushed each other, jockeying for position, in some sort of collective dance. The morgue ambulance waited to one side, pulled by stolid, pensive horses.

I wanted to see the corpse, but the crowd was impenetrable. Arzaky made his way over to me, shouting.

'You, the Argentine, come here.'

I elbowed my way over to an area that was only accessible to a chosen few. I wouldn't have been able to break through the crowd if Arzaky's voice hadn't cleared the way, pulling me towards him like a rope. The photographers' flashbulbs exploded over the dead man's face and the air was filled with the bitter smell of magnesium.

'Now I have a case, but I don't have an assistant. I am the only detective without one. That may be a custom in your savage country, but in my city it is an oddity. I want you to work with me. Observe everything carefully. Any comment that occurs to you, make it: there is no greater inspiration for a detective than the frivolous words of the hoi polloi.'

'What happened?'

'Darbon was investigating the tower's opponents, who had recently sent hundreds of anonymous letters and caused some minor incidents. He came here at night, alone, following a clue; he fell from the second platform. We don't know anything more. Do you accept?'

'Do I accept what?'

'Working as my assistant.'

'Of course I accept!' I exclaimed, surprised. Without meaning to, I had shouted my reply and, in spite of the racket, everyone turned to look at me. I had become an acolyte thanks to Craig, who had sent me to Paris, to Alarcón, who gave his life, and thanks to Arzaky, who accepted me; but also thanks to Darbon who was now being lifted off the ground by the morgue employees (grey uniforms, flannel hats) with a mixture of ceremony and annoyance, to be transferred to the realm of deciphering and dissection.

NINE

Two hours later we managed to get permission to enter the morgue, leaving behind the journalists and onlookers, who were crowded together behind the railing, waiting for some extraordinary revelation. Arzaky knew the building well. I would have got lost in the labyrinthine series of hallways which always turned to the left and stairs which always went down, but the Pole moved forward with giant strides, exuding that crazy joy of a detective on a case. It was as if, with each step, he was taking the world by force. But when he entered the room he lowered his head, as though he were in a cathedral. His face reflected both humility and defiance, like a saint who finds dissipation in temperance, overindulgence in moderation, ecstasy in renunciation.

There were nine empty gurneys and one that was occupied lined up beneath the greenish light of the lamps that swung from the very high ceilings. A strong smell of bleach and maybe camphor hung in the air. Darbon's body, already undressed, had a lunar whiteness to it that was marred by the lacerations and bruises caused by his fall. Of his numerous authoritative features (his imposing voice; the gravitas that never deigned to smile, unless it was ironic; the gaze that dissolved any obstacle) the only surviving one was his white beard.

The forensic doctor was a tiny man, named Godal. He greeted Arzaky with a familiarity that was not returned. The Detective of Paris (now without any rival to dispute the title) half-heartedly introduced his colleagues that were also there: Hatter, Castelvetia and Magrelli. I was the only assistant in the room.

'It is an honour for me to have members of the Twelve Detectives here,' said Dr Godal, looking at everyone except me.

'I imagine that this case is something new for you, as it is for us. No one has ever fallen from so high,' said Hatter with the air of an expert.

'What are you saying, Hatter?' said Arzaky, in a very rude tone. 'Do you think there are no bodies in the crevices of the Alps?'

'There must be . . . but no one has ever seen them.'

'I have.'

Godal began to point out the marks from the fall.

'Observe the destroyed legs; this proves he was conscious when he fell. His feet plunged into the earth. Halfway down he hit some kind of protrusion, which tore his skin at the height of the thorax but didn't kill him.'

Castelvetia was ashen and looked around as if searching for a window.

'Come closer. When I was young, we practised autopsies outdoors. We had to rush to make use of the sunlight, before night fell and erased all the details.'

'Do bodies come in every week?' asked Hatter.

'Every week? Every day. A thousand a year: suicides, accident fatalities, murder victims. Lately there has been an increase in poisonings: we've done about a hundred and forty autopsies already this year. We have to be very careful with poison: in the old days they stuck to arsenic, which we can easily identify, but now they're forever coming up with new poisons.'

Arzaky picked up the dead man's hand. He pointed to one of the fingernails. There was something black underneath it.

'Louis Darbon was fastidious about his appearance. Why are his nails dirty?'

'I'm sorry, his hands were black with oil, and it took us a lot of work to clean them. But there's always a trace left behind!'

'A trace left behind? Everything is supposed to be left behind. How can we work if you clean up the evidence?'

'I didn't think it was important. It was oil. He fell from the tower, and I imagine that that horrible tower is full of machine oil.'

Arzaky was going to say something, but he held himself back. When he left the room, furious, I followed him. He banged his head against the wall several times.

'Incompetent! That damn Dr Godal was always on Darbon's side. He's a forensic doctor who ought to have been an undertaker. What do you think we should do?'

I was surprised that he asked for my opinion. What value could my thoughts on forensic practices have?

'I think we should go to the tower, to the place where Darbon fell. And see where that oil came from.'

'No, no. You are supposed to be an assistant. You should embody common sense. For example, you should say: "The oil isn't important. At the tower everything is oil-stained."'

'But I don't think that's the case.'

Arzaky hit his head against the wall one more time, but lightly.

'Tanner was always spot-on with his comments. Craig failed in his school for assistants. Wasn't there a professor of common sense?'

'I know I'm not as good as the other assistants, but I'll try my best to keep up.'

'The others? Don't worry about emulating your colleagues. The black man is a thief; the Andalusian, a liar; Linker, an imbecile; the Sioux never says anything. I don't even think he's real, I think he's a wax figure from Madame Tussaud's.'

'And Castelvetia's acolyte? I still haven't seen him.'

'You have just mentioned an awkward mystery. No one has seen him. I would leave it at that, but it's inevitable that someone will bring him up at our meetings. And between you and me, I don't think that fop Castelvetia has an assistant. If he does . . . he must not be the same kind of assistant the others are. You know what I mean. That's a mystery you could solve.'

His anger vented, Arzaky went back into the room. Dr Godal had turned the corpse over and was pointing to a wound on his back. Castelvetia, passed out on a metal chair, was being tended to by one of Godal's assistants, who was trying to bring him around with smelling salts.

'I swear, gentlemen, this is the first time this has ever happened to me,' he declared as soon as he came to.

Arzaky looked at me.

'I miss Craig,' he said.

TEN

That night the detectives reconvened in the subterranean parlour of the Numancia Hotel. Between those four walls their grief took strange forms: without removing his white hat, Jack Novarius took long strides from one side of the room to the other, while his Sioux assistant remained immobile; Castelvetia laughed openly; Hatter waited for the meeting to start while taking apart a small mechanism that looked like an artificial heart; Sakawa was arranging flowers in a vase, pulling out some petals and letting them fall on to the table. They were detectives, crime was their lifeblood, they couldn't be blamed for not shedding tears.

Only Arzaky seemed to be grieving.

'When Castelvetia goes out, follow him. I want to find out the truth about his assistant today.'

It was a job for a lackey, but I accepted it, even though

I didn't like the whole business. I didn't want to get involved in the gossip between detectives.

Arzaky took centre stage. The shelves of the glazed cabinets had begun to fill with objects: a giant magnifying glass, a microscope, a small metal filing case with photographs of delinquents, a pistol that shot tranquillizer darts, a hypnotizing machine. Off to one side, away from the other objects, was Craig's cane, its powers concealed. Arzaky spoke.

'As we all know, Louis Darbon died last night, falling from the stairs that led to the second platform of the tower. For the moment, nothing points to it having been anything but an accident.'

'And the railings?'

'They had been found to be defective and were being replaced.'

'Come on, Arzaky. Who can believe it was an accident?' said Hatter.

'I am going to be in charge of the case and when I know anything for certain, I will tell you.'

Caleb Lawson, tall and stooped, cloaked in the smoke from his pipe, stepped forward.

'I don't think you should be in charge of this case. We all know that Darbon despised you. If anyone is a suspect, it's you. Inspector Bazeldin has already been asking questions around here.'

'Shut up, Lawson!' said Magrelli indignantly. 'Arzaky is one of the founders of our order, along with Renato Craig. You can't go accusing him just because that idiot,

Inspector Bazeldin, was asking questions. Have you never read Grimas's magazine?'

In the pages of *Traces*, Inspector Bazeldin was always the butt of jokes. The clues he followed up on, which were the most obvious ones, always ended in failure.

'Darbon was also one of the Twelve Detectives,' said the Englishman. 'And someone pushed him from the tower. What's more, Arzaky, his death left all of Paris to you.'

Arzaky shrugged his shoulders. Sakawa, who rarely spoke, said, 'Arzaky should be in charge of the case. This is his city. What right do we have to investigate a crime in Paris? If someone was thrown from a tower in Tokyo, I wouldn't let any one of you investigate who incited the victim to jump.'

'In the West no one invites anyone to jump with flicks of their fan or seventeen-syllable poems, Sakawa,' said Lawson. 'Here, when someone wants to throw someone off a tower, they push him. We know that we have to investigate those who stand to benefit from Darbon's death. Why shouldn't we suspect Arzaky?'

The Japanese detective responded serenely. 'I am sure that if Arzaky is the murderer, he himself will follow every single one of the clues that lead to him and he will accuse himself of the crime.'

What Sakawa said didn't make any sense, but as often happens, nonsense is harder to refute than logical opinions.

Arthur Neska let his voice be heard.

'Arzaky hated my mentor, Louis Darbon. If you leave

the case in his hands, the guilty party will never be punished. Or an innocent man will pay.'

'The assistants must ask for special permission to speak, which is granted by their mentor,' said Hatter. 'Those are the rules.'

'My mentor is dead. I speak in his name.'

'It's okay, Hatter. Let him speak,' said Arzaky. 'These are exceptional circumstances. We can't always go by the rules. I'm going to be in charge of the case: I am not asking for your permission, because that is not incumbent on the Twelve Detectives. If you want to make inquiries on your own behalf, you may do so. But we shouldn't compete amongst ourselves. We should share our discoveries.'

There was a suspicious murmur.

'We don't know each other, Arzaky,' said Caleb Lawson. 'If there's one thing you can't ask of us, it's that we share what we know. For many long years we have cultivated secrecy and solitude; it is too late for us to become a Commune.'

Neska always had a gloomy air about him, and now that appearance was substantiated. He didn't speak with the humility appropriate to the acolytes. He even dared to give the detectives advice.

'You would be wise to watch your backs. I don't think anyone who finds out anything will live to see the dawn.'

'Be careful. Don't let your grief make you reckless. We have rules about expulsion as well,' warned Hatter.

'What are you going to expel me from? I no longer

have a detective to assist. The murderer has already expelled me.'

Arzaky, who until that point had spoken softly, now raised his voice.

'I am not going to respond to your foolish words. But I need Darbon's papers in order to begin my work. I want to know who he was investigating.'

Neska smiled defiantly at Arzaky.

'I left the whole lot in the hands of his widow. If you can convince her to give it to you, you'll have everything.'

Neska left the room without another word. We all, detectives and assistants, remained there in silence. And that moment was the only tribute that Louis Darbon received, the only moment in which his death weighed on the detectives' lives, not as an enigma, not as a morsel for their insatiable curiosity, but as a loss. With a solemnity that competed with the others' silence, Arzaky spoke.

'Perhaps Darbon did fall accidentally, perhaps it was some old enemy with a score to settle. But we have to consider another possibility. We have gathered here, in Paris, to display our trade among the other works of Man. And it is possible that one of our secret partners has taken this opportunity to challenge us. And thus display, not only the art of investigation, but the art of crime.'

PART THREE

The Tower's Opponents

ONE

The tower flaunted its blend of grandiosity and futility at the grey sky. It was made for cloudy days, to be seen through drops of rain, from far away. A few years later, at the 1900 World's Fair, surrounded by automobiles, it would already seem old, but as it was being built the tower projected an air of extravagance and surprise. It wasn't just its height that was exceptional, but the promise of its demise. That something so gigantic could disappear without some kind of cataclysm. Its transitory nature cast a shadow of fantasy around it; whispering in our ears that we shouldn't take life too seriously.

There is something coffin-like about lifts, a tendency towards the worlds below (volcanoes, mines, the dirt on Pluto). But the tower's lift rose effortlessly. It amazed me that it didn't fall. On that day the mechanism that went up to the second platform wasn't ready yet, so we got off at the first and continued our ascent to the scene of the crime on foot. Arzaky went ahead, and I struggled to keep up with his swift pace. I was very inexperienced back then, but even now, after having seen hundreds of crime scenes, I can say that nothing seemed further from a murder than the silence and tranquillity of that platform. I know that a match, a drop of blood, a stain on the wall, or a newspaper clipping can be signs that lead to the killer, but my first thought upon arriving at a crime scene is the utter meaninglessness of everything that remains in the face of death.

'Well, it seems we are dealing with a locked-room case,' said Arzaky. He wasn't even out of breath. 'In this case, the locked room happens to be outdoors. No one saw the killer come in or out.'

I remembered the now-deceased Alarcón maintaining that it made no sense to speak of a 'locked room'. I barely managed to put together a coherent sentence as I gasped for breath, but Arzaky seemed to understand.

'What authority are you citing?' he asked.

'Alarcón, Craig's original apprentice.'

'Did he solve many crimes?'

'No, he died on his first case.'

'Oh yes, I remember, he was killed by the magician. With all due respect for the dead, why are you repeating such foolishness? The locked room is the essence of our work. It doesn't matter if the room doesn't actually exist. We must accept its metaphorical power.'

We arrived at the second platform and went up a few more steps. After finding a flaw in the smelting, they had removed the protective railings and hadn't yet installed new ones. It was easy to see where Darbon had slipped and fallen, because the steps were covered with the same thick black liquid that Arzaky had found beneath the detective's nails.

'Be careful what you touch and where you step,' said Arzaky. 'There's oil everywhere.'

'And broken glass. Do you think the killer broke a bottle of oil over his head?'

'The killer made sure to be far from here when Darbon fell. He was an old man and had a lot of trouble climbing stairs. He used a cane, which only hid a small sword, not the myriad of surprises that Craig's has. The killer proposed a meeting up here, promising information about the attacks on the tower. Darbon was anxious to close that case before our next meeting.'

'But Darbon only took on the most important cases, murders; a few anonymous letters sent by a lunatic . . .'

'You're new to this city and you don't understand. You've barely seen anything of Paris besides this tower. To you, Paris is the tower. But those of us who live here have been watching its slow progress for two years. These struts and vertical irons have filtered into our dreams. Everyone feels compelled to shout either "yes" or "no!" about this matter, particularly because no one has asked their opinion. For some it is evil, for others the future, for the most pessimistic, it's both evil and the future.'

I didn't know where to lean, where to step. Everything was covered in black oil.

Arzaky's voice sounded remote, almost as if I were dreaming.

'If Darbon managed to solve this case, although it seemed simple on the face of it, his name would be in all the papers again; tied to the heart of Paris itself. He would have achieved the definitive victory over the interloper . . .'

'The interloper?'

'Me. He also used to call me "the damn Polish traitor".'

Arzaky reached into his pocket and pulled out a tiny pair of tweezers, tiny scissors, and a tiny metal box. They looked as if they belonged in a dollhouse. He carefully took a sample of the glass shards. I prayed he wouldn't get any oil on him, because then I'd have to put up with his bad temper. He pointed out a cord that was almost completely soaked in the black liquid, and cut off a piece with his miniature scissors. Arzaky put the cord and the glass into the metal box, which he then returned to his pocket.

'Do you understand the nature of this trap? The killer put a bottle of machine oil on the stairs. It's very thick oil, and made the steps impossibly slippery. Darbon went up without a lantern, perhaps according to the instructions of the killer himself, who must have set up this meeting with him. We should look for evidence of his correspondence. When Darbon's foot hit the cord, the bottle tipped over, spilling its contents on to the steps, causing him to slip and fall.'

'And how could someone get up here and set the trap without anyone seeing him?' I asked.

'At six o'clock the workers leave for the day and only the night watchman remains. Everyone knew that he liked to drink, and that afternoon he received a gift of two bottles, addressed to him from an anonymous benefactor. He drank them and passed out. He didn't see or hear anything.'

I pointed to a small puddle of oil a few stairs further up. Arzaky shone his lantern on it.

'I think the killer first considered placing the bottle higher up,' I said. 'He calculated the trajectory of the fall and decided to move it. In the process he accidentally spilled a little.'

Arzaky looked at me distastefully, as if it was annoying to him that I was pointing out some imperfection in the murder. But then he said, 'All the better for us. The killer must have stained his clothes, gloves or shoes. Have you got all this down?'

'You mean the bottle, the cord and the oil? I remember it perfectly.'

'And my words? Don't you think you should write down what I say?'

I hurried to find a notepad in my pocket. As I hastily took out a pencil it slipped from my fingers, bounced and fell into the void. I was suddenly aware of how high up we were. I peeked over the edge, and seeing how far below the ground was made my stomach turn and my hands and forehead began to sweat.

I tried to play off the loss of my pencil as an intentional experiment.

'They say that if you drop a coin from this height, the force of gravity increases the speed of its fall so much that it could go through a man's skull.'

'Don't be an idiot, you're forgetting about the air's resistance. And now what are you going to write with?'

I pointed to my forehead.

'Like a steel trap.'

'Old Tanner responded to each and every one of my sentences with an amazed "Oh" or a "That never would have occurred to me." You don't even pay attention. What are you looking at?'

I didn't answer right away.

'The whole city. Do you realize that I'm incredibly lucky? I just arrived in Paris and I'm observing it from a height that even those born here have never seen.'

'Get away from the edge, before you get even luckier: you could be the first foreigner to fall from up here.'

Avoiding the oil slick, we began our descent.

TWO

On the way back Arzaky seemed discouraged.

'Do you think this is a difficult case?' I asked him.

'Even the easiest case can get complicated. What worries me is not that it can't be solved, but rather that it will be solved in a trivial way. That in the end the solution will be something absurd. An indignant lover, a jealous husband, a crime of passion . . .'

'Don't you like crimes of passion?'

'No. I prefer envy, ambition, revenge – especially revenge, for something silly that everyone thinks has been forgotten. Even suicides that have been covered up. But not murders committed out of lust or insanity. There's nothing admirable in them. Those cases are purely formulaic. They have no poetry.'

Every once in a while, a passer-by turned to look at the great Arzaky, whose photograph often appeared in the newspaper. Arzaky walked briskly, oblivious to the attention.

'Now what are we going to do?'

'I don't know what *you're* going to do, but I'm going to rest. At six I have a meeting with the people from the Fair's organizing committee. And as for your other assignment, have you figured anything out?' I shook my head no and he continued, 'I was told that Castelvetia wrote the name Reynal in some hotel's register, but no one has seen him yet.'

'And what do you suspect?'

'Castelvetia was the last one to join the Twelve Detectives. Craig insisted on it. I was against it. Caleb Lawson detests him; they harbour a mutual grudge. When we issued the invitations, I double-checked his resumé. Most of his cases are impossible to verify. He could be an infiltrator, a journalist putting together information for an exposé of us, or an envoy from the European police's annual secret meeting.'

'A spy?'

'Who knows? We detectives are men with shady pasts. We can invent our histories, because our career has no supporting institutions, like doctors or lawyers. We are self-made men in every sense of the word.'

We had arrived at the point where our paths separated.

'As soon as you can, follow Castelvetia and find out his secret,' Arzaky ordered me. 'Right now, when all eyes are on us, I don't want any surprises.'

* * *

Faced with Arzaky's insistence, I had no choice but to follow Castelvetia. Of course it's not easy to follow a man who is a specialist in tracking, since he could easily discover what I was up to. Craig had taught us to become invisible; the first thing one had to do was think about something else, move as if sleepwalking, get closer as if by accident. I followed Craig's teachings so obediently that I forgot I was following the Dutchman and I bumped right into him in the middle of the street. I shouted out an apology, in an intentionally high-pitched voice so he wouldn't recognize me. He was so wrapped up in his thoughts that he didn't even look up, and immediately went into the Varinsky Hotel.

I distanced myself a few paces. The Varinsky was a hotel for tired travellers who aren't choosy: it was part hostel and part brothel. Like all the hotels and all the pensions in Paris those days, it was completely full, since the committees of visiting countries had already begun to arrive. I waited outside until he left. Then, instead of following him, I resolutely entered the hotel. A near-sighted young man came out to assist me, which is to say, to get rid of me. I put some coins into his pockets as I mentioned the name Reynal.

'Room 12,' he said.

Craig had warned me: sometimes investigations are complicated and tiring, and other times we solve them immediately. A detective must be willing to work, but even more willing to receive a revelation. I was certainly willing: I knocked on the door and it opened, with no delay or questions. Inside the room there was a young woman: she looked as if she had just got out of bed. Ever since that moment, I have always adored women who've just woken up and are still somewhat in sleep's clutches. She wore a distracted smile as she stretched languidly. I didn't quite know what this situation meant for the Twelve Detectives, but I was even more confused as to what it meant for me. Castelvetia's assistant was a woman: this was unprecedented. I tried to replace the entranced expression on my face with a shocked one.

I had ended up here by following Arzaky's orders, and I had to speak for Arzaky.

'Don't tell anyone who I am,' said the young woman, as if I could possibly know who she was.

She invited me in, so we wouldn't be seen together in that hallway travelled by fabulists: the shady men who were the electricians that would light up the Fair; the discreet ladies who would welcome foreigners and justify the city's reputation; the young men who seemed quintessentially Parisian but were actually South American journalists drunk on absinthe.

'I didn't know the rules allowed . . .'

'Where are the rules written? Have you ever seen them?'

'Nowhere. In the detectives' hearts.'

'But they only have brains. They don't have hearts.'

I sat on the edge of a chair, as if I was about to leave at any moment. I wanted to be shocked, but my ability to be shocked was dulled by intrigue. *Wait till I tell Arzaky*, I thought.

She washed her face in a basin.

'My name is Greta Rubanova. I'm Boris Rubanov's daughter. My father left Russia when he was twenty years old and he met my mother, a Frenchwoman, in Amsterdam. She died giving birth to me. When my father started working for him, Castelvetia was practically still a child. They had an office in Amsterdam, which Castelvetia rented from a shipping company. Together they solved dozens of cases. My father taught me everything he knew. But he had a weakness for women, especially dangerous ones. And when he walked out on a Hungarian woman, she said goodbye with her knife. When Castelvetia found him, my father was dying. Castelvetia asked him who had done it. My father's reply was that some cases shouldn't be solved. Castelvetia respected his last wish. At his funeral I asked Castelvetia to let me work for him. He accepted, at first out of sympathy, but later took me seriously.'

'And how did Castelvetia manage to keep you hidden all this time?'

'Detectives are fame seekers, and they know that their renown is an essential part of investigative work: before arriving in a city, their name precedes them, and it's the talk of the town. Sometimes this helps their work, and other times it's an impediment. When a detective is around, fantasies multiply. Castelvetia, on the other hand, always sought anonymity. Since joining the Twelve Detectives, his obsession with secrecy has become even greater. In Amsterdam there are few crimes: we are too polite, too accustomed to ignoring one another. We are so distanced from each other that we never reach the point of murder. There's no need. So Castelvetia and I often have to travel. That helps our cases to go unnoticed. Castelvetia has renounced fame for me: many doubt that he is a true detective, but he did it all to keep me hidden.'

She came closer to me. She smelled of fresh clothes dried in the sun.

'We were confident that during this meeting things could finally be cleared up. Castelvetia was planning to ask that I be recognized as his assistant.'

'A woman? Never,' I said indignantly.

'Who are you, the keeper of the rules?'

'I'm simply the bearer of common sense.'

'Don't get too alarmed, it's not going to happen after all. Things have become complicated, and Castelvetia has changed his mind. Now all the detectives are plotting against each other, they even suspect that Darbon's murderer may be among them. If he presented me now, he would have everyone at his throat. Caleb Lawson hates him, he would take full advantage of the situation.'

'Why does he hate him?'

'Lawson considers three of the Twelve Detectives his rivals: Craig, Castelvetia and Arzaky. Craig and Arzaky are his enemies because he wants to run the Twelve Detectives. Craig has already quit the race, so now only Arzaky, the more skilled and more difficult, remains. Lawson hates Castelvetia because, on a trip to London, Castelvetia solved the Case of the Princess in the Tower.'

'I'm not familiar with that one.'

'No? You can ask Lawson about it. He likes to reminisce about old times. And now that you've seen me, you can leave. Or did you want something more?'

'What use is an assistant who has to be hidden away?'

'I can go places that men can't. Doors have opened for me that you couldn't dream of walking through.'

'I'm sure I'd rather not walk through them.'

'You see? In men, curiosity is laborious, something borrowed and, in the long term, a pretence. Men ask questions that they think they already know the answer to. I ask what I don't know.'

'And you never leave here? Castelvetia has you locked up?'

'I go where I like. We meet in secret.'

'Like lovers?'

'Like conspirators. Like revolutionaries. Like father and daughter.'

'Father and daughter,' I repeated incredulously.

'Father and daughter. Can I trust you?'

'No one has ever doubted my honour.'

'I am completely dependent on that dubious honour. Imagine the consequences of the scandal, now that the investigative arts are on display in full view of everyone. Who would maintain their faith in the Twelve Detectives?'

I had to leave, but it wasn't easy; I was comfortable in my discomfort. For a second I saw things from a distance. The detectives, the rules, the hierarchies, murder itself: it was all just a game. And I was like a stamp collector who comprehends, in a flash, that he has been playing with worthless little slips of paper.

'Now I will ask that you keep our secret, and that you leave. I have to finish getting dressed.'

I got up from the chair that I had barely occupied. I was going to say something, but she brought her fingers to my lips. She knew how to ask for silence.

THREE

I had solved my first mystery, but I couldn't tell anyone about it, not even Arzaky. In Madame Nécart's hotel, at breakfast, the other assistants looked at me enviously. I had a case while they just sat around smoking, drinking and chatting. The Japanese assistant, Okano, was always silent, and only once in a while sat at the desk to write a letter in his language that looked like little pictures. Linker and Baldone argued over the possibility of making a rule about the relationships between detectives and their assistants.

'We live in an era dominated by science,' said Linker. 'Everything has a system, and we should have one too. The Twelve Detectives should be organized just like any science academy or association. We can't appear to be of nebulous origin like the Knights Templar.'

'I've seen too much to believe that everything can be explained. Reality is immune to explanations. I think that we are Templars, and like the Templars we'll eventually die out.' Suddenly Baldone addressed Novarius's assistant in a mocking tone, 'What do you think? Should we have a rule?'

The Sioux remained silent. He was cleaning his knife: a large blade with a horn handle. He didn't even look up.

Baldone noticed my presence. 'The only lucky one. He just got here and already he has a case. Unlike us . . .'

I spoke humbly. 'The other detectives are going to investigate this case too, not just Arzaky.'

'But it's a foreign city. They don't have informants, and they have trouble speaking the language. Arzaky's chances of solving the case are much better. I think that all of the detectives would have preferred to continue their discussion on the art of investigation, rather than actually conduct one. And meanwhile the killer is still at large.'

I didn't want to give myself superior airs, so I stayed with them for a while, as if I were off duty too. I was hoping that if Arzaky sent me any instructions they would arrive discreetly, so that no one else would notice. I had almost managed to convince the others that Arzaky had chosen me just to handle the paperwork, when a tall, robust messenger with a soldierly air burst into the room and asked for me in a loud voice. He brought a note from Arzaky: I was to accompany the detective to Madame Darbon's house.

'Orders?' asked Baldone. I nodded, not wanting to

reveal anything. 'Meanwhile we just sit here. Luckily we have the Sioux here to liven things up.'

I didn't say anything. I just left the room amidst envious gazes and set off to find Arzaky at the Numancia Hotel. He was already waiting for me at the door.

'Darbon hated me, but his loathing was nothing compared to his wife's. If the old witch gives you something to drink, don't taste it. Don't even accept a mint from her.'

We took a car to a yellow house. The housekeeper made us wait in an anteroom filled with armour and shields, and swords. It was clear that the owner had wanted to live in the midst of a legendary past. He had achieved fame as a detective, but perhaps in his dreams Darbon didn't imagine himself solving the case of the century, but rather recovering the Holy Sepulchre. I know, from my own experience, that no one is who they dream of being. We all aspire to something else, an ideal that we don't want to sully by bringing it too close to our real lives. The orchestra conductor would have preferred to be an Olympic swimmer; the renowned painter, a skilled swordsman; the writer famous for his tragedies, an illiterate adventurer. Fate is nourished by errors; glory feeds on regret.

Darbon's house, where he had raised his three daughters, had many rooms. It had a piano, heavy furniture, and objects that had been handed down through the generations. Everything pointed to the past, to roots, to tradition. Arzaky, on the other hand, had never married; he lived in the Numancia Hotel; he had no possessions. He devoted all of his time to investigation. He lived like a foreigner who had just arrived and was about to leave.

'I am Polish, and everything that implies,' he used to say in the adventures Tanner recounted. And he also said it in real life. It excited me to hear with my own ears the same phrase I had read so many times, the refrain that served as a prologue to his escapades.

The house seemed deserted, but there wasn't a speck of dust, which was a sign that the walls hid an unflagging domestic staff. I heard the distant noise of a door being opened and then slammed shut, and then other successive doors, closer ones, and finally Mrs Darbon arrived. She looked like a woman who had been widowed long ago and had already recovered from the shock and grief. She didn't even glance at me: she walked directly to Arzaky, with the decisiveness of someone about to commit murder. I feared she was hiding a stiletto in the sleeve of her violet dress. Arzaky watched her warily, like someone studying a dangerous beast in a cage.

'My husband hated you, Arzaky,' she said in greeting.

'Your husband hated everybody.'

'But you most of all. Did you come to give me your condolences?'

'I am investigating Monsieur Darbon's death. His assistant, Arthur Neska, told me that you have his papers. I want to know what leads he was following on his last investigation.'

Any other person would have adopted a conciliatory

tone with that furious woman, but Arzaky spoke to her arrogantly. Here comes the moment when she kicks us out, I thought. But the widow said, 'Let's go up to my husband's study.'

Louis Darbon's office was nothing like the piled-high chaos of Craig's. The walls were lined with metal filing cabinets, the kind used in accountants' offices. On a large table were microscopes and magnifying glasses and five bronze lanterns with coloured glass that might have been for discovering blood or poison stains. In one corner there was a camera. The wall that faced the window held a complete library of books on forensic medicine, dictionaries, and a copy of *Vidocq's Memoirs*. There was also a portrait of Paris's famous chief of police. Darbon had considered himself his heir. The study was as much a laboratory as it was an office and reading room.

'It still seems as if my husband has just gone out and is about to come home,' said the widow.

Arzaky let out a slightly exaggerated sigh. I was about to start laughing, out of sheer nervousness.

On the desk there was a cardboard box, the type used for mailing, with the inscription *Eiffel Affair*.

'May I borrow that?'

'I knew you were going to come. I prepared it for you.'

Arzaky took the widow's hand between his. The woman immediately pulled it away. The detective, somewhat confused by the woman's reaction, said, 'I am being sincere. I assumed that you would ask me to quit the case and let one of the other detectives solve it, or Captain Bazeldin, who was such a good friend of your husband's. Now I see that your interest in knowing the truth is more important to you than any old enmity.'

The widow laughed so abruptly that Arzaky shuddered. It was a warning.

'That old enmity didn't disappear with my husband's death. Quite the contrary: it has deepened. Before, I hated you because my husband did; now that you have caused his death, I despise you myself.'

'I didn't force Monsieur Darbon to climb the tower in the middle of the night.'

'But if he hadn't loathed you so much, he'd still be alive now. He climbed that tower thinking of you; it was your image that gave him the strength to go up those stairs in the middle of the night, in spite of his leg and his respiratory problems. He climbed with your name on his lips; he thought that no other enemy mattered, and that's why he lost his concentration.'

'Then why are you giving me his papers?'

'Because I want you to find the killer. I want him to feel hunted. To tremble with fear when he hears your footsteps and to take action. If he could best my husband, he can best you.'

FOUR

Arzaky had an apartment on the top floor of the Numancia Hotel, for which he paid a monthly rent. The first room served as his office, where he received clients and kept his archives. It was littered with papers. It was impossible to avoid stepping on the pages that completely covered the floor: forensic reports, outstanding debts, unanswered correspondence, letters from women. That jumble of papers, which seemed to have acquired a life of its own, climbed as high as the desk drawers and the table, hiding firearms, bottles filled with dead insects, handkerchiefs stained with blood from who knows what distant murder, a mummified hand, tickets for the theatre, for transatlantic voyages, for trips in hot-air balloons.

'Reading documents bores me. Why don't you look for clues in Darbon's papers? While you're at it, organize them without making any changes.'

'I'll do my best. But you know, my inexperience . . .'

'Experience can be deceiving. It teaches us that at one point we already did what we are doing now. Nothing could be more false. Approach everything as if it's for the first time.'

Arzaky went out, leaving me alone with the papers. He said he had to go supervise the progress of the exhibition about the Twelve Detectives. It seemed absurd to me that in the middle of a criminal matter he would bother with canes and other artefacts abandoned in dusty glass cases. But detectives are like artists. In the life of every actor, musician, singer, or writer there is always a moment when they begin to play the role of themselves, and everything that they do in the present is merely a ceremony with which they evoke something from their past. And life becomes, for the artist or the detective, the incessant fine-tuning of their own legend.

At first I feared that Darbon's widow had tricked us, that she had manufactured the documents herself to send us off on false leads and towards real dangers. But that wasn't the case: the pages were a compilation of Darbon's methodical work. There was a diary, where the old detective recorded the progress of his investigation. He pursued more than one case at a time, but he had devoted more energy to the Eiffel affair than to any other.

His investigation had begun seven months earlier. From the beginning, the tower's construction had numerous enemies who claimed it was destroying the city's beauty. At first these were relatively harmless, those who didn't want the wrought-iron monument cohabiting with the old palaces. Eiffel had been attacked by associations of war widows, scholars of the city's history, and museum and monument conservators. But then a radical group had joined the battle: the anonymous letters became threatening; the threats, actions. A rose with poisoned thorns was sent to the engineer Eiffel, and a miniature Statue of Liberty with a bomb inside that hadn't been triggered. The most unique attack involved poisoning the pigeons that perched on the tower, so that hundreds of birds dropped dead at once on to the construction site, paralysing the lift motor and frightening the unsuspecting workers.

Louis Darbon was convinced that a group of intellectuals that he called 'crypto-Catholics' was responsible. Most of his observations referred to someone named Grialet, to whom he attributed the formation of a Rosicrucian cell.

'Grialet is a tireless seeker of the esoteric, from astrology to magic, from alchemy to Rosicrucianism. Like so many others, he's more fascinated by the hierarchies and the initiation rites than by the mysteries themselves. These types are always like that. They spend their lives suspicious of one another; they barely establish any rules; they emerge out of schisms and heresies. The schism becomes the rule and a new heresy springs up. Grialet is the soul of that process of continuous disintegration, that constant movement that seeks to create, in everything, the sensation that something is hidden within.' Darbon considered Grialet the main suspect. The papers included the names of two possible accomplices: the writer Isel and the painter Bradelli.

I was immersed in those documents, trying to understand the principles of that circle of esoteric writers, when someone knocked on the door. I opened it. It was a tall woman with black hair. She smelled of a mixture of perfumes, and the scent changed with each step, as if it were a complex mechanism of sleeping substances that suddenly awoke according to the stimulus of light or the passage of time. She was surprised to see me.

'And Monsieur Arzaky?'

'He's gone out.'

'You . . .?'

'I'm his assistant.'

'I didn't know he had an assistant. I thought he'd never resign himself to replacing Tanner. Didn't he leave a message for me?'

'No. If you tell me your name, I'll let him know you came by.'

'I am Paloma Leska, but you can call me the Mermaid, like everyone else. That's my stage name.'

'Your stage name? Are you an actress?'

'An actress and a ballerina. Haven't you heard of the Night Ballet?'

'I've only just arrived in Paris.'

'There are certain things that people should do as soon as they arrive in a city, while they still have money.

Later their pockets are empty and they have to become respectable. We are going to do a piece called *In the Ice Mountains*. Arzaky has already seen the rehearsals. If you're new to the city, I can assure you you'll never see anything like it. Does the cold bother you?'

'Yes, but it's springtime.'

'In the piece, I plunge naked into a lake of ice. It might give you shivers. Do you think you can take it?'

I looked at the woman's bare arms. Her corset was a bit too tight; she was the one wearing it, but I was having trouble breathing.

'Arzaky never told me he liked the ballet.'

'He doesn't just come for the ballet.'

I jotted *The Mermaid* down on a piece of paper. I had to struggle to place one letter after the other instead of all on top of one another. She had been born in Spain, which was why her name was Paloma, Spanish for dove. But she was the daughter of two Polish actors. She considered herself Polish.

'As Polish as Arzaky?'

'More so. I long for Poland, and I travel to Warsaw twice a year. He doesn't. He wants to be a good Frenchman. He won't even touch Polish food. It doesn't matter though. To his enemies he'll always be that damn Polish traitor or, to his more intimate enemies, simply that damn Pole. You're working, I don't mean to interrupt . . .'

'Don't worry about that. It's dead letter . . .'

I don't know if she heard me. The woman had disappeared, as if I had only dreamt she was there. Her perfumes, that had come in gradually, left in order, one by one. Finally I was alone again, with the scent that came off of the newspaper clippings and the yellowing dossiers.

FIVE

When Arzaky arrived I told him about the ballerina's visit.

'So you've met the Mermaid. Paris's finest. What did you think of her?'

'She told me about the ballet.'

'She always has some crazy new thing going on. You should see her, sunk deep in the ice. I don't know where they get those blocks from. Sometimes they even have frozen fish inside them. She's the kind of woman that drives men crazy.'

'Does she drive you crazy too?'

'Me? No. I'm like the lake of ice she plunges into. What did you find in Darbon's papers?'

I told him about Grialet, Isel, and Bradelli.

'Darbon always loved false leads. He searched where it was easiest to search, where there was nothing hidden. Do you know the joke about the drunk who came home late? He drank so much that he couldn't get the key into the lock, and eventually he dropped it. About ten feet away there's a streetlight, and the drunk starts looking there. His wife hears him and sticks her head out of the window, saying, "Did you drop your key again?" "Yes," says the drunk. "Well, why are you looking for it by the streetlight instead of by the door?" And the drunk replies, "Because there's more light here." That joke is Darbon's professional biography: he's always right by the streetlights. Electric light would have made his job even easier.'

At my insistence, Arzaky finally agreed to visit Isel.

'All right, let's go, if it'll make you happy. We're going to wind up switching roles; in the end I'll be your faithful acolyte. The devotion that Tanner had for every last one of my opinions! He thought I was infallible, and he liked to make mistakes just so I could correct him.'

'Mistakes lead to the truth.'

'Mistakes only lead to mistakes, and skill leads to the truth.'

A carriage took us to Isel's house. It was a gloomy castle on the outskirts of the city. It had two or three incongruent architectural blocks, which looked as if they had been built in different periods, or in one very fickle period. They were a series of failed attempts to give the building a medieval air.

'You knock on the door. Convince me that there's something of interest within these walls.'

A servant let us in. He was tall and bald, with Oriental features. He moved with his eyes closed, like a sleepwalker. We entered a vast monastic room, where everything appeared to be missing. There were marks where paintings had hung, where rugs no longer covered the floor, where furniture had been taken elsewhere. The statues had gone, but the pedestals remained. We sat in hard chairs, like the kind you find in a church.

'They're dismantling everything,' I said. 'Do you think Isel's dead? No, the servant would have told us.'

'Servants are no longer allowed to give such news. If the master has died and someone comes to visit him, they leave the person waiting in the living room, with some information left where they can find it – a newspaper, or a death notice – that fills them in on what happened. If the visitor doesn't think to have a look at those papers, the waiting continues indefinitely. I remember a certain count who was so offended at being made to wait that he challenged the deceased to a duel. Of course, the duel couldn't be fought.'

Someone coughed a few steps away.

'That's not the case, gentlemen. This mausoleum houses a living man.'

Isel appeared before us in a tattered yellow robe. He wore round eyeglasses and a grey beard covered his face. From his neck hung an exaggeratedly large gold crucifix.

'Have a seat, please. I'll sit as well.'

For a few seconds the three of us were silent. Since the chairs were next to one another, and all faced the same direction, the situation was a bit ridiculous. We looked like passengers waiting for a train. Was the silence deliberate? Was it part of Arzaky's strategy, or was he shy, or distracted? I coughed, and realized that I was the only one made uncomfortable by the silence. For different reasons, they were each used to provoking unease.

Arzaky finally explained what we had come for, and then he asked if Isel had known the man who fell from the tower's heights.

'Yes, Darbon came here. He began by asking me about my youthful exploits. It is true that we founded groups and sects, and we ordered books from abroad and each had a library filled with banned volumes. But now I use those books to keep me warm in the winter. Although they're not even entirely good for that, since the leather covers smell terribly when they're burned.'

'Who else was a part of your group?'

'Their names aren't important. Pseudonyms abounded. Names with alchemical or Egyptian echoes were the most common. There were many, they came, they left, they founded new churches . . . For most of them I was depravity incarnate. They blamed the devil for my sins. If there were a copyright office for vices, I would have registered mine there so that no one could attribute my inventions to the devil.'

Isel stood up and pointed to the mark a large painting had left on the wall.

'You see this painting? These are my parents. I inherited a fortune from them and never worked a day in my life. I spent my time studying and collecting. I had exotic birds brought from abroad, which I often either freed or killed, depending on my mood. I had a large music box built, and I hired a blind girl to dance for me, repeating the same mechanical movements over and over. She danced naked, and never knew how many eyes were upon her. I would invite my friends to the meetings, some of which were held in the dark, and make them smell perfumes, sip drinks, and taste food without knowing what they were. When the lights came on, the real surprises were waiting for them. I was sick, I couldn't handle real life. I searched for corners where life still held an air of strangeness and artifice. Now I've stopped all that, now I devote all my energy to the Church of Truth.'

'What brought about your change?' asked Arzaky.

'Three years ago, a young man who called himself Sinbad joined my domestic staff.' He pointed to another mark on the wall that had been left by a small painting. 'I painted his portrait myself. He had Arab features and called himself Sinbad for a circus act he had once performed. I let him keep it; it didn't bother me. He was dark, reserved, he cheated at every game, and I became interested in him. I had the strange idea of making him into a gentleman, because I sensed that, beneath his wild exterior, there was a hidden god. The statue within the marble block. I hired a tutor to acquaint him with mathematics, Latin and the French classics, particularly the funereal orations of Bossuet. He learned to fence, and I took him to museums and cathedrals. Meanwhile he helped me to maintain order in this castle where I keep, all muddled together, marvels and misfortunes. I had trouble getting him to enter my natural sciences room, where I kept stuffed birds, some turtles, and several tanks of fish brought from Brazil. Those fish devour anything that's put before them, and he trembled at the sight of them just cutting through the water with their fins.

'I don't know what happened to him. Perhaps my efforts weren't enough, or he missed his old life, because one day he fled. I was undone; I felt that my masterpiece had been completely ruined. My good servant Joseph, whom you saw, was glad that the young man had disappeared. I thought of tracking him down and killing him; I thought of killing myself; I thought about burning the house down . . . Fortunately I'm not a man of action – except for the act of collecting – so I returned to my studies, my dusky evenings and my disappointments.

'One day I heard a rumour that a two-headed lamb had arrived in the market; I set out immediately to buy it. But something distracted me on the way: in the crowd I saw Sinbad, juggling for pocket change. He juggled the monkey skulls he had stolen from my collection. I hid my rage, which was also joy, and I embraced him without a second thought. I convinced him to come back with extravagant promises, which I didn't make to him so much as to myself. Once he was back at the house, it only took me a few minutes to notice how his French had been corrupted, how his manners had changed, how his gaze had become sidelong and given to surreptitiousness and betrayal. I could see it in his eyes: I was just an old eccentric he could get enough money from to run away again. It terrified me to think of him disappearing and I made Joseph lock him in the natural sciences room. With no windows and only one door, there was no way he could possibly escape. Sinbad begged me on bended knee not to lock him up, but he used such common words that I was reminded of how his foolish flight had nearly ruined my work.

'I never knew if he slipped or if he threw himself into the water of his own volition. I heard a terrible scream in the middle of the night, the truest sound I have ever heard in my life. The words we use are nothing more than disguises to cover that scream, which is the essential expression of our soul. In the red water there was incessant motion, boiling. Incapable of moving, I stood staring at the depravity of nature, which was symmetrical to my own illness. When the movement stopped, I was empty, hollow. The great experience that life had in store for me was over. I didn't leave my room for ten days. I smashed the perfume bottles, I drank all the cocktails I had brought for him, I used up my supply of hashish. I destroyed that abominable tank. Then I pulled out all my collections, every little pleasure meticulously catalogued, and I buried them in the basement of this house. The emperor's cabinet of wonders would envy what I have stored here! I had nearly reached the most perfect of all experiences; it no longer made sense to continue. Now I devote myself to a different kind of pleasure.'

'Crime?'

'No. Louis Darbon had nothing against me. He considered me an enemy of the tower. Why would I care about something whose existence I don't even recognize? Could that tower compare with the bloody visions I see in my dreams? Darbon didn't understand. We are not men of action. We are a school of contemplators. We are the immobile, the useless, those who read books about men of action. I wish there were a true criminal among us. It's better if Grialet explains it to you. Grialet, now he has a golden tongue. But, of course, Arzaky, you know that full well.'

I had mentioned Grialet when I told Arzaky what I had read in Darbon's papers, but he hadn't told me he knew him.

'I haven't seen him in some time. Where is Grialet these days?'

'I don't know where he lives, but I doubt he's stopped going to Dorignac's Bookshop. That is the port through which all banned books arrive. Paris is filled with sects that are out to kill each other, but Dorignac's Bookshop is a sort of common ground, a neutral zone where enemies observe each other from a distance.

'I miss Grialet. I used to take nighttime walks with him. He took me to see the many perversions the city has to offer, and I paid the price. Now I prefer other sights. Once in a while I travel to see far-off oddities; in Naples I saw a church made entirely of human skulls. I go to see local miracles: in one chapel there's an intact cadaver, as fresh as if he'd died just moments before; in another, further away, I watched a corpse decompose in seconds, right before my eyes. These are the only wonders that fill my free time these days. I'm consumed with death, because, after Sinbad, I don't deserve any new pleasures. I've renounced everything.'

Arzaky didn't seem to take Isel's confessions very seriously, because he asked him, 'And don't you want to renounce your servant as well, to make your contrition complete?'

'Get rid of Joseph? Oh, please no. I might be insane, Monsieur Arzaky, but not so insane as to think one can get by without servants. What's more, he keeps me alive. On my nights of insomnia he tells me, in infinite detail, of Sinbad's spasmodic movements as he fell into the water, he describes how his face lit up with terror. He fills my sleepless hours with those few dreadful seconds. How could I go on living without that bedtime story?'

SIX

Six days had passed since Darbon's murder, and the halls of Madame Nécart's hotel were no longer filled with leisurely, waiting assistants. The armchairs were empty, and even the Sioux had set off on some mission.

'Where are they? How would I know where they are?!' replied the owner. 'Finally those savages are out of the drawing room. If my husband were alive, he never would have stood for having a redskin in our hotel.'

The flight en masse had me worried. While they were there, I felt privileged to have a case. But with them out in the city, I couldn't help thinking that they were the ones with the real clues, and that I was left walking in the shadows.

Arzaky didn't seem to trust the information we had either, because he sent me to look for Grialet and Bradelli on my own.

'Grimas, the editor of *Traces*, knows them well. He published several magazines for them. Ask him where they are.'

'But,' I protested, 'you can get the truth out of suspects with just a look. I'm a foreigner, I'm inexperienced, I'm only an assistant . . .'

He dismissed my arguments with a contemptuous wave of his hand.

'Detective's apprentice, son of a shoemaker: don't be so sheepish, just go and distract Grialet.'

'I'm better at distracting myself than anyone else. And even if I manage to, what do I do then?'

'What do you think? Look for oil-stained clothes or gloves or shoes, of course.'

'If Grialet is the killer, he's had time to get rid of those things.'

'You are an Argentine spendthrift. No good Frenchman would ever throw away a pair of shoes, not even if holding on to them could send him to the gallows.'

Adrien Grimas's publishing house was located on the first floor of a building in the Jewish quarter. There was a haberdasher's below. Grimas was eating a bowl of soup when I came in, and as soon as he saw me he hurriedly tried to hide the large blue notebook where he kept his accounts. The editor was supposed to give a percentage of his profits to the Twelve Detectives, but he claimed to have recorded a loss. Later, I mentioned to Arzaky that it seemed very strange to me that the wisest men on the planet, capable of finding a killer from one hair or a cigarette butt, could be taken in by that little bespectacled man, who made only a cursory attempt to cover his tracks. He replied, 'It's a well-known tale: Thales of Miletus was walking through the field, looking up at the stars, when he fell into a well. A Thracian slave who saw him laughed and asked, "How can a wise man know so much about the distant stars and not notice the well that's in front of him?" Well, in our case, we are twelve men who all fell into the well at the same time because we were looking up at the stars.'

Once Grimas had hidden his ledger book, he went back to finishing his soup of onions and meat.

'Arzaky won't speak to me,' he said. 'I wanted to meet you so I could give you some copies of *Traces* and remind you to take notes as you go along, so you'll be prepared when it comes time for you to write the story of Arzaky's case. I will ask that you maintain Tanner's style.'

'I don't have enough experience to be able to tell Arzaky's adventures, much less in Tanner's style. Besides, I can't write in French. I'm just a temporary assistant, until Arzaky can find someone permanent.'

'We're all temporary, Monsieur Salvatrio. We are all awaiting our replacement.'

I asked the editor about Grialet and Bradelli, and he in turn asked me, 'Arzaky's following up on the Hermetic lead?'

'Are you surprised?'

'No. I knew that Louis Darbon was on the trail of

the tower's enemies. Occultists are like detectives: they investigate the lines that join the macrocosmos to the microcosmos. But while detectives look for signs in corners, at the bottom of drawers, between the floor-boards, the occultists do the opposite: they search in gigantic things, in monuments, in the shapes of cities, or the pyramids. Then they try to find a relationship between those enormous things and their own private miseries. Detectives go from the tiny corner to the world, occultists from the world to the tiny corner. That's why the tower has made such an impression on them. Where others see beauty or ugliness, the steel or the height, they see the symbolism.'

'I thought they were only interested in the great monuments of the past. I wouldn't have thought that the Eiffel Tower would attract their attention . . .'

'The Eiffel Tower is not Eiffel's tower, it's the tower of Koechlin, his assistant, who had to work long and hard to convince Eiffel to get on board with the project. Maurice Koechlin, an engineer like Eiffel, was the one who made the first sketch and later designed the structure. Now everyone talks about Eiffel, but you'll see – in a few years it'll be called the Koechlin Tower. You want to make a bet? Koechlin is Swiss, maybe that's why he doesn't like to draw attention to himself. He first thought of devoting himself to medicine, and studied anatomy in Zurich. When he designed the tower he was thinking of the organization of the fibres in the femur, which is a very strong, lightweight bone, the longest in the human body. Pythagoras was also obsessed with the femur, he found its relationship to music and, as a result, a link between that bone and the universe's hidden arithmetic. So our occultists are convinced that Koechlin is a Pythagorean devotee who divulged his greatest secret. The tower has always been a symbol of the centre of the world, which is why these occultists believe ours is a false centre that they must expose. Also, lately they've been leaning more towards the Catholic Church, and they don't like the fact that the tower is taller than St Peter's. It doesn't really matter though; it's a mistake for Arzaky to investigate them. I know them well, they're harmless, I've published several of their magazines. Everything goes fine through the second issue, and then the in-fighting starts. It's hard to work with people who want to publish their exploits and keep the secret at the same time.'

Grimas ate the last drop of soup and moved the plate away on to a pile of papers. Caleb Lawson's name was on the top page. It seemed sacrilegious to treat the Twelve Detectives' material that way.

'Well, I'd still like to know where Grialet and Bradelli are.'

'Of course, the more moves Arzaky makes, the more pages you'll write for me, isn't that right?' I shook my head no, but he ignored me. 'Arzaky's adventures are the most chaotic, but our readers love them – who knows why. Tanner brought out the best in Arzaky. There was always a moment in his adventures when Arzaky seemed confused, about to admit defeat, sometimes he even disappeared for two or three days, and

Tanner narrated the details of his absence with a master hand. He described his empty study on the top floor of the Numancia Hotel, his unopened correspondence, and the dust that gathered on his desk. Then Arzaky would make a triumphant return and resolution would come swiftly. Christ also had to spend a good while in the desert before allowing the prophecies to be fulfilled.'

Grimas stretched out his arm and handed me some back issues of *Traces*. It was obvious that it was a relief for him to be able to get rid of some of those papers.

'So you can familiarize yourself with Tanner's style.'

'Thank you very much. I'd love to have them, although I'm already very familiar with Arzaky's cases.'

'You already know them? Oh, of course, the *Key to Crime*.' Grimas said the name of the Argentine magazine disdainfully. He looked at the clock on the wall and leapt from his chair. 'You'll have to excuse me, but I must go to the printer's. I'm sorry I haven't been much help with the two occultists. After involuntarily becoming one of the protagonists in the Case of the Magnetizer, Grialet went to live in Italy.'

'He was involved in a criminal investigation?'

'Yes, the detective was Arzaky. Didn't he tell you anything about it? Ask him, or look for the case in issue 45 of *Traces*, which I just gave you. The one with the green cover. As I said, Grialet went to Rome to live for a while. He became involved with the widow of a general, who gave him large donations for the Hermetic cause. I think the ruse he used was the publication of the complete works of Fabre d'Olivet. Once he had the money, he returned to Paris, but he hasn't been seen much since he got back. And, of course, he hasn't published even a brief treatise. I don't know where he lives now, but he's not hard to recognize: his right ear is missing, lost in a fight at the now defunct Pythagorean Society of Paris. And as for Bradelli, he died three months ago.'

'A natural death?'

'Natural for a man with his sombre disposition. He poisoned himself. During the last few years he had tried to apply his knowledge of alchemy to painting. His frequent use of mercury provoked fits of madness and finally poisoned him to death. Three years ago he had promised the Autumn Salon a painting in which he had created new colours never seen before. To heighten anticipation, he published an article in one of Grialet's magazines, *Anima Mundi*, where he refuted Goethe's theory of colours as well as Diderot's. He announced the names of the new hues, which were a mix of Latin, Catholic liturgy, alchemy and even necromancy. They were designed to alter the viewer's perception and provoke sensations in him that transcended the subject matter. Painting, he said, must be a secret message; in the colour one finds true meaning. When, after much beating around the bush, and many announcements and retractions, he finally presented his paintings, he pointed out the new colours: diabolical topaz, larva yellow, mandrake green and silentium blue, and a dozen more. We saw only greys and blacks, and large areas where the white of the canvas hadn't even been touched. That was Bradelli's last work.'

I followed Grimas down the stairs and we said goodbye at the door.

SEVEN

With Bradelli dead, I needed to find Grialet. The Dorignac Bookshop, like everything in Paris, was hidden. If I hadn't written the address down, I would have walked right past it. There was a main room where history books, innocuous new arrivals, big volumes with pictures of military uniforms, and anatomy guides were gathered on large tables. But all those books were the façade behind which Monsieur Dorignac carried out his true mission: the chosen few had to go down some stairs and to the back of the shop to find, behind a worn velvet curtain, the real bookshop.

Two other people were there when I entered, a tall, elegantly dressed lady who wore rings with snakes on them, and a gentleman who had rather greenish skin. Apart from his colour, he seemed to be in perfect health. The grey-bearded bookseller completely focused on assessing a shipment of used books that had arrived in a trunk. The lady feigned interest in a dictionary, which she set aside quickly, and made a gesture to the bookseller with her head. He responded with a nod of approval, and the lady vanished behind the red curtain. Minutes later, after leafing through a thick book by Michelet entitled *Bibles of the World*, the green gentleman made the same sign of complicity and received an identical response. I waited for the gentleman to disappear behind the curtain and then I perfectly imitated the seriousness of the gesture. I was about to go past the threadbare curtain that separated me from the Mystery, when the bookseller stopped me.

'Who are you? Where are you going?'

I shook the hand that he put in my way, and I introduced myself.

'Monsieur Dorignac? My name won't mean anything to you. I am Monsieur Arzaky's assistant.'

'Arzaky is an enemy of everything here.'

I drew close to his ear.

'Monsieur Arzaky is having a crisis of faith. He has poured himself into reading the occult texts, but he has no discipline. He wants it all at once: alchemy, spiritualism, black magic. He mixes stills with crystal balls, sulphur with Haitian dolls. I'm afraid he's heading for disaster. And that he'll end up like . . .' Just then the green gentleman left the bookshop empty-handed. He had spent no more than a minute in the forbidden section.

'Poor Serdac, so persistent in his experiments. He comes here to look at the cover of the most expensive book I have. It's enough for him to know that it's here, and then he leaves. He doesn't look good, but he's in better health than he was when his skin was white. Similar methods have greatly reduced the clientele of our bookshop. The ones that don't end up in a hospice blow themselves up. The ones that don't die in an explosion end up with sulphur poisoning. Suicides are the order of the day. I'll confess that lately I've been hiding the most dangerous books, so I won't go bankrupt for lack of readers. As for Arzaky, I can't help him. I'm sure your detective already has the books he needs.'

'One never has the books one needs: one has too many or too few. That's why I was looking for Monsieur Grialet. I trust that he can help me get Arzaky back to his cases.'

'And why would I want Arzaky back on his cases?'

'Do you want them to accuse the Martinists of having driven Paris's great detective crazy? Or the Rosicrucians? Or you yourself, nourishing all those impressionable minds with your books?'

'He's not the Detective of Paris, Darbon is.'

'He was, but Darbon was murdered while investigating some of your customers.'

'Don't think you're telling me anything I don't know. I run a bookshop, but I read the newspapers too.'

The curtain opened slightly and a woman's hand, adorned with an assortment of rings, waved the bookseller over. Did she want to know the price of a book? Was she looking for some title that wasn't on the shelves? Dorignac's haste in attending to her made me think that it was something more mundane than the search for knowledge. From what I had been able to observe, good booksellers invariably waited on customers in an offhand manner, convinced that everyone would eventually find the book they wanted without any help. If a bookseller takes care of a customer, it's not about a book.

Dorignac, rushing to help the woman, found a pencil and jotted down the name of a street that I wasn't familiar with.

'I recently sent him a package at this address. Grialet devotes his days and nights to searching through thousands of pages to find the perfect quote, the one that will save him. Then he gets rid of the books. He believes in these things.'

'And what do you believe in?' I asked as I put the piece of paper in my pocket.

'Surrounded by dangerous books as I am, I believe that our only hope is in forgetting the quote that we once read, the one that will lead to our downfall.'

Dorignac vanished behind the red curtain.

EIGHT

Although there were no books in Grialet's house, the house itself was a book. The building, I found out later, had belonged to an editor named Fussel, who had the door and windows built to look like book covers. The spiral staircases crossed through the building like arabesques, unexpected rooms appeared here and there like footnotes, the hallways extended like careless margin notes. On the white walls there was writing, in some places it was like calligraphy, and in others scribbled with the haste of sudden inspiration.

I knocked on the door and Grialet appeared and immediately invited me in. He was about forty years old, and of average height. The contrast between his very white skin and black beard gave him a theatrical air, as if at any moment he might take off the beard and moustache and reveal his true face. Grialet wore his hair a little long to hide the fact that he was missing half of his right ear. With his mouth closed, he looked weak and shy, but when he opened it, he was transformed. There was something animal about his large yellow teeth. He was dressed in a blue wool suit, which was too warm for the season. He had his reasons: the house was cold; not the gentle coolness that some homes have in the summer, but the dank cold of long abandoned houses.

'Arzaky sent me.'

'I know.'

'You do?'

'Don't be alarmed, I was warned. Predicting the future isn't one of my talents.'

'Who warned you? I haven't talked to anyone.'

'We all keep track of Arzaky's movements, along with those of his informants and servants.'

Grialet had said that to see if I would be offended and back off. I acted as if I hadn't heard a thing. He led me into a room with yellow walls, on which the black words continued. There was malignancy in that writing, as if it were an incurable disease, a corrupting decay that would soon bring down the walls and bury the occupants. It would have been impossible to sleep in that house without fearing contagion, without the fear of waking up between the closed pages of a book.

'If I can stand one unexpected visit, I can stand two,' said Grialet.

It was then that I noticed there was someone else in the room. I think it took me a few seconds to recognize, towards the back of the room, by the piano, Greta

Rubanova, as still as a statue. We looked at each other with the mix of kindness and lack of interest strangers adopt when forced to greet each other. Grialet didn't introduce us, as if he had guessed that we already knew one another.

'It is an honour to be suspected by all of the Twelve Detectives. But I promise the tower is not among my concerns.'

'If you were a suspect, Arzaky wouldn't have sent me, he would have come in person. He only wants to end this matter that Darbon started, prove that the old detective was on the wrong trail . . .'

'And one of the trails led to me?'

'The trails lead in many directions; one of them is here.'

Grialet waved his hand, brushing aside my investigation as something to be dealt with later, and looked over at the young woman.

'You didn't finish telling me why you're here. Don't tell me that you work for the Twelve Detectives too.'

He said it sarcastically, of course.

Greta approached him as if she were going to whisper something in his ear, but she spoke out loud. 'I come as a representative of a certain countess whose name I cannot mention. She asked me to tell her what quotes you've written on the walls that surround you. She admires you and is very impressed by your aversion to books. A man who rejects books must be a saint.'

'Often names don't mean anything to me,' replied Grialet, 'but when one is withheld, I know immediately who it is. Tell your countess that I take only what I need from each book; I don't want those extra pages tormenting my nights. I stroll through the house as if it were my memory, one day I sleep here, another there. Every book has unpleasant sentences, ideas that attack the main structure, words that cancel out other ones, and I want to eliminate all that. The path to the perfect quote is winding and takes years to travel, but when one arrives, it justifies all the unhappiness that reading gives us.'

'Can I go through the house, copying down the quotes that strike me as appropriate?' Greta asked Grialet. 'My mistress would be very happy to have just a tiny part of your vast treasure.'

It was clear that Greta was too quick for me. She was poised to find the oil-stained boots or clothes before me, guaranteeing Castelvetia's victory. But Grialet advanced towards her and for a moment I thought that he was going to bite her with his big yellow teeth.

'No, those quotes are mine alone. The countess has to find her own. These only have meaning for me; outside of this house, they're worthless.'

Greta had already got Grialet's attention with some new lie. She didn't even have to talk much, since Grialet couldn't take his eyes off her. She was wearing a blue dress that showcased the whiteness of her bosom, which was the only space in the room that wasn't covered in letters. Grialet was distracted, just as Arzaky had asked, but I couldn't simply go looking for oil-stained shoes. Besides, I felt absurdly jealous about leaving him alone with the girl. The sentences surrounded me and held me back, as if they were obeying a secret signal from their master. On the wall, two feet above a dusty piano, I read, *Nothing survives except secrets* – SEFER HA-ZOHAR.

Next to that phrase, in a careless hand, Grialet had written, *The day will come when God will be a meeting between an old man, a decapitated man, and a dove* – ELIPHAS LEVI.

There were quotes in Greek, Latin, and German. Some were attributed to well-known names, like Holderlin or Novalis, but other names were completely foreign to me: Stanislaus de Guaita, Laterzin, Guillaume de Leclerc. On the closed piano there was a messy pile of papers. I also saw a postcard, with an image of a woman swimming in a lake of ice. She was naked, covered by only a few well-placed ice blocks. When I realized that the woman was the Mermaid, I hid the photograph in my clothing. I didn't know then why I took it, and I still don't know. I instantly regretted it, but there was no turning back. I consoled myself by thinking that it was probably just publicity for the performance and that Grialet wouldn't miss it.

One entire wall was devoted to a poem by Nerval, '*El Desdichado*' [The Disinherited]:

Je suis le Ténébreux – le Veuf – l'Inconsolé,
Le Prince d'Aquitaine à la Tour abolie:
Ma seule Étoile est morte – et mon luth constellé
Porte le Soleil noir de la Mélancolie.

Dans la nuit du Tombeau, Toi qui m'as consolé,
Rends-moi le Pausilippe et la mer d'Italie,
La fleurqui plaisait tant à mon cœur désolé,
Et la treille où le Pampre à la Rose s'allie.

Suis-je Amour ou Phoebus? . . . Lusignan ou Biron?
Mon front est rouge encor du baiser de la reine;
J'ai rêvé dans la Grotte où nage la Sirène . . .

Et j'ai deux fois vainqueur traversé l'Achéron:
Modulant tour a tour sur la lyre d'Orphée
Les soupirs de la sainte et les cris de la Fée.

I knew the poem, because a Central American poet had published a translation of it on *The Nation*'s literary page. I remembered the first verse of the sonnet by heart.

I am the Gloomy One – the Widower – the Unconsoled
The Prince of Aquitaine, at his stricken Tower
My lone Star is dead, – and my star-spangled lute
Bears the black Sun of Melancholia.

Perhaps Grialet had lost all hope of my leaving, because he turned away from the girl and came over to me.

'Gerard de Nerval hung himself from a streetlight not far from here, on Vielle Lanterne Street. Everything he wrote had a coded message. I spent many years discovering new meanings to the words of this poem.'

'I don't know if it's because I'm foreign, but I have trouble understanding it.'

'The keys are in tarot and alchemy. The speaker is not the poet, but an alchemical Pluto who represents the philosophical earth, matter prior to its transformation. The tarot is also mentioned. The fifteenth card belongs to the Devil, who is the prince of darkness and, in this case, the Prince of Aquitaine. The sixteenth card is the tower in ruins. And the seventeenth, the star.'

I read the second verse out loud.

In the night of the Tomb, you who have comforted me,
Give me back Posilipo and the sea of Italy,
The flower that so pleased my desolate heart
And the trellis where the branch and the rose meet.

'I understand even less of this one,' I said.

'I'm not surprised: detectives get lost in the written word. They can read what isn't written, but when letters come into it, they go astray. The night of the tomb means the same as the black sun and melancholy: darkness, the rotting of the matter which will then be transformed. Posilipo is a red stone, which is to say, sulphur, alchemists' material of choice. And the sea of Italy is mercury. All in all, the entire poem speaks of the transformation of matter, the second alchemical operation.'

The sonnet continued:

Am I Eros or Phoebus? . . . Lusignan or Biron?
My forehead is flushed from the Queen's kiss;
I dreamt in the Grotto where the Mermaid swims . . .

And twice victorious I crossed the Acheron:
Modulating alternately on the lyre of Orpheus
The saint's sighs and the fairy's screams.

'I'm not going to overwhelm you with the secrets contained in each and every word; every night I find new possible interpretations. But I want you to observe how the dark, star-spangled lute of the first verse turns into Orpheus's luminous lyre at the end. Nerval set out to tell the story of an alchemical transformation, but here, in the penultimate verse, we see what really matters to him: when matter and work become art. Orpheus is the poet capable of creating an allegorical version of alchemy and its mysteries; he is the artist capable of putting into words those other secret arts. And the result of that verbal operation is as important, if not more so, than its contents. Nerval didn't need to tell us the secret; he was interested in pointing out a puzzle that couldn't possibly be solved.'

I read the poem again and then said to Grialet, 'But what's interesting about enigmas is that they hint at the possibility of an answer. I like your interpretation, even though I don't completely understand it. I like knowing that, just as mysteries exist, so do solutions, even if I can't figure them out. When I was a boy I used to read about the detectives' great exploits and I loved the cases that seemed impossible, a locked-room case, for example, did have an explanation. The enigma only exists for the moment in which the detective unravels it with the strength of his reasoning.'

'You said it: Arzaky and his finds want to unravel mysteries, not complete them with the revelation of the enigma. If they embraced the mystery instead of confronting it, don't you think they would come to a better understanding of their cases? Arzaky always finds the killer, but he loses sight of the truth.'

'Arzaky is a detective; like a scientist he only believes the evidence.'

'Do you believe that the evidence leads to the truth? Evidence is the truth's enemy! How many innocent killers has Arzaky sent to the guillotine? It's not just crime that makes us guilty, nor the lack of it that makes us innocent.'

Grialet had raised his voice, surprising Greta, who moved closer to me. Then the occultist started to circle us, pressing us against one another.

'I was partially deaf until they hacked off half my ear with a butcher's knife. Since then, I hear perfectly.' Grialet moved his greasy hair aside to show us his wound, whose irregular edges appeared to have been bitten rather than sliced by steel. 'With this pretty little ear I can hear your thoughts. I know what the detectives don't. They don't dare come here, sending you instead. Who do you work for, miss? For Lawson, or Castelvetia?'

Greta, pale, bit her lips.

'But your detectives don't know what they're doing,' he continued. 'You are more than servants, more than assistants. Each of you will be the downfall of your mentor.'

I felt that the accusation was directed at Greta, not at me, so she was the one who should respond.

'You're wrong,' said Greta. 'And don't speak to us as if we were some sort of a team. We just met, it's only a coincidence that we're here at the same time.'

Grialet had lost all meekness. He left his slashed ear in view and, far from being a weak point, it seemed triumphant, a point of pride, a mark that signified that he belonged to a chosen circle. I couldn't take my eyes off his big yellow teeth.

'I'm wrong? I recognize the voices of those who are due for a transformation. I see the pride that can't be concealed by false modesty. You suspect me. It is you who are the suspects. You, who pretend to be the acolytes, the messengers, the assistants, the shadows . . . Now, leave. You'll find nothing more here than obscure phrases and obsolete verses.'

NINE

We left the house upset and confused.

'My performance was perfect. Grialet would still believe my lie, if you hadn't shown up.'

'He knew who we were before we came in. Grialet pretended to believe you just so he could get a good gawk at your bosom.'

'I used my bosom to distract Grialet, so that you could look around. Why didn't you check the other rooms? Then we might have something now.'

I shrugged. 'I didn't want to leave you alone with him. I thought he might bite you.'

'I'm used to –'

'Being bitten?'

'To this job. I've dealt with men much worse than Grialet, men that wanted to do more than look at me. Now we're not going to be able to get in again. Instead of looking for clues, you just stared at the walls . . .'

'There was writing on them.'

'But the clue wasn't going to be there, on the wall, in plain sight.'

'With everything that was written there, the wall could have easily read, "I killed Darbon" and neither of us would have even noticed.'

'Brilliant observation. And now we're leaving empty-handed.'

I took the photograph of the Mermaid out from where I had hidden it in my jacket.

'I'm not leaving Grialet's mansion completely empty-handed.'

She looked at the image, her eyes wide.

'It's trick photography. No person is capable of such things. It must be some play of light and cameras –'

'I've seen her.'

'Like this?'

'Dressed.'

'I still maintain it's impossible.'

She turned the photograph over, as if she expected to find some confirmation that it was fake on the back. In green ink, a woman's hand had written, *I dreamt in the Grotto where the Mermaid swims . . .*

'There are so many photographic tricks these days; they can make women look as perfect as statues.'

'That photograph isn't painted.'

'Only fools fall for optical illusions.'

She gave me back the photo and left, offended. But Arzaky was even more upset when I showed it to him.

'How dare you enter a house using my name and

steal a photograph? The idea is to send criminals to prison, not for them to send you and me there.'

'I thought it could be a clue. Perhaps the woman's handwriting indicates –'

'It's the Mermaid's handwriting – no secret there for me. She's known Grialet for some time. I asked her to help in an investigation a while back, that's all.'

'The Case of the Fulfilled Prophecy?' I showed him the magazine that Grimas had given me.

Arzaky looked at me, annoyed.

'Old cases are no concern of yours. Your job is to ask questions and, if it's decided that we continue following up on this Hermetic lead, search for some oil-stained shoes. You don't need to steal anything. I don't know what strange things Craig taught you, but the assistant is a spectator, not an actor. The assistant watches life pass in front of his eyes, without getting involved. Now close your eyes. Imagine that life is a theatre. Did you imagine the curtain, the orchestra, the actors? Good, now imagine yourself seated in the last row.'

I told him about the conversation I had with Grialet, but it was difficult explaining exactly what went on without mentioning Greta. Arzaky listened to me without interrupting. I told him of the writings on the walls, and the phrases written on them, I recited part of Nerval's poem and I told him Grialet's interpretation of it. But when I got carried away and acted like an expert as I explained the second of the three verses, Arzaky had a fit of anger and began banging the floor with Craig's cane.

'Okay!' I said to him. 'I won't recite any more! And be careful with that cane, it could go off.'

Arzaky wiped his forehead with a handkerchief. 'I can't stand poetry.'

'Maybe it's my foreign accent . . .'

'Your foreign accent isn't the problem. It's your mind; it's foreign to all reason. Put all this in order. Gather these things into the glass cases and start writing out placards that explain the function of each object. And go to the parlour to see if you can find my colleagues and demand the objects that are still missing. The Japanese detective, Castelvetia, Novarius, Baldone . . . And did you find out anything more about Castelvetia's assistant?'

I shook my head no, without looking at him, as if I barely realized what he was asking me. Arzaky gave an indignant snort and I thought he was going to have another fit, but he sat down, dispirited.

'I'm sorry to be so irritable. Grialet brings back bad memories.'

'Because of the unsolved case?'

'It was solved. But perhaps that case is the prologue to this mess we're in now.'

Arzaky took the magazine out of my hands and quickly reviewed the story, as though he had trouble remembering the names. Every once in a while he smiled bitterly, as if mocking those pages Tanner had written. For the first time I suspected that there might be quite an abyss between the published versions of the cases and the real investigation.

'The Case of the Fulfilled Prophecy was the first time I had contact with Paris's Hermetic sects. The victim was a professor at the Sorbonne who had one paralysed leg. His name was Isidore Blondet. He lived alone in a large house, shut in with his books. He had spent his youth in Lyon, where he had contact with a Martinist order, a spiritualist group that he soon abandoned. Once he was living in Paris, he became obsessed with the myth of Atlantis, and began combing through histories of remote cultures for references to islands swallowed up by the sea.

'One of Blondet's most loyal friends was Father Prodac, a former seminarian who experimented with poisons and liturgical elements. He fed communion Hosts to rats and kept track of how long it took them to die of starvation. From his bodily fluids he extracted poisons that were said to be extremely powerful and could kill on contact. Blondet eventually got tired of Prodac's experiments, and he kicked him out of his house.

'This was the first enemy that the cripple Blondet made, but he soon discovered that constantly creating enemies was entertaining – an amusing way to fill his empty Sundays. He founded a satirical newspaper in which he was the sole writer and editor-in-chief, making fun of the leaders of the Paris Hermetic scene. His favourite target was Grialet and, of course, his former friend Prodac. In those days Prodac claimed to be a prophet. His prophecies were fairly banal (a storm on St Peter's Day, a vague shipwreck), but one day he made a prediction with a name and date: on 18th September, Isidoro Blondet was going to die.

'Blondet, a bit frightened by the prophecy (not because he believed that Prodac could see the future, but because he feared that he was plotting to kill him), didn't leave his house the whole day, didn't open the door to anyone, and only picked up the newspapers and the post. Nevertheless, when the maid came in the next day, she found him dead, seated at his desk, with his head resting on a large book.

'For a few days Prodac enjoyed his fame as a prophet. Businessmen and ladies of leisure visited him at his house so he could predict their luck in investments, gambling and love. It didn't last long. Blondet's autopsy, which I attended, revealed that he had been poisoned with phosphorus. I helped the police with their investigation, and found that the last book that Blondet touched was impregnated with phosphorus. Blondet had climbed a staircase to get the book, gone back down, and looked through it. Then, when he slammed it shut, a cloud of dust rained out from its pages and poisoned him.

'Prodac was arrested immediately. It was obvious that the murder had been well planned. He eventually confessed to the judge that, before leaving Blondet's house, five or six months earlier, he had poisoned the book. Then he waited for him to consult that particular volume.

'The police were satisfied with the chain of events, but for me there was a missing element. How could Prodac know that Blondet was going to take out that book on that precise day? It was this investigation that led me to Grialet.

'The book that killed Blondet was a thick volume about the Hermetic movements during the Renaissance. I combed through the newspapers from that day looking for some information about what could have awakened Blondet's interest in consulting that particular book. One of the papers at Blondet's house was *The Magnetizer*, which was run by Grialet. After reading it over and over, I found, on a footnote signed by someone named Celsus, a common pseudonym in the Hermetic circle, a mention of Marsilio Ficino, the philosopher to whom we owe the revival of Plato's thinking in the Western canon.

'At that time Blondet was preparing the definitive edition of his work on Atlantis. The author of the footnote, this Celsus, pointed out that Ficino (the son of the Medicis' doctor, who had founded his own academy and was vegetarian and chaste) had written a book about Atlantis, the fable created by Plato, when he was twenty-three years old, but later destroyed it. According to the note, Ficino had found earlier sources than Plato, which proved that Atlantis hadn't been a chance invention by the philosopher. And it cited as bibliography the thick volume steeped in phosphorus. I realized that this footnote was the fatal weapon. As soon as Blondet read the false information, he sought out the work on Renaissance Hermeticism to see if the citation was true. He didn't find it and, slamming the volume shut, was enveloped in the phosphorus cloud.

'I asked the district attorney to arrest Grialet, the editor of the magazine, but he defended himself, saying that the article had arrived in the post and he knew nothing about the author. To prove his innocence he showed an envelope postmarked Toulouse. The plan was too complex for Father Prodac's limited imagination. I sent the Mermaid after Grialet. Although she managed to become his friend, she never found a single piece of evidence that linked him to the phosphorus, to the murderous citation, or to Prodac himself. As a last resort I went to see the killer at the Salpetrière Hospital (the judge deemed him insane due to his fits of rage); on the day I arrived Prodac had been found hanging from the ceiling. He didn't leave a note, nothing that implicated Grialet in the crime.

'That's why Grialet's name brings back bad memories. With time, solved cases fade, diminish, disappear. But unsolved cases come back again and again, convincing us on sleepless nights that this collection of question marks, uncertainties and errors is our true legacy.'

TEN

I returned to the hotel disheartened, with the feeling that Arzaky didn't trust me and was only using me for minor tasks. He had kept the fact that he knew Grialet from me and he hadn't told me anything about his plans for the investigation. I locked myself in my room to catch up on my correspondence. Even though I addressed it *Dear Mother and Father*, I couldn't help but think that I was really only addressing my mother, as she was the one who took a real interest in my letters. I told her about everything around me but I altered it, trying to restore the original patina, the glow of things seen for the first time, to this world that had begun to tarnish.

After dining in a seedy bar, whose weak light was in cahoots with the chef's dark arts, I went to the hotel drawing room to see if I could find Benito or Baldone. Only the Sioux warrior was there, seated in an armchair rigidly gazing out into space. I greeted him with a nod.

Tamayak took out a packet of cigarettes and offered me one. I had heard that some tribes smoked hallucinogenic herbs, and a scandal in Madame Nécart's drawing room was the last thing I needed. It would have been the final straw that made Arzaky send me back to my father's shoe shop. Maybe Tamayak noticed that I was looking at his cigarettes suspiciously, because he said, 'Don't be afraid, they're from Martinique. I bought them right here in the hotel.'

I was surprised that the Sioux spoke French, and I boldly told him so.

'Four years ago Jack Novarius began studying French so he could join the Twelve Detectives. Knowing French is a prerequisite to anyone aspiring to be a full member. It's not required for assistants, but he made me learn as well so he would have someone to practise with. And how's it going with Arzaky? Becoming the acolyte to the Detective of Paris should make you proud, but you just seem unhappy.'

'I'm not a real assistant. I'm sure he has a plan, but he's keeping quiet about it. He doesn't trust me.'

'But his silence is good. When I started working with Novarius, for the Pinkerton Agency, he almost never spoke to me. Once in a while I would make some comment, but he always reserved his words for the final surprise.'

'He never disclosed anything about the investigation?'

'Not a thing. Our first case took place in a circus, in the Midwest. They had killed the Human Cannonball right in the middle of a performance. The acrobat had commenced his usual routine, greeting the audience, showing his helmet and asking, "Is it shiny? Is it shiny?" And then he stuck himself into the cannon. But instead of shooting out and landing a few paces further on, he blew straight through the circus tent and disappeared into the night.

'The cause of death was clear. The cannon had two mechanisms: an explosive charge to make noise, and a spring, which was the real force that propelled the Human Cannonball. The killer had filled it with gunpowder, turning it into a real cannon.

'Jack showed me a lamp that gave off blue light that he always carried with him, which allowed him to detect fake bills. With that lamp, he told me, he would catch the killer. Gunpowder, explained Jack, remained under the fingernails of anyone who touched it for ten days. Washing your hands was no use, said Jack. The only way to get rid of the powder was to burn it. He asked me to repeat the explanation to anyone who wanted to listen.

'Jack announced that the following night he would perform his great experiment, making everyone who worked with the circus show their hands under the light. At nine o'clock, after the show, we gathered everyone in the arena and we stayed there in the dark, lit only by the blue lamp. No one's hands shone and the detective apologized with a heavy heart. The circus artists, one by one, left the tent. The last one, a trapeze artist named Rodgers, I'll never forget his crazy smile, had burns all over his hands, and the police officer stationed outside the tent arrested him immediately.

'Later we found out the details of the case: Rodgers's wife, who worked as a horseback rider, had been planning to run off with the Human Cannonball. Rodgers found out and increased the cannon's charge to get the Cannonball out of his marriage, and his life. Mrs Rodgers confessed to Novarius that, when they were in bed, in the dark, he had asked her to look at his hands under the moonlight. And he asked her, "Are they shiny? Are they shiny?"'

'Then Novarius tricked you too.'

'Yes, but my own faith in the trick had been essential to it coming off successfully. If I had been suspicious, if I had employed my cunning, I might have given away his plan. That's why I'm telling you, my dear Salvatrio, that while you're here, feeling ignored and neglected, you may actually be the key piece of Arzaky's secret plan. It could ensure your own success as an acolyte as well.'

As if Tamayak's words were a premonition, the next morning I was awakened by Mrs Nécart banging on my door.

PART FOUR

The Fire Sign

ONE

'Come on, Salvatrio! Get up! There's a message for you!'

I staggered over to open the door. The first thing I saw was Mrs Nécart without her makeup; it was not a good omen for the rest of the day. I snatched the message from her hands and read:

Come to the Galerie des Machines as soon as possible.

The yellow paper was dirty with soot, and stamped with Arzaky's big black fingerprints.

The machines were grouped according to function inside the palace of glass and iron. But often a machine belonging to one sector was sent to another, since the boundaries of man's disciplines have always been unclear. The operators moved them around, trying to place them according to blueprints that were constantly being produced, and then continuously modified by other blueprints brought by messengers sent from the Organizing Committee. The messengers were very young and wore blue uniforms and leather caps, and they sometimes had to consult the blueprints they were carrying to keep from getting lost amid all the pavilions and corridors. One wrong turn and they would be walking in circles for quite a while; because of this, it was common for a messenger who had left first to arrive after a later one, so an already established decision could be taken as a last-minute change. The dockyard workers, made up largely of foreigners, complained about the excessive work, and threatened to halt operations. In order to resolve the conflict it was decided that the machines that hadn't been correctly placed when they arrived would be sent to a special area. There they joined others, no longer united by their function but by the circumstances of delays and confusion. So a digger used for mining was positioned next to an electric piano and Graham Bell's metal detector. This area was the most popular with visitors to the World's Fair because of its variety. That variety represents the world, filled with too many different things for anyone ever to be able to see them all. There must be a point at which strict classification finally crumbles and confesses that everything is just a dream. All alphabets are letters that don't have a proper place, or that are hardly ever used, and could easily be overlooked. Their function isn't so much to represent a sound as to unshackle the alphabet from the constraints of perfection. (In Spanish we have the x, which we use to name what isn't there and to cross things out.) Loose bricks and twisted beams are the foundation of every building.

At the entrance to the Galerie des Machines I had presented my safe-conduct – a sheet of paper with the official seal of the Organizing Committee, but also the round seal, always in red ink, of the Twelve Detectives. The guards stared at the seal, unsure whether or not to believe it was real. Everyone had heard of the group, but no one knew for certain that it actually existed; the red seal was like a postmark from Atlantis.

Since I was in a rush to meet with Arzaky I couldn't stop to look at the machines, but caught a glance at them as I walked past. The more esoteric the object's utility, the more brilliant and successful it seemed; it was magnificent to see the bronze chimneys, and the oiled gears, and the watches with blue hands that measured God knows what pressure, speed or temperature, and the levers and little control switches. There was a strange effect created in the palace: as in so many other glass monuments, the sun that filtered in showed the myriad dust particles floating in the air. The machines, while at odds with each other, seemed to be united by the dust that floated above them, confusing the connections and controls, the clocks and pistons, the cords and spark plugs into one common realm, as if the entire palace was inhabited by one single, sleeping, machine.

I walked through the corridors admiring the infinite fields of knowledge that I would never master. At the back of the pavilion a group of policemen were waiting, and Arzaky was with them. At that end, in an almost hidden area, were the latest – and, to my mind, most bizarre – innovations in the funereal industry: the corpse cannon, which sent the dead to the bottom of the sea; the excavating coffin, which dug its own grave with the cadaver inside and disappeared below ground; and various cremation ovens.

Arzaky shook hands with a man who had just arrived; he was as tall as the detective, with a big nose and professionally dressed in a black suit.

'Monsieur Arzaky? My name is Arnesto Samboni; I'm a representative of the Farbus Company. They got me out of bed at dawn to tell me that someone had turned the oven on.'

The oven was built of firebricks and iron, and looked very much like a house. The controls and the emblem with the company's name were on the front. On one side there was a tray and on it lay a blackened body. The features were burnt away. It reminded me of a stone idol, a god exhumed in the farthest corner of Asia by some archaeological expedition. The head seemed to be separated from the body; it was hard to believe it had ever been human.

'It's a campaign oven,' explained Samboni, with the same tone he used when making a sales pitch. 'It reaches extremely high temperatures very quickly. It can run on gas, with wood or liquid fuel. One of our ovens, I'm proud to say, was used to cremate the body of the poet Percy B. Shelley, after he was shipwrecked on the Ligurian Coast.'

‘It’s supposed to reduce the body to ashes, and this corpse is merely blackened. Did something go wrong?’

‘It was turned off too soon. Otherwise, Monsieur Arzaky, there would be nothing left but dust, and you wouldn’t have a single clue to start your investigation.’

‘Don’t be so sure, Monsieur Samboni. Even ashes can hold clues.’

Arzaky took out a pencil and scraped at the skin of the body around the abdomen. The surface gave way and I could see something that looked like scorched wool.

‘Who else knows how to use this oven, Monsieur Samboni?’

‘It’s very easy, anyone who has read the instructions could do it. But it was already set up, because we were planning to do a demonstration on opening day.’

We didn’t get to find out what type of demonstration one would do for a crematorium, because a commotion interrupted Samboni. Alarmed, the policemen who had been watching Arzaky as if spellbound, moved away from us, as if they didn’t want to be associated with the Polish detective or his dark assistant. The newcomer was wearing an oversize plaid overcoat, and sported a gigantic moustache that seemed to precede him, as if to say, *Watch out for the guy behind me*. He looked at the body, took a momentary pleasure in the effect his appearance had caused, and then pulled out a notebook.

‘Step aside, Arzaky. From now on I’ll ask the questions.’

For a few seconds it looked as if the two men were going to fight a duel with their pencils. The newcomer was Bazeldin, Paris's chief of police. I recognized him from his picture in the newspapers. Since Darbon's death, he had appeared in *The Truth* saying that there were no legitimate detectives outside the official police force, and that the Twelve Detectives would be wise to disband.

Arzaky stepped back a few paces, distancing himself from the body and Samboni.

'Before interrogating this man,' Bazeldin pointed to Samboni, 'I'd like you, Arzaky, to tell me how you found out about this murder.'

'What murder?'

'The body right here.'

'I'm investigating Darbon's death. I was returning from one of my evening walks when I saw a commotion at the door to the Galerie des Machines. We still don't know if someone killed this man.'

'Do you think he's still alive?'

The policemen laughed at their boss's joke, and briefly shook, as if in spasms of mirth.

'You'll have plenty of time to laugh when we've found the guilty party. Now, go through the pavilions, see if anyone is missing.' Then Bazeldin addressed a plain-clothes policeman who never left his side. It was no secret that Bazeldin wanted to be like the detectives in every way; he even had an acolyte. 'Rotignac, you guard the body until someone from the morgue comes to pick it up.'

'I want to point something out, Captain,' Arzaky interrupted. 'The head seems to be almost detached from the body.'

'You are always giving me false clues, Detective. You want to send me off on a wild-goose chase. But I am going to conduct this investigation my way, and we'll see who solves the case first. Just because Darbon is dead, that doesn't automatically make you the Detective of Paris. It's a responsibility one must earn. In the meantime, consider yourself the Detective of Warsaw – assuming they don't already have a better one.'

Arzaky moved away from Bazeldin, feigning indignation, and took me aside. While the chief of police continued giving orders, the detective said to me, 'I'll stay here. If I go anywhere, Bazeldin will have me followed, and I don't want to tip him off about my suspicions. You are to go the Taxidermists' Pavilion and ask if they are missing a body.'

'You mean this wasn't a murder? That the dead man . . . was already dead?'

'That burned smell is too caustic for an ordinary cremation. You come from a country where they raise sheep, so you should know that in the spinning process they separate a very coarse type of wool called unbonded wool, which is used to stuff cushions and dolls. It's also used by taxidermists when embalming bodies. I think someone stole an embalmed body and burned it.'

'Why would anyone do that?'

'How should I know? If my job were that easy, anybody would be able to solve crimes, even Paris's police chief. Right now, the only thing that concerns me is that Bazeldin sees me here. I'll ask some more questions to keep him occupied.'

As I left the Galerie des Machines I found one of the messengers who worked for the Organizing Committee. He gave me directions to the Taxidermists' Pavilion. As I walked there I spied several of the Twelve Detectives heading over to see if the news bore any relationship to Darbon's death. I saw Hatter, with Linker by his side. I also saw the two Japanese men, who pretended to be distracted by the machines, but I could tell that they were completely focused as they moved forward with a determined stride. Baldone, almost breathless, followed Magrelli, the Eye of Rome.

At the entrance, Novarius tried to get the Sioux in, but the guards insisted that he had escaped from a tribe of South American Indians that were set up on a piece of land on the other side of the Fair, and they wanted him to return. To avoid being followed, I entered other pavilions and exited through side doors. I stopped to see the globe they had just finished putting together, and then I sidetracked towards the Palace of Fine Arts. When I was fairly sure no one had followed me to that point, I continued on to the Taxidermists' Pavilion. Before I went in I saw a young woman waving to me from a distance. It was Greta, looking at me through binoculars. I waved back, embarrassed at being exposed, and casually entered the pavilion, which was built to look like an Egyptian temple.

TWO

At the entrance to the temple I was greeted by a stuffed bear, whose open jaws welcomed me to his world of simulated immortality. On glass shelves and large black wood tables nested birds as small as insects and insects as large as birds. A giraffe from Paris's zoo, whose death had been announced in the newspaper six months earlier, was still in the wooden box that had been used to transport it, sticking its neck out into the world at last and forever.

A short, stout man passed by me, dressed in grey overalls. I asked him for the taxidermists and he muttered between his teeth the name 'Dr Nazar' and pointed to a closed door.

I knocked, and without waiting for an answer, opened the door. A doctor in a white coat was writing a letter, with his back to me. Next to him there was an empty gurney.

'Rufus, wait a second, I'll give you this letter, it's for the Organizing Committee . . .'

I stepped forward.

'I'm not Rufus, Doctor. My name is Sigmundo Salvatrio, and . . .'

He put the pen down and turned to look at me. Nazar had a long beard and eyes reddened by long nights of work.

'I'm busy right now. Perhaps in the future I'll be taking on apprentices . . .'

'I don't want to be an apprentice. I was sent by Detective Arzaky.'

I assumed he would throw me out, but he stood up enthusiastically, as if I had uttered a magic word.

'That's exactly what I need – a detective! A body has just disappeared. It was our best work and someone took it in the middle of the night.'

'That's why I'm here,' I said with a smug smile.

Nazar stared at me.

'But how could you know that, when I haven't reported its disappearance yet?'

'We are aware of everything that goes on at the World's Fair,' I replied, happy that someone, in the midst of so much confusion, deemed me useful.

'Your accent and your arrogance are familiar to me,' said Dr Nazar in perfect Spanish. 'Are you Argentine? Me, too.'

Doctor Nazar came closer as if he were going to hug me, his lab coat stained with chemical products, blood and other substances I was not keen on coming into close contact with. Frightened, I backed up with the agility of a fencer and extended a tentative hand. The deferred embrace evaporated. Anyone who saw Nazar's exuberance would have thought that it was extremely rare to find another Argentine in Paris, when in reality the city was full of us.

'So you're working in Paris?' I couldn't avoid Dr Nazar's presumptuously giving me a pat on the back.

'Just for a short while. I was sent by Detective Craig, for the first meeting of the Twelve Detectives.'

'I met Craig at a meeting of the Progress Club five years ago. He gave a masterful lecture on the difference between deduction and induction.'

'One of his favourite topics.'

'It was brilliant. I didn't understand a thing, but I could tell he was a cut above. I understand that, in recent years, he has given up detective work.'

'Because of his health problems.'

'And because of the Case of the Magician. Well, you should know better than me.'

I was speechless. I often forgot that I wasn't the only person who knew about the Kalidán case and Alarcón's death. When that old business came to light I felt horribly ashamed, as if I had squandered an opportunity. Guilt, in many cases, has no relation to actual events. We feel responsible for things that have nothing to do with us, and don't give a thought to our real sins. I abruptly returned to the matter in hand.

'I came because a body was found, and we believe it is the same one that was stolen from you.'

Nazar's face lit up.

'I knew it couldn't have gone far. Is it in good condition?'

I shook my head.

'Did they take the head off?' he asked. 'It's going to take a lot of work to get that head back where it belongs.'

'I'm afraid, Doctor, that won't be necessary.'

Nazar breathed a sigh of relief.

'They burned it.'

Crestfallen, Nazar sank back into a chair.

'What day is it?'

'Thursday.'

'The Grand Opening is in a week. A week! And I've had to do everything myself; this whole pavilion, getting the permits . . . The authorities from the Argentine Pavilion didn't want to give me any space. The only thing they care about is showing their horses, their sheep, their wheat, and especially their cows – they have an unhealthy obsession with cows – but they don't want my art displayed there. Life, life, they told me. Life, they kept repeating, rolling their eyes. But do they even know what life is?'

He shook his head slowly and stared at his fingertips.

'I'm the one who knows what life is. I'm the one who knows the decomposition process. I am the one who can stop it. Oh well, I'll have to go and see the disaster. Show me the way.'

'It won't do any good. Besides, if you go now, they'll

keep you there with questions. Captain Bazeldin will call you into police headquarters and you'll have to spend a whole afternoon waiting for them to question you. You're lucky that Arzaky still hasn't told the police that the body is one of yours. Don't you have other things you can show at the opening?'

'I suppose I do. Come with me.'

Nazar led me into the back room, filled with the animals that hadn't yet been classified. There was a lion with its jaws open, a stork, a large crocodile, and an ostrich. In the corners, there were many minor pieces: foxes, otters, pheasants, snakes. Some had no eyes, others had come unstitched. Each had a yellow card attached with a thread, showing its origin, a date, and the taxidermist's name.

In the middle of the room there were four gurneys, holding three bodies. The first was a mummy; the second, a stone statue; the third, a woman who seemed to be made of dust and about to vanish into thin air. The last gurney was empty.

'We were thinking about showing four bodies in different states of embalming. Now we'll have to make do with three. This one, as you can see, is an Egyptian mummy, which we reproduced strictly following the traditional procedures. We even recited the ancient incantations. If you are interested, the jars with the entrails are around here somewhere . . .'

He got up to look for the jars in a cupboard, but I assured him it was unnecessary.

'This other body was embalmed using an ancient

Chinese method that uses volcanic lava to convert the body into stone. The method is interesting but the results are highly debatable. It looks just like stone, you see? There are taxidermists who don't believe me when I tell them that it's a human body, they think it's a sculpture.'

'How'd you get the lava?'

'We made it artificially, heating mud, limestone and sand to high temperatures. It was an absurd amount of work. There wasn't a single day that I didn't burn my hands. Guimard, my closest collaborator, is still in the hospital. I hope they discharge him soon so he can come to the opening.'

Nazar approached the third gurney and delicately touched the woman's skin. She wore a white dress and still held the ribbon that had tied some flowers, long since disintegrated. Her hair, streaked with grey, looked exactly like that of a living woman. Nazar gestured to me, inviting me to touch her leathery skin, but I recoiled.

'This isn't my work; it was executed by time, weather conditions and chance. The third method, which often keeps the bodies that are stored in churches intact, is the reduction of humidity inside the coffin. We bought this woman from a dealer in relics. She died half a century ago, but looks as if it were only yesterday.'

Lastly, Doctor Nazar pointed to the empty gurney.

'But Monsieur X, preserved using the traditional, Western method, was our most exquisite model. He had been executed by guillotine and we were able to reattach his head and almost perfectly restore him.'

I pulled a black notebook I had recently bought out of my pocket. Its pages had a grid, like graph paper, just like the one Arzaky used. And without realizing it, I was imitating the way he wrote, with the notebook half shut as if I were afraid someone would peek at my notes.

'How could they have got the body out of here?'

'They forced the lock and took it on a wheelbarrow. At the Fair, people work all night long, especially now that opening day is so close. No one would have looked twice at someone transporting a bulky load in the midst of hundreds of carts and wheelbarrows filled with construction materials, machines, statues, animals . . .'

'Where do you get the bodies you work on?'

'From the city morgue. This pavilion depends on the Ministry of Public Health.'

'And that's where Monsieur X's corpse came from?'

'Yes, of course.'

'Why do you call him that? Monsieur X? It would be helpful to know his real name.'

'Is that important to the investigation?'

'Of course. The person who incinerated him may have borne a personal grudge . . .'

'We don't know his name. We never know any of their names. It's easier to work on anonymous bodies, you understand? That way one can forget they once walked the earth, that someone gave birth to them, that someone misses them at the dinner table, or in bed. Anyway, it's a waste of time to search in that direction. This was an attack directed at me by rival taxidermists!

It was my job to accept the pieces you see here and reject the ones you don't. We are a vindictive lot: one of them sends a poorly sewn rabbit, with buttons instead of eyes, and when it's rejected, a hatred that lasts a lifetime is born. In our business, what's best preserved is resentment.'

THREE

I didn't want to continue the investigation without further orders from Arzaky. I looked for him first in his apartment and then in the subterranean parlour of the Numancia Hotel. Arzaky was sitting on a chair with a stack of papers. He grabbed his head in a theatrical gesture while a tiny man with a pointy beard shouted.

'So, Arzaky, you think your problems are bad? It's never the dead people that are the problem, it's the live ones! Messengers knock on my door day and night, my wife is threatening to leave me and, what's worse, my cook too! The government's decision to have the Fair this year, as an homage to the Revolution, forces us to constantly exchange information with other countries. A few months earlier or a few later, and the whole thing would be solved. But now, the crown heads of Europe don't want to participate officially because they don't think it's right to celebrate a king's decapitation.

They don't like to see the words "guillotine" and "majesty" in the same sentence. But their diplomatic advisors, their industrialists, and their technicians have come, and are filling our hotels. Men that we call "informal civil servants" pay us visits; hordes of characters with a conspiratorial air ask to meet with everyone and hand out business cards, so hot off the presses that they stain your fingers. And we never manage to discern informality from impersonation. The day before yesterday I threw a lout out of my office, and he turned out to be an envoy from the British Embassy. My secretary had to spend all morning writing letters of apology. Last Saturday, the minister himself was talking for two hours to a German, supposedly a representative of the Swabian industrialists, who turned out to be the con man Dunbersteg, wanted for the Swiss bond scandal. Your murdered detective and incinerated corpse don't seem like such great problems to me.'

Giant Arzaky looked at him with what seemed to be fear. I must say, I've often noted that very tall people are completely disconcerted by very short ones, as if they belong to a quicker, more intimate, more complex world.

'We are doing everything possible, Dr Ravendel. If you had hired me instead of Darbon, this never would have happened.'

'I didn't hire Darbon. It was the Organizing Committee; they were frightened.' Ravendel threw down an envelope filled with banknotes on to the table. 'I brought what we agreed on, Arzaky, to serve as incentive. The other half when the case is solved. We have managed to get the press to portray Darbon's death as an accident. That's cost more money than anything else so far. Bribing politicians is much cheaper, because they're naturally dishonest; but journalists are always expensive, because they try to pretend that they're willing to take their scruples to the limit. Our coffers are not bottomless, we're not like those ostentatious Argentines that felt they had to build the Taj Mahal.'

Ravendel stormed out without saying goodbye. Arzaky's gaze followed him as if making sure he was really gone. Then he stuck his hand into the envelope and took out a banknote.

'Is your information worth one of these?' he asked me.

'I'm not sure.'

'Did the body come from where I thought it did?'

'Yeah, the Taxidermists' Pavilion. The taxidermist that prepared it is named Nazar. It was a body donated by the morgue. A guillotined man. Nazar was very proud of having reconnected the head.'

'Let's go to the morgue then. We have to beat Bazeldin's foot soldiers.'

Arzaky, not convinced that I deserved it, gave me the money.

An hour later we were walking across a square stone courtyard. Arzaky sent me to buy a bottle of wine, some cheese, and cold meats, and I was carrying the box with the provisions. There were two green ambulances in the courtyard, with yoked horses, ready to go out to the furthest reaches of the city in search of a body. We went down a staircase to the autopsy room. As we passed an open door, Arzaky signalled for me to keep quiet, but I couldn't help peeking in. The forensic doctor was talking to Bazeldin and a couple of policemen.

'Right now they are finding out what we already know. We've got the upper hand,' said Arzaky in a whisper. And when I smiled complicitly he warned, 'But one should never, NEVER, rely on that.'

We opened a door that revealed a deserted room: the morgue's archives. The shelves held cardboard boxes and file folders with papers coming out of them, tied with green ribbon. On the wall there was an engraving of an anatomy amphitheatre, with medical students and curious onlookers surrounding a professor as he dissected a cadaver. On the desk there were photographs of faces and bodies, and judicial orders with the hospital seal and doctors' pompous signatures. Arzaky, who knew the archive well, searched through a cabinet that, because of its proximity to the desk, was the most likely receptacle for more recent papers. After much searching he triumphantly pulled out a page.

We heard heavy footsteps approaching. I was scared, but Arzaky didn't even look up.

An immensely fat man entered the archives. He wore an administrative staff uniform, but his shirt had been mended so many times he looked like a beggar.

'Arzaky! If the doctor finds you in here, he'll fire me. Do you want me to starve to death?'

'That would break my heart, Brodenac.'

Arzaky signalled for me to put the box I was holding down on the desk. Brodenac examined the bottle, the cheese and the cold meats, and smiled with satisfaction.

'There are better places to shop, but the Bordeaux isn't bad. What are you looking for?'

'I've already found it.'

Brodenac studied the sheet of paper Arzaky had in his hand.

'You too?'

'Who else was here?'

'That red-headed girl . . . the dead guy's sister.'

Arzaky looked at me.

'The dead guy didn't have a sister. Someone else got here before us.'

'You already know who the dead guy is?' I asked.

Arzaky took the paper from Brodenac and showed it to me.

'Jean-Baptiste Sorel,' I read. The name meant nothing to me. 'Who is he?'

'An art forger. Imprisoned for stealing paintings, and for murder.'

'Did you know him?'

'I met him under unpleasant circumstances.'

Brodenac had taken out a wood-handled knife and was already cutting off a piece of cheese. 'Unpleasant circumstances? Well, they were unpleasant for Sorel . . . It was Arzaky, the great detective, who sent him to the guillotine.'

FOUR

Night had already fallen and Arzaky asked me to go with him into a narrow café that stretched out towards a smoky back area. He ordered absinthe and I was going to ask for the same, but he stopped me.

'An assistant's mind always has to be sharp. You shouldn't get clouded up on this poison.'

A short waiter, practically a midget, brought us our drinks: a glass of wine for me, and for Arzaky a glass filled with green liquid, a slotted spoon, and a lump of sugar wrapped in blue paper. Arzaky put the sugar in the spoon and poured water over it until it dissolved. As it lost its purity, the absinthe turned opalescent. When it was still, before the water was completely stirred in, it seemed to turn into green-veined marble.

'Sorel was a small-time forger,' Arzaky told me. 'His speciality was academic painting, all those big canvases with mythological figures, a little tree over here, some ruins over there, and a naked lady in the middle. But that went out of style, and Sorel found there was no market for his fake Bougeraus and Cabanels any more. He was broke, and he spent his days sinking deeper in debt in the backroom of the Rugendas Café. One night Sorel met Bonetti, a Sicilian smuggler, among the other lost souls at the café. They became friends, discussing art, reciting the names of their favourite paintings, and exchanging information about which famous works in France and Italy's great museums were actually forgeries. Within six months Bonetti knew everything about Sorel, who was a very talkative chap, and he was able to convince him to steal a painting that hung in the house of one of Sorel's old clients. The former client was a textile manufacturer who had profited from the sale of overpriced uniforms to Belgian army detachments sent to the Congo. Sorel got into the house under the pretence of selling him a painting, and Bonetti, dressed as a gentleman, came in with him. Sorel introduced Bonetti as an expert from the Vatican gallery. Bonetti cased the house and discovered there was almost no security. Fifteen days later they pulled off the heist, entering through an open window.'

'That's not enough to send somebody to the guillotine. Did they kill someone?'

'No. They were thieves, not murderers. Bonetti knew what he was after: several books had been published on *The School of Athens* by Raphael and, at that time, minor painters were benefiting from the renewed interest in paintings with philosophical subjects. Bonetti was planning to sell the painting to the president of the Platonic Society, but he never got the chance.'

At the back of the café, in front of a mirror, two men were arguing loudly. I looked in that direction and saw my reflection. I barely recognized myself. At that distance and with all the smoke, unshaven and bleary-eyed, I looked older. In that moment I wanted to go back to Buenos Aires and, at the same time, never wanted to go back, ever. But if I did return, who would I be? The shoemaker's son sent by Craig with a cane and a secret, or the tired man that looked back at me from the mirror?

Arzaky waited for the men's shouting to stop before continuing.

'Sorel had only one serious fault: he was very jealous. Bonetti foolishly took the liberty of sleeping with Sorel's common-law wife, a pale, consumptive-looking woman. Sorel attacked Bonetti with the knife he used for cutting canvases and left him in the street so that it would look like a mugging or a drunken fight. When the police found him, Bonetti was still alive and conscious, but he refused to name his attacker. Five days later Sorel sold a forged painting to one of his clients, unaware that the police were on his trail. The owner of the painting, who was abreast of the matter, asked me to examine the painting. In one corner of the canvas I found a bloody thumbprint. It was so easy to prove his guilt that I won't even bother boring you with the details that led him to the gallows. They found the stolen painting in his studio.'

'Had he harmed the girl too?'

'No, he hadn't even beaten her. He loved her too much. I saw her recently; she was selling violets on the street. I bought a small bouquet and paid far too much for it, leaving quickly before she could recognize me because I was afraid she would refuse to accept the money. I didn't like sending Sorel to the guillotine, but we detectives strive to know the truth, and when we find it, it no longer belongs to us. It is the other men – the police, the lawyers, the journalists, the judges – they decide what to do with that truth. I hope that young woman hasn't found out Sorel's body was defiled and burned.'

'And the stolen painting?'

'The businessman got it back, but shortly afterwards went bankrupt and sold it to the Platonic Society, exactly what Bonetti had planned on doing. It still hangs there. It's called *The Four Elements* and, according to what I've been told, it depicts Plato, Socrates, Aristotle and Pythagoras. How can anyone tell? In paintings, all philosophers look more or less the same: tunics, beards and pensive eyes.'

FIVE

When I arrived at Madame Nécart's hotel, the assistants were all gathered there. I never saw them in groups of three or four; it was all or nothing. Perhaps they had agreed behind my back when to appear and when to disappear. Baldone shouted at me from a distance, with his Neapolitan terseness: 'The Argentine, finally! Come here, come here!'

I felt uncomfortable. I wanted to disappear, but instead I took a seat beside the Japanese assistant, who looked at me harshly. I greeted him with a nod, which he returned, somewhat exaggeratedly. Tamayak and Dandavi were missing from the group.

'And what does Arzaky say about what happened in the Galerie des Machines?' asked Benito, the Brazilian.

I was honest: 'Arzaky doesn't know what to think.'

'Magrelli says that the two incidents are related. They both happened on a Wednesday,' Baldone said smugly.

'Your Roman detective has a distinct tendency to find serial murders in isolated cases,' interjected Linker.

'That's our mission, isn't it?' said Baldone. 'Finding a pattern in the chaos. The police see isolated events, then the detectives connect the dots, creating constellations.'

'Good for Magrelli. When he retires from investigation he can take up astrology, which is, I've been told, a much more profitable business. At least in Italy.'

Baldone chose not to respond. Benito seemed to agree with Linker: 'But there's no sequence here. In one case a murder, in the other, the theft and incineration of a corpse. If it is a series, it's going backwards: burning a body, unpleasant as it is, is not as serious as killing. What next? Stealing a wallet? The killer could finish off his list of crimes with a final act: leaving a restaurant without paying.'

'Or leaving the Numancia Hotel without paying,' said Linker. 'The Twelve Detectives are a club, but they're also rivals. It's inappropriate to mention it, but we know that many of them hate each other, and we shouldn't rule out the possibility that the killer is among us.'

'Among them, you mean,' corrected Baldone.

Linker's round face turned red. I don't know if it was because he had suggested that one of the assistants could be mixed up in the case, or because he had included the detectives and the assistants in the same group.

'Among them, of course.'

There was an awkward silence. Everyone wanted to discuss it, but nobody dared to start the conversation.

'I'd like to know who hates who,' I said to get things rolling.

'There's plenty of hate to go around,' said Baldone. 'But the real animosity, the most serious . . . well, it's best not to talk about it.'

'Don't I at least deserve a clue?'

Benito came closer to my ear and whispered, 'Castelvetia and Caleb Lawson.'

Linker turned red, this time with indignation.

'You're taking advantage of the fact that their assistants aren't here, to speak ill of them.'

Benito shrugged his shoulders.

'You brought it up, Linker. Besides, it's not our fault that the Hindu is never around and that Castelvetia has an invisible assistant.'

'That is an old subject and it makes no sense to dig it up again. The Argentine is young and the impressions formed now will stay with him for the rest of his life.'

'He has plenty of time to forget everything he runs the risk of learning here,' said Baldone.

'I want to find out everything I can about the detectives,' I insisted. 'Besides, it isn't fair for me not to know what you all do. I might say something inappropriate in front of them.'

They looked at each other in silence. There were two possibilities: they could either include me in the group so that mutual loyalty developed, or they could completely exclude me. If I were somewhere in the middle, I might hear some careless comments, and repeat them to the detectives. They had no way of knowing for sure that I wasn't a snitch. They had to decide if I was truly going to be part of their group or not. After exchanging glances with those who hadn't yet spoken, Linker said, 'Okay, then I'll tell him myself. I'm impartial, and I hate Baldone and Benito's gossiping. When this happened, Caleb Lawson was already a famous detective and prominent member of the Twelve. Castelvetia, on the other hand, was a complete unknown. The case that made them enemies for life was the death of Lady Greynes, whose father had been president of the North Steamboats Company, a shipping business. Lady Greynes suffered from a nervous condition. Francis Greynes built a tower to support her voluntary isolation from the world. The townspeople called her the Princess in the Tower. Lady Greynes very rarely left her refuge. She said that she couldn't stand contact with other people, that they might infect her with fatal contagious diseases. Her husband managed the family fortune, but he couldn't do anything without his wife's signature. One stormy night, the woman fell from the window of her tower. Her head hit a stone lion, and she died immediately.'

'And her husband?' I asked.

'He was several miles away, at a party in Rutherford Castle. As a social event it was terrible, not enough wine, champagne or food, but there were plenty of witnesses. They were very reliable (no one got drunk with such a shortage of booze) so Lord Greynes wasn't considered a suspect. But rumours of his involvement in his wife's death spread by word of mouth and were printed in the newspapers. Francis Greynes wanted to clear his good name and honour, so he called his old Oxford buddy, Dr Caleb Lawson, and asked him to investigate the case and absolve him of any guilt.'

'Agreeing to help an old friend and then accusing him of murder is behaviour unbecoming to an English gentleman,' I said. 'I hope Lawson didn't do something like that.'

'Of course not,' continued Linker. 'Lawson interviewed the servants, the doctor who had treated Lady Greynes, and Lord Rutherford's dissatisfied guests, and he confirmed Greynes's alibi. He declared it a suicide. Everyone knew that Lawson was the most famous detective in London and the judge wouldn't question his opinion. And yet this judge, a provincial civil servant, decided to keep the case open. He felt he had to.'

'Had Caleb Lawson changed his mind?'

'No, that wasn't it. Caleb Lawson has never, not in his entire career, ever admitted to making a mistake. But Lady Greynes had a sister, Henriette, who didn't believe the suicide theory. Henriette was married to a Flemish painter who knew Castelvetia, and he enlisted his help. At that time, Castelvetia worked with a Russian assistant, a remarkably strong man named Boris Rubanov. Boris had acquired the habit, on every new case, of engaging the domestic help in conversation, without interrogating them. He let them talk about their families, about their little everyday complaints, he bought them drink after drink, and after a few days of increasing trust and alcohol, there were no secrets between them. Thanks to Boris, Castelvetia solved a case which, outwardly was not a mystery.'

'Castelvetia contradicted Caleb Lawson?' I asked.

'Contradicted him? Castelvetia almost ruined Lawson's reputation! After that, Lawson's assistant, Dandavi, had to force him to practise those breathing exercises that Hindus do so they won't succumb to dizzy spells. Boris had gathered the following information: before the crime, a cook and a coachman had heard the sound of furniture being moved around in a room of the tower. Those nighttime noises were what enabled the Dutchman to solve the case. Castelvetia maintained, before the judge, that Francis Greynes had planned his wife's murder long before it happened. He had the tower built in such a way that there were two identical windows, one facing east and the other west. One opened on to a small stone balcony, the other on to nothing. Architecturally, the room was completely symmetrical. Every night the cat would meow and Lady Greynes would go out to the balcony and tend to her. That night, Greynes doubled his wife's medication so that she would fall asleep in the dining room. When he carried her to the tower in his arms, he had already switched the furniture around, so that the window that faced east, instead of being on the left side of the bed, was on the right. Then he went to Lord Rutherford's castle, so he would have an alibi. That night the cat meowed, as always, and Lady Greynes, disoriented by the medication and the rearranged furniture, went out the wrong window.'

'The poor woman,' I said, because I didn't know what else to say.

'Poor Lawson,' continued Linker. 'The press had a field day with him, they even talked of bribery, and he swore undying hatred for Castelvetia. Before Castelvetia had time to report the results of his investigation, Francis Greynes was tipped off and escaped. They say he fled to South America. That flight saved Lawson, because the press paid much less attention to the trial than they would have if the accused were there in the courtroom. Trials in absentia are even more boring than executions in effigy.'

The animosity between the two detectives was a delicate and unpleasant topic, and the assistants were silent, pondering the consequences of that distant episode. I felt slightly ashamed for having taken the conversation in that direction.

Luckily Benito broke the silence. 'But they are also divided by theoretical concerns. I've heard that Castelvetia maintains that an assistant, under certain circumstances, could be promoted.'

'That's enough, Benito, we've already discussed that,' said Linker. 'Don't dream the impossible dream. They are the Twelve, not the Twenty-four. Who's ever heard of an assistant who was promoted? Nobody.'

'But maybe the laws state that –'

'And who's ever seen the laws? They're unwritten; the detectives only make veiled references to them when they're alone. They won't tell them to you, or to me. It doesn't make any sense to argue about something we've never seen, and never will.'

'But I have seen them,' said Okano, the Japanese assistant. His voice, in spite of being barely the whisper of silk paper, made us all jump. 'I've seen the rules.'

Linker attributed his claim to a language problem. 'Do you know what we're talking about?'

Okano responded in perfect French. He was more fluent than Linker.

'My mentor is very methodical, and any time he receives correspondence about the laws, he writes it in a separate place. I had a chance to read the papers, before he burned them.'

'He burned the laws?'

'So no one else could see them. He burned them in the garden of an inn where we were staying during an investigation in a southern town. It was summertime and the cicadas were singing. My mentor burned the papers in a stone lantern.'

'Do you mean to say that you read something about an assistant becoming a detective?'

'That's right. My mentor didn't ask me to keep it a secret, so I'll dare to speak. I even think Sakawa allowed me to read those papers on purpose, so I would know that the remote possibility exists, and so someday you all would know it as well. Knowing that means we have to be better assistants. Not because we have ambitions of becoming detectives, but because the mere fact it could happen exalts us.'

This was much more than the Japanese assistant had said in any of the other sessions, and now he was visibly short of breath. He was drinking a glass of pure absinthe, which was probably the reason for his sudden loquacity. But now the green fairy seemed to have abandoned him. Linker grew impatient.

'Come on, tell us. How is it done?'

Okano squinted his eyes, as if he were recalling something that had happened long ago.

'Four rules have been established for the promotion from assistant to detective. The first is that the detective, on his voluntary retirement, has to nominate his assistant as his replacement. He must be willing to give him his good name and his archives as well. The assistant would carry on his mentor's work, as if he were the same detective. Nine of the eleven other members must approve the appointment. That's the rule of inheritance.'

'And the second one?'

'The second tenet is called the rule of unanimity. That is when all the detectives agree to fill an empty chair by naming an assistant that they deem exceptional based on his performance.'

'And the third?'

'That's the rule of prepotency. When a mystery has stumped three detectives and there is an assistant who is able to solve the case, he can present his application for membership. Their incorporation into the club is subject to a vote in which two thirds of all the members, not just those present, must agree.'

Benito smiled, pleased with his victory.

'What now, Linker? Was I right or not?'

Linker looked at him with irritation.

'But those are hypothetical situations. Pure theory. In practice, none of those three rules have ever been applied. But . . . didn't you say there were four?'

Okano now regretted that he had said so much. Baldone held up the little green bottle and Okano looked at his empty glass. He had to talk to get his reward.

'There was a fourth rule, which my mentor called the rule of inevitable betrayal. But Sakawa didn't write anything more on that sheet of paper, as if he found it so shocking that not even the burning flames could remove the stink of sacrilege. All of the clauses are secret, but that one is twice as secret.'

Everyone had fallen silent. Baldone poured two fingers of absinthe into Okano's glass. He drank it straight. Soon he fell asleep.

'Dream,' said Linker. 'Dream of secret clauses and rules whispered into ears. Dream of papers burning in the stone lantern of a Japanese garden.'

I said goodnight to the acolytes and I went up to my room.

SIX

The next morning I was awoken by banging on the door.

'Get up, assistant! You only have the right to sleep late when you've been out investigating all night.'

It was Arzaky's voice. I jumped out of bed and started getting dressed. I told him to come in because I didn't want to make him wait outside.

'I envy those gleaming boots.'

'I shined them last night.'

'I have mine shined, but they never look that good.'

'I polish my boots with a special cream that my father makes. It's his secret formula.' I opened my shoeshine box and showed him the jar, whose blue label showed a picture of a shoe and the name Salvatrio. 'Do you want some? It's perfect for when it rains. My father says that it can cure injuries too.'

The detective took the jar, opened it and breathed in the cream's smoky odour.

'You put shoe polish on a wound? I don't trust your father that much.'

Arzaky moved some papers off of the only chair in the room and sat down.

'I can make your boots shine like mine.'

'You can? Please do.'

I looked in the shoeshine box for a blackened rag and a sable-hair brush. I sat on the floor and covered the boots with polish and then brushed them vigorously. They soon shined with the blue gleam characteristic of Salvatrio polish.

'I think deep down you're ashamed that your father is a shoemaker.'

'He works hard. I have nothing to be ashamed of.'

'But you don't mention it either. Do you think all the other assistants come from aristocratic families?'

'I suspect not. If they did, they wouldn't be assistants. They'd be detectives.'

'Is that what you think? The detectives don't come from important families either.'

'Doesn't Magrelli come from Roman aristocracy? I read that somewhere. Castelvetia has a noble title, count or duke; and the Hatters own the largest newspapers in Germany –'

'Counts, dukes, millionaires, relatives of the Pope . . . I'm afraid we fall very short of your fantasies. Magrelli's father was a Roman policeman. Zagala grew up in a fishing village and his mother died in a famous storm that destroyed half the ships in port. Castelvetia gave himself a title, but it's fake. The Hatter family used to own a small press in Nuremberg; they printed commercial stationery and wedding invitations. The others I can't recall, I don't know them as well, but I can assure you that Madorakis isn't the heir to the Greek throne, and that good old Novarius used to hawk newspapers on the street. And as for me, I'm a bastard.'

I started, almost imperceptibly, but Arzaky noticed it.

'Don't worry, I'm not going to tell you any big secret that might threaten your sense of decency. My mother, when she was very young, had an affair with the town priest. The priest stayed in his parish, but she was forced to leave, taking her sin along with her. The boy was never baptized. After she moved, my mother had to make up a last name for me. She thought about killing herself, cutting her wrists with the sharp knife she always carried. She read the brand engraved into the steel and that was the name she gave me: Arzaky. Arzaky knives were very common in those days. I understand that in Argentina you are very Catholic . . .'

'The women are; we men are free thinkers . . .'

'Then I hope your mother doesn't mind that her son works for an unbaptized detective.'

We went out on to the street and I quickened my step to keep up with Arzaky.

'Aren't you going to ask me where we're headed? Or have you already guessed?'

'I'm in no condition to guess.'

'You don't seem to care either.'

'In ten minutes, after a cup of coffee, I'll start caring about things again.'

Arzaky walked briskly in his newly shined boots. He was wide awake at night and in the morning too. I don't know when he slept; I'm not even sure he did. We walked fifteen or twenty blocks and we stopped in front of a building whose bronze plaque announced: THE SOCIETY FOR PLATONIC STUDIES.

Arzaky rapped with the door knocker, a bronze fist. A butler opened the door; he was an old man with eyes so pale that he looked blind.

'The secretary of the society, Monsieur Bessard, told me to expect you. It's about the painting, right?'

He led us up a staircase. He was so old that I wouldn't have bet money on his being able to climb the stairs. But he had gone up and down them so many times that he and that staircase had become friends, and the oak steps pushed him upwards; his steps were light, while ours sounded like heavy marching. The staircase led us to a meeting room: a large table, dirty curtains, library shelves. On one of the walls was the painting of four men walking among ruins and olive trees. I guessed that the most broad-shouldered one was Plato, although they were fairly indistinguishable in their tunics and beards. One carried a torch, another a pitcher, the third a handful of dirt, and the fourth was blowing a dried leaf.

'Here it is, *The Four Elements*. Stolen by Sorel.'

'A painting that sent a man to his death,' I said.

'No; if you remember correctly, it was the woman, not the painting, that sent him to his death. If he had killed someone for the painting, Sorel would now be in crime's gilded archives. But instead he ended up on the endless, grey list of all those who kill for love, for jealousy, out of blindness. Love inspires more crimes than hate and ambition do.'

I stared at the solemn, static painting.

'I wanted to find a relationship between Sorel and Darbon,' said Arzaky, as if he were talking to the figures in the painting.

'Did Darbon have anything to do with the recovery of the painting?'

'No, nothing at all.'

'So?'

'So, nothing. The first fact: Darbon's death. The second: Sorel's cremation. What do those two men have in common?'

'I don't know.'

'There is one thing. They were both my rivals. I'm searching for the missing piece of the puzzle that connects Darbon and Sorel.'

'You said that an investigation was nothing like a jigsaw puzzle.'

'Did I say that?'

'You agreed with the Japanese detective. He said that investigation was like a blank page. That we think we see mysteries where there may be nothing at all.'

'I'm pleased that you remember. If I manage to solve this case, you must write up the account of it. I don't remember any of my own words, but I remember what everyone else says. So then we won't search for a puzzle piece, we'll search for a line on a blank page.'

I approached the painting.

'The victims may not be connected through their rivalries with you. Darbon could have been killed by the crypto-Catholics and Sorel could have been burned by someone from his past, someone related to his crime.'

'Perhaps you're right. Our minds always search for hidden associations. We like things to rhyme. We can't accept chaos, stupidity, the shapeless proliferation of evil. We're more like the crypto-Catholics than we think.'

Since we were spending so long in front of the painting, the butler came over to check on us.

'Has anyone else been to see the painting?' asked Arzaky.

'A young lady. She was pretty and seemed very determined.'

'Did she mention her name?'

'Yes, but I don't remember what it was. She just stared at the painting and I stared at her. Her hair was the colour of fire.'

'A philosophy enthusiast,' I said.

The old man, to my dismay, shook his head.

'Women never come here, only old men, sometimes even older than me. And all of sudden this young lady comes in. She told me not to tell anyone that she had been here.'

'So you're betraying her secret.'

'That's true. But ever since she came here I've been asking myself if it was just a dream. Now that I see this young man's face, I can tell that it wasn't.'

Arzaky looked at me sternly.

'Do you know what he's talking about?'

'No. Maybe he's right and it was a dream. Why would a young woman come here?'

The old man seemed to be weighing my words.

'Then it was a dream,' he said. 'That's not such a bad thing. After all, a dream can recur.'

We went down the stairs. Standing at the door, we thanked the old man for his kindness.

'The pleasure is all mine,' said the old man. 'I got to meet the great Arzaky. They say he is the only living Platonic philosopher.'

'I'm afraid that, for a detective, that description isn't a compliment. It's my enemies who say that.'

'You yourself said that enemies always tell the truth and only slander does us justice.'

'If I said that, then I'm more of a Sophist than a Platonist.'

I was anxious lest Arzaky would question me about the woman, but as soon as the door closed he hurried off; he was expected in a meeting.

As I walked towards the hotel, it occurred to me that my silence about Greta was a betrayal of Arzaky's confidence. This is the only thing I'll keep from him, I promised myself. When I arrived at the Nécart Hotel the concierge handed me a note folded in two. The ink was green, and the handwriting a woman's.

I know you took that photograph from Grialet's house. If you haven't mentioned it to Arzaky, don't. I want to

see you tonight, at the theatre after the show. The rear door will be open. Go up the stairs.
The Mermaid

It wasn't even noon, and already I had found another occasion to betray him.

SEVEN

The Grand Opening was four days away, and Viktor Arzaky had already filled the glass cases of the parlour with a variety of objects lent by the detectives. Louis Darbon's widow had donated a microscope with a slide containing a shiny drop of blood. Hatter was displaying some of his toys, including a wind-up soldier that counted metres while he walked. The best Novarius could come up with was the Remington revolver he had used to kill Wilbur Kanis, the train robber, on the Mexican border. At first Arzaky had opposed the idea of showing such a common weapon; it seemed to be the exact opposite of what a detective represented. But since there was so little time left, he gave in.

'"Don't you have something to display that reflects your thinking?" I said to Novarius, and he replied: "That is how I think."'

Magrelli had filled several shelves with his portable

criminal anthropology office, which didn't look particularly portable at all. It was comprised of endless comparative charts, a photographic archive, and several instruments made of German steel that were designed to measure the length of a nose, the circumference of one's head or the distance between one's eyes. Some of the objects needed an explanatory card, such as the one Madorakis displayed from the Case of the Spartan Code, which was a short cane on which you could attach a strip of fabric containing a message. Only someone with a similar cane could decipher it. Castelvetia had chosen a set of five Dutch magnifying glasses, with different gradations.

Benito interrupted my tour through the cases.

'Did you read the news from Buenos Aires?'

'No.'

'Caleb Lawson has been spreading it around everywhere. In Buenos Aires they're accusing Craig of murder.'

I was shocked for selfish reasons. Even though I was now working for Arzaky, I was Craig's envoy. Anything that stained Craig's reputation would stain mine. Mario Baldone had a newspaper. I took it out of his hands.

'Relax, Salvatrio. There was an accusation, but Craig will take care of disproving it.'

The news was written up in vague terms: the police had stopped searching for the magician's killer in the gambling arena. They then began to look for an avenger in the victim's circle. Alarcón's family hadn't hesitated in pointing a finger at Craig. The newspaper said there was no proof that implicated the detective, but that he, due to his convalescence for an unspecified illness, had refused to defend himself.

'You look pale,' said Baldone. 'Here comes Arzaky. The Pole will take care of putting a stop to Caleb Lawson's attack on Craig.'

I was looking at the cases, but my mind was elsewhere. There was the large chest of disguises belonging to Rojo, the detective from Madrid, which was chock full of makeup and wigs and fake beards; and Caleb Lawson's anti-fog spectacles that he used to work at night in London; Zagala's wardrobe and nautical instruments that he carried with him when he boarded ships with their flags at half-mast, or boats abandoned in the ocean. Arzaky had only contributed a series of black notebooks filled with his tiny handwriting, which were displayed open. An empty case awaited Craig's cane.

'I'm leaving it till the last minute,' Arzaky had told me. 'I want to use my friend's cane for a few days. As if he were here with me.'

It made me nervous to see the impulsive Arzaky handling Craig's cane, loaded and ready. I feared an accident.

The Japanese detective had chosen to show a wooden square filled with sand, accompanied by black and white stones. He called it the 'Garden of Questions', and he used it to study the relationships between circumstances and events. When anyone asked him what it was, he responded, 'I sit on the floor and contemplate it, and I move the stones as my thoughts move inside me. Then I take away the stones and I see the shape traced by their movements. That drawing sometimes tells me more than all the evidence and eye-witness accounts and clues, and all those other annoying details we detectives have to deal with.'

All the detectives were now in the centre of the room, seated in armchairs. And we stood around them, their satellites, with one exception: Castelvetia's acolyte.

'Hey, Baldone,' I said. 'That fellow over there, who can't seem to make up his mind about coming in, isn't that Arthur Neska?'

I pointed to a man dressed in black who stood behind a column. Baldone wasn't surprised to see him.

'He keeps hanging around the hotel. They say he was sent by Darbon's widow to see how the investigation is going. But I don't think that's true. If it were, he would try to make conversation, try to get us talking. And he hasn't said a word. He just stands around staring at the detectives, especially at Arzaky. As if the acolytes didn't exist for him.'

Neska's situation perplexed me. And at the same time, in spite of the fact that I didn't like him at all, it made me sad.

'If his detective dies, can an acolyte still keep coming to meetings?'

'No one has relieved him of his post. He's like a ghost Darbon left behind. Besides, in these chaotic times, who would dare to throw anyone out? I would assume that the events here in Paris will lead to new rules.'

'Or perhaps he hopes to be named as Darbon's successor,' I dared to say.

Baldone shook his head.

'No, nobody ever really liked Neska. He has that kind of negative charisma that causes people to dislike him before he's even opened his mouth. Wherever he goes, women stop laughing and birds stop singing.'

Neska had now approached the cases and was looking at Darbon's microscope as if it were a religious relic. Arzaky was asking everyone to be quiet, so Baldone had to whisper in my ear.

'I used to hate him, but now I feel sorry for him. He wants to cling to his old job; he wants to believe that he still has a mission. When the symposium ends, and everyone returns to their own countries or to some city that murder leads us to, he won't have anything to do except tearfully put his mentor's archive in order.'

EIGHT

Arzaky loudly asked everyone to come to order again. Magrelli was the first to speak. His words struggled to impose themselves upon the scattered conversations that continued. Everyone knew that the important stuff was what was said in the corners, not in the centre of the room. The truth is a secret, and secrets are whispered.

'When we had our first meeting, seventeen years ago, only five of us were present. Craig was among us then, even though he's not here today. We agreed on proposing "locked-room" cases as the highest art in our field, but those types of crimes are now a thing of the past. These days they don't attract anyone's attention. I want to propose, without forgetting the glory and prestige the locked room has given us, that we add the serial crime to the list of our greatest challenges.'

'I was there on that occasion, Magrelli,' interjected

Lawson, 'and I'm not willing to change what we established with so much effort and what made the formation of the Twelve Detectives possible. We founded an order, an orthodoxy, a set of rules. If we change one, we'll end up unravelling them all.'

'Come on, Lawson,' said Castelvetia's voice. He hadn't stood up, and the fact that he was speaking from his armchair added a defiant note. 'Ever since the Case of the London Ripper you just don't want to hear anything about serial murders.'

For a few seconds there was perfect silence. We knew that it was a difficult subject for Lawson, but for Castelvetia to be the one to mention it – he who had almost ruined Lawson's reputation in the past – made us all feel in that moment that the Twelve Detectives was at risk of dissolving. What association, what club, could contain such wrath amongst its members – the hate in Lawson's gaze, and the disdain that Castelvetia's words implied? Like so many other associations, the Twelve Detectives had functioned perfectly from a distance, through correspondence and reports. It had functioned well as long as there was the promise of a future meeting, a sum of handshakes and embraces sent over the ocean waves. But now, face to face, the Twelve Detectives' fragility was showing.

We all knew that Lawson had worked with Scotland Yard on the investigation of the infamous murders by Jack the Ripper, who, to this day, is remembered, reviled, and destined to live in infamy – every wax museum contains a hypothetical image of the killer. But in spite of his efforts to help the police, not one single well-founded arrest was made. There were plenty of suspects, but they all paled in comparison to the murderer's audacity and savageness.

Caleb Lawson exchanged a look with his acolyte, and kept quiet, as if obeying the Hindu. Why was he silent? Why didn't he respond to Castelvetia's attack? It was clear to all of us that Caleb Lawson's silence meant he had some sort of surprise in store for the Dutchman. The ace up his sleeve, I would find out later, was me.

'I don't see why we can't also include serial murder among our greatest challenges,' said Arzaky. 'The series and the locked room complement each other perfectly. The locked-room crime happens on a very limited stage, but one with a very high potential significance, since any seemingly circumstantial element can end up in the evidence box: a packet of cigarettes, a key, a torn-up letter, or rope strands as in the case Castelvetia told us about during our first meeting. Serial crime, on the other hand, can spread throughout an entire city, one corpse here and another there, or even over a whole country, or the world. But the chain of signs is limited and one has to find a common pattern created by the killer's obsession or intelligence. In a minimal setting, there is the maximum possibility of combinations; in a maximum setting, the minimum possibility of combinations. I propose that we consider both variants from now on, and that we don't deem inferior the intelligence of a detective who takes on the challenge of a series of crimes to that of one who faces the famous locked door.'

'And what do you have to say about this series, Arzaky?' said a raspy voice. Madorakis, short and stout, had stepped forward. He was smoking a cigar and wore a garish threadbare jacket. He held tight to some sort of worn leather attaché case, tied with a cord (the catch was broken), from which yellowing papers, unbound books and mended gloves struggled to escape. Surrounded by gentlemen, he looked like a travelling salesman. Arzaky was a good two heads taller than the Greek detective.

'And what series is that?'

'I'm talking about Louis Darbon, and your friend, Sorel, who you sent to the guillotine.'

A murmur of surprise was heard. Several of those present weren't aware of the identity of the cadaver incinerated in the Galerie des Machines.

'That's not a serial crime. A series has to be based on a scene that the killer has imagined, inspired by a desire for revenge or by the criminal's childhood. The murderer seeks to repeat that ideal image. There is none of that here.'

Madorakis laughed.

'That is pure Platonism, and I thought that you were in favour of exiling Plato from investigative work. There is no original, archetypal scene that the criminal seeks to replicate. He starts out committing crimes by chance, until he finds an element that strikes a chord with him, and then in the crimes that follow he tries to repeat that element. So if there is something that resembles the archetype, we'll find it at the end of the series, not at the beginning.'

Arzaky moved towards him defiantly, using his height to his advantage. Madorakis didn't back off.

'Don't think you scare me with your so-called philosophy. That's applying the third-man defence. You think that the chain of similarities between one crime and another, and the vague model that inspires them, means that the true crime is nowhere to be found, the total crime that is the killer's full expression and therefore –'

'Therefore,' Madorakis interrupted, 'all the pure murderers – and history shows us this – have kept killing until someone stopped them.'

'And what sort of link can there be between these two crimes without rhyme or reason?'

Madorakis adopted a mysterious air. 'When the third one happens, you'll know.'

'You sound like a fortune teller. First you're a philosopher and now the Delphic Oracle. No one understands your message.'

'I'm sure that you do, Arzaky.'

Madorakis and Arzaky weren't enemies, but they were looking at each other as if they were. What was it in the air that was cancelling out past alliances? Was it the electricity of the World's Fair, the thousands of lamps prepared to make life go on even after nightfall? Arzaky himself seemed shocked by Madorakis's aggressiveness. Going up against Caleb Lawson or Castelvetia didn't bother him, or having a shouting match with his friend Magrelli, but the Greek's outburst had disconcerted him.

I took my watch out of my pocket and checked the

time. The argument continued, but I had to leave. I made my way through the acolytes, who didn't even look at me because their attention was on the detectives' increasingly heated discussions. Only the Sioux nodded his head in acknowledgement. As I passed Neska, he pretended not to see me.

NINE

Although no one could have any interest in following me, I walked through the night looking back every couple of steps, like a conspirator. It was late: that time of the night when we no longer check our watches, and the only people we pass on the street are entirely joyful or entirely melancholy. I was so distracted I almost got hit by a carriage. I heard an insult, but by some strange auditory hallucination it seemed as if it was the horse and not the coachman who shouted at me. It was such a deep voice and a sensible tone: one couldn't help but agree. We should take a cue from horses, they never shut their eyes.

When I arrived at the theatre, the last audience members were leaving. In opera, or any kind of theatre performance, light or profound, you see the same phenomenon: the first audience members leave the theatre chatting and laughing, eager to abandon the world of fiction and re-enter the real, where they feel at home. The last ones to leave, on the other hand, have to be forced out by the ushers or the lights going up or the silence that follows the applause. If it were up to them, they would remain there in the imaginary world the performance offers them. These last stragglers came out without saying a word, grieving over having to abandon the Mermaid's island. They didn't know their place in the world outside; in real life the seats aren't numbered.

I found the side door mentioned in the note and entered without knocking. Dusty sets, papier-mâché statues, armour and costumes from other shows. I was reminded of the Victoria Theatre, where the murderous magician had performed. I thought that in some way all theatres are the same, as if their architects fill them with nooks to show that to create just one stage of illusion you need hundreds of wooden artefacts, moth-eaten curtains, and costumes covered in cobwebs.

I followed the sound of a woman's singing down a hallway. Her voice was so sweet that I longed to stop right there, not wanting to break the spell. I had been to the opera a couple of times and once to a concert, and all three times I fell asleep. I prefer unexpected music, the music one hears without seeking it out, that's unaware that I'm listening.

My footsteps made the woman's voice grow quieter; by the time I was in front of her door and read her name, the Mermaid, she had already stopped singing. She received me with a nervous smile and peeked out into the dark hallway to see if anyone had followed me. She was dressed in a green mermaid costume; some sort of oil made her hair shine as if it were wet.

'Did you bring the photograph?'

I had expected a greeting, some friendly conversation, not just an urgent demand. Once I handed over the photograph, I had no power. I held it out to her but I didn't let go of it immediately and she had to tug at it a bit. I was ashamed by my hand's attitude, acting on its own, without even consulting me. The Mermaid looked at the photo to make sure it was the one she was looking for, turned it around and read her own handwriting: *I dreamt in the Grotto where the Mermaid swims.*

She stared and stared at the green writing.

'Does Arzaky know about this postcard?'

'No,' I lied.

'You are a gentleman, and you did the right thing by returning it. I am eternally grateful.'

'I'm not a gentleman. A gentleman wouldn't have stolen it.'

'Why did you? Did you think it would help you solve the crime?'

'No. I don't know why. I've never stolen anything else in my life.'

'Now that I don't believe. There's never a first time, we've always sinned, hinting at what's to come.'

The Mermaid had barely spoken those words when I remembered another slight infraction: two months before my trip, I had gone into the Craig family kitchen and found a pile of Mrs Craig's clothes on top of the wooden table, fresh off the line and still warm from the sun. I hadn't stolen anything, but I had stroked the garments for a few seconds before I heard the footsteps of the cook approaching. If someone had caught me, what would I have been able to say to them? What worried me about these acts was not that they were my most shameful, my most illicit, but rather that they seemed more truthful than all my polite words and kind gestures.

'Are you going to tell Arzaky about our conversation?' The Mermaid's voice pulled me from my thoughts.

'No,' I answered.

'It's better that way. Remember, I work for Arzaky too, but I can't tell him everything. Arzaky wouldn't know what to do with all the things I find. He sends me to the grottos and caves so I can bring him the clues that are submerged, the worn-out pieces of sunken ships.'

'Did he send you to Grialet?'

'Arzaky has his agents. But sometimes he doesn't trust us. Viktor believes that Grialet killed Darbon.'

'And that's not true?'

'No.'

I felt her hand on my arm.

'Come towards the light. Your boots are so shiny. Is that Argentine leather?'

'Yes, but that's not why they shine. I polish them with a cream my father makes.'

'It's raining. But your boots still gleam.'

'And my father says that this polish also cures wounds.'

'I could use a bottle of that.'

'I'll send you one when I go back to my country. Do you have black shoes?'

'No, but I'll have to get either some shoes or a wound so I can test the cream's effectiveness.'

A creaking noise was heard in the dressing room. There was a coat stand, a shapeless mountain heaped with garments. For a moment I was afraid that she had led me into a trap because it was obvious that someone was hiding there.

'You can come out,' said the Mermaid.

I thought maybe it was a hidden lover, I thought maybe it was Grialet, maybe even Arzaky, but it was Greta. I felt a mixture of rage and relief.

'These theatres are labyrinths. She can show you the way out.'

I was sorry that the show ended so soon. I was starting to be like the people who always leave the theatre last. The Mermaid closed the door to her dressing room. Greta and I walked out together.

'Are they hiring performers? It's a good idea to try a new career. I don't think Castelvetia can keep you much longer as an acolyte.'

'The detectives have more important things to worry about,' she said in an untroubled voice. 'Castelvetia's secrets aren't a pressing subject.'

'Caleb Lawson is going to go after him, sooner or later.'

'Castelvetia doesn't care about Caleb Lawson or his Hindu. He beat him once and he'll beat him again. He's worried about Arzaky.'

'Why Arzaky?'

'He wouldn't tell me. But he talks about it in his sleep.'

It seemed as though she regretted having told me. I didn't dare ask her how she knew so much about Castelvetia's dreams. Did she secretly go to the Numancia Hotel for clandestine meetings? Or was he the one who came to her?

We arrived at the hotel but had to keep a safe distance away because the detectives were talking at the entrance. The acolytes were getting ready to march, in formation, towards the Nécart.

'Why did you go to see the Mermaid?' I inquired.

'I wanted to ask her about the Case of the Fulfilled Prophecy.'

'That's an old case.'

'It's still unresolved. Castelvetia thinks that Grialet was the guilty party that time, but even though Arzaky sent the Mermaid over to investigate Grialet, they weren't able to prove anything. Perhaps the Mermaid protected Grialet then. Perhaps she's protecting him now.'

'And what did she tell you?'

'Nothing. She talked about Arzaky and she sang a song, the song she had sung the night they met. I thought after that she might be willing to talk. But something interrupted her.'

'What?'

'The footsteps of an idiot.'

Now Greta looked at the detectives and assistants, who were disappearing into the night.

'Is this the first time you've seen them?'

'No. I've been here before. I like to watch them, to imagine the day when I'll enter the circle of acolytes. If I can become a member, it will be as if my father did too.'

I didn't raise any objections to her fantasies. Who was I to pass judgment, among the ambitions and worldly matters, on what was possible and what was impossible? Greta took a step back and the streetlight illuminated her; but her face shone so brightly that it looked as if she were the one illuminating the street-light. It was the face of a girl looking through a shop window at a shiny toy she knew she would never possess.

TEN

The next day, at ten in the morning, I was in front of the theatre again. Some acolytes were with me, as well as their respective detectives: Magrelli, Hatter, Araujo. Then Zagala arrived, wearing a hat that exaggerated his nautical air. He was complaining, saying that Benito should have been there but he was still sleeping. A policeman tried to keep the group from getting through, but Magrelli, accustomed to wrestling with the carabiniere, had no problem getting rid of him. He flabbergasted him with convoluted pronouncements of authority, constantly pointing upwards with his index finger, indicating his friendship with very important civil servants, and showing him papers affixed with bureaucratic-looking signatures and seals.

'You always have to show the police some piece of paper. They are very sensitive to written documents,' he explained to us later.

Inspector Bazeldin went white when he saw the detectives burst into the room and climb the stairs towards the stage. I followed their impatient and happy march like an automaton. The fights had been forgotten and they were once again a cohesive group, now that crime had called to remind them that they had a purpose in life.

'The show is cancelled,' said the inspector. 'We don't need any actors.'

But he couldn't stop them; they surrounded him like a chorus, all questioning him at once, heaping on the praise and flattery just to distract him. On the stage, large blocks of ice created a sort of frozen grotto. The Mermaid's body was sunk into a circular lagoon in the centre. Her black hair floated around her. Blood had traced streaks in the water, like veins in marble. Her eyes were closed. Her lips were black, holding on to the kiss of death. I looked at her without sadness or horror, as if there were no relationship between the cold scene before me and the splendid woman I had spoken to the night before. I could still smell the mix of perfumes in her dressing room. I looked at my hands, the hands that had touched the photograph. I wondered if it wasn't that photograph that had been the passport to the frozen place she now inhabited.

The inspector, who was unable to contain the detectives, tried one last gesture of authority, and austerely gave the order for the body to be taken out of the ice. Four policemen knelt down and, after rolling up their sleeves, plunged their arms into the water. They reached hands and ankles and pulled up, insecurely and brusquely. The Mermaid hadn't lost her beauty in death; one could imagine that all her arduous insistence on green costumes, grottos, and her stage name had been the preparation for this perfect scene of underwater sleep. But when she was pulled out of the water, with her hair oily and sticky and her slack limbs taking on the slapdash poses of a broken doll, we were keenly aware that she was no longer the Mermaid; she was a corpse. Bazeldin knelt down out of pity, wiped a handkerchief over her face, cleaning it of oil, hair and blood. Her lips were now white.

The rescue manoeuvre had left the nape of the Mermaid's neck showing. It was covered in blood. Without realizing what I was doing, I took a step forward and almost fell into the water. Benito, who had just arrived and was still buttoning his shirt, held me back.

'What's going on? Did you know her?'

I managed to say, after much effort, 'No.'

'And Arzaky?' asked Magrelli. 'Where is he?'

'He was the first one here,' the chief of police responded with annoyance. 'I was ready to throw him out, because his arrogance aggravates me, but luckily that wasn't necessary. He left on his own. As soon as he saw her, he took off with those giant strides, as if he had urgent business to attend to. This case has nothing to do with you detectives, so if you don't mind I'm going to have to ask you all to leave. The World's Fair is expecting you.'

'Of course it has something to do with us,' said Hatter. 'This woman was Arzaky's lover.'

Inspector Bazeldin started to say something, but when he opened his mouth no sound came out. He dropped the handkerchief he had used to clean the Mermaid's face. Perhaps he was thinking about all those agents he had sent to follow Arzaky, all those reports that piled up on his desk, all the informers he had bought useless information from that weren't even able to tell him the name of Arzaky's lover.

Zagala made a murmur of displeasure. He didn't want Arzaky's secrets aired in front of the police. Hatter realized he had said too much and tried to defend himself.

'What? We all knew it. That's why we came as soon as we heard the news.'

Baldone made the sign of the cross, very quickly, so that no one would notice. I imitated him, unashamed: the detectives could fight with positivism, but we acolytes were allowed to be religious. I knelt down for a few seconds beside the body to pick up the handkerchief Bazeldin had just dropped. I said two our fathers in a soft voice: one for the Mermaid's soul and the other for the chief of police not to discover my sleight of hand.

Madorakis stepped forward and bent down beside the body. He touched the Mermaid's oiled hair with one finger.

'First Darbon, Arzaky's adversary. Then Sorel, who Arzaky had sent to the guillotine. And now this young lady dressed up as a mermaid, Arzaky's lover. The Polish detective finally has his series.'

PART FIVE

The Fourth Rule

ONE

In the days following the Mermaid's murder, no one saw or heard from Arzaky. I am sure that it had been the shock of seeing her body that made him disappear. He had gone to the theatre, alerted by one of his informants on the police force; he had looked in to see the Mermaid's drowned body and then, without saying a word, he had completely vanished. After a few hours, the detectives began to worry. Gathered in that room at the Numancia Hotel, they were now ensconced in an uninterrupted conclave. Caleb Lawson recommended that I wait in Arzaky's study, in case he happened to show up.

Arzaky's absence had caused more worry than the crime itself. The next day representatives of the Fair's authorities began to arrive, with urgent messages that I piled into a cardboard box. What I had seen of Arzaky was a negligible portion of his real life, of the people he dealt with, of the numerous tasks that kept him busy: his absence made that hitherto buried world come to light. A parade of people came through the office: desperate women, men who owed him their lives, wives of the falsely accused and imprisoned, people selling secrets. I tried to get rid of them all calmly and quickly.

'Monsieur Arzaky will be back any minute.'

I grew tired of waiting and I went out to look for him. I visited all the bars the detective frequented, I found informants who told me about other, more secret, spots; I left absinthe territory for opium dens. The more I asked around, the further Arzaky seemed. I wasn't worried about the lack of clues, but rather the abundance of them. Arzaky had argued with a Hungarian, Arzaky had hit a woman, Arzaky had grabbed a dagger from a Chinese cook, that shadow on the wall is Arzaky's shadow. A blind man, high on opium, opened his white eyes and said, 'Arzaky is dead, and you are the one who killed him.'

I couldn't go through those lairs without tasting what they offered me, so the more debased the places were, the more debased I became. First the wine, then the liqueurs improvised in secret stills, adulterated absinthe, which made me forget life's troubles, and finally opium, which made me forget everything. In a few days all my money was gone. Everything Arzaky had paid me I had spent searching for him.

In my travels I noticed that what was said about Arzaky could have been said about anyone. A woman had whispered in my ear that Arzaky was sleeping in a brothel on the outskirts of town. When I went in, a drunken old man from Marseille attacked me with a butcher's knife. I escaped, but the next night I came back again to ask for Arzaky. 'He was here last night; a man from Marseille attacked him with a butcher's knife,' they replied.

Aware that my stupor was clouding my good judgment, I spent an entire day in my hotel room, cleansing my system. There was no reason to think that Arzaky had given in to his grief. He could be working in secret, going back over old clues. At dusk, finally lucid, I decided to pay Grialet a visit. He opened the door himself, dressed in some sort of long black outfit. I wondered if I had interrupted a ceremony.

'Ah, my friend, the one who steals photographs. You'll have to forgive me, I'm fresh out.'

'I'm ashamed. I already returned that photograph to its owner.'

'I was its owner. What are you looking for now?'

'I wanted to ask you about Arzaky.'

'Arzaky? They say he's gone, disappeared, that he's dead.'

'Did he pay you a visit?'

'I didn't have the pleasure.'

'The Mermaid was Arzaky's lover,' I told him, somewhat defiantly. He didn't bat an eyelash.

'I know. She was my lover too. He sent her to investigate me. And now he's sending you.'

'I'm here under my own steam.'

Grialet laughed.

'The more we think we are acting on our own, the more we are being manipulated by unknown forces. Come in. We're all friends here.'

There were three other men gathered in the living room. I recognized Isel's bird-like profile. He greeted me with a nod of the head, leading me to believe that he remembered me too. Near the piano there was a man who wore a priest's habit. His face was round and childlike, without any trace of a beard. The other, a younger man, wore a white shirt, open at the neck, and he looked around with the anxious eyes of a consumptive.

'Here we are: Darbon's bêtes noires. You've already met Isel; the others are Father Desmorins and the poet Vilando. Desmorins was expelled from the Jesuits for dabbling in necromancy, but he hasn't accepted that decision and still wears the habit.'

Desmorins spoke in a high-pitched voice: 'The Pope should go back to Avignon. Now, more than ever, the Catholic Church is not a stone, nor a cathedral, nor the nave at the heart of every cathedral. It is a broken bridge leading nowhere.'

'Desmorins insists on writing those kind of things. He started out as the superior of the order's libraries, and his job was to burn all the inappropriate books, but some time ago he gave up the fire and gave in to the temptation of that literature. Young Vilando, on the other hand, has followed the opposite path: he once belonged to the circle of Count Villiers and Huysmans, but now he spends every night writing poems and then burning them. He wants them to exist only in the mind of the unknowable God.'

Grialet paused. The four men looked at me. They enjoyed being observed by others. They had spent their lives cultivating secrets, and now they wanted their faces, their slightly outlandish outfits and their conspiratorial gestures to illustrate the power of everything they were keeping secret.

'These are the enemies of progress, the enemies of the tower and the World's Fair,' continued Grialet. 'The disciples of the secret teachings of Christ. We're not so dangerous as Darbon suspected. Don't you agree?'

He pointed me to an empty chair. I sat with them. Soon there was a glass of spiced wine before me.

'We are against the World's Fair. At least Darbon wasn't wrong about that,' said Grialet.

'Why?'

'Because we believe that secrets make the world exist. The city of Paris has been a refuge for esoteric knowledge for many years. Now they've decided to illuminate it. Electric light, positivism, the World's Fair, the tower: they are all part of the same thing. Science no longer strives to collect answers, but rather to obliterate the questions.'

I drank to the bottom of the glass. Since I wasn't a born drinker, I liked the sickly sweet taste, the scent of cinnamon, and the other overlapping flavours that I couldn't name. When the rock crystal cup was empty, Grialet refilled it.

'For years we initiates fought amongst ourselves.

Gnostics, Rosicrucians, alchemical nostalgists, Valentinians, faithful of the Martinist church, Christians, anti-Christians. But now we are united. Now we all have a common enemy. Positivism, the desire to understand everything, to explain everything, is the modern disease. The tower, from which one can see the whole city, and the World's Fair, which wants to display everything that exists, are nothing less than the symbols of a world without secrets. And your detectives encourage the builders, they encourage the scientists; they don't know they too are alive because secrecy exists, and when it disappears, they will too.'

Isel brought his birdlike profile close to mine. 'Grialet speaks the truth. The detectives have become, unwittingly, the most flagrant sign of the philosophy that everything can be explained. They cannot be saved. None of them, except Arzaky.'

'Why Arzaky?'

'Because he's Polish,' said Isel. 'Because he hasn't renounced his faith in Christ, even though he hides it. Because he believes in the dark forces and in the limits of Reason. But that battle takes place in his heart and it will eventually destroy him. He thinks he's a rationalist, a materialist, but he is a soldier of Christ.'

The wine had begun to make me woozy. For a few seconds I feared it was a bewitched potion. I tried to put some order to the words that floated around in my mouth; I slowly translated them into French.

'Darbon was investigating all of you. Darbon knew

that you wanted to use the tower to disseminate your beliefs.'

'Disseminate?' Grialet laughed. 'Do you think we're journalists?' He said the word with unbounded disdain. 'We've done everything possible to hide our beliefs. Christ preached to us, but his true message was a secret one: we are the target of that message, and we transmit it according to our rules. It doesn't matter if they illuminate the world with electric light: the more light there is, the more shadows it creates. We hide ourselves in the darkest corners, like the Christians in the catacombs.'

I wanted to jolt Grialet out of his superior posturing. I wanted to bring him back to the world of accusations, evidence and alibis.

I asked him, 'When was the last time you saw the Mermaid?'

Grialet stood up. I assumed that I had offended him and that he would kick me out right then and there. But he answered with the saddest voice I've ever heard.

'If only that were the case. If only I had stopped seeing her. I can't stop seeing her. I go to the window and I think she's about to show up.'

'Did you kill her?'

'Me? Why would I kill her?'

'Out of jealousy over Arzaky. Because she worked for him.'

'The Mermaid died of what all mermaids die of: the call of a world that doesn't understand them.'

Grialet's voice had begun to crack. He moved away from us and towards the window. Father Desmorins listened to everything with his gaze lowered, and didn't interfere. The consumptive poet fixed his large damp eyes on me. It seemed that he was about to say something and he raised his hand, as if we were in school and he was awaiting the teacher's approval, but then he lowered it quickly and regretfully. It must have been true that he burned his manuscripts because the tips of his fingers were blistered and scarred.

Isel dug his claw-like fingers into my arms.

'It is true that we are dark men, and that our rituals eventually leave us with a certain distaste for life that sometimes leads us to lose our way. Among our predecessors, the suicide rate is higher than for other men. "Lucky are those that die a quick death, a death that the Church condemns," wrote the Baron Dupotet. But don't think that your detectives are men of the light. With the risks they run, they too, unsuspectingly, seek out a death worthy of their legend. Or hadn't you noticed how frequently they put their lives in peril for no good reason? And then there is the other temptation: crossing the line.'

'What line?'

'The one that separates them from the murderers,' said Isel.

Grialet called to me from the window. I freed myself from Isel's grasp.

'You think you are looking for Arzaky? I think Arzaky's following you. Come here.'

I looked through the glass at a man who was trying to hide in the darkness. He looked without daring to enter. His hair was a mess; he hadn't changed his clothes or shaved in days. The man who used to be Reason incarnate was now seeking refuge in the shadows. Behind me, the wall whispered in black ink:

I am the Gloomy One – the Widower – the Unconsoled
The Prince of Aquitaine, at his stricken Tower

I felt a mixture of happiness and disappointment. While I was relieved to have found him, I had hoped that Arzaky was on his way to a revelation, a solution to all of the enigmas. And the man that was there below, clumsy and dishevelled, didn't even look as if he knew where he was.

By the time I made it out on to the street, he had disappeared.

TWO

It was 2nd May: three days before the Grand Opening. The Numancia Hotel was a constant hubbub of travellers coming and going; many had come to the Fair some time ago – secret delegates from the European crowns, technicians intent on investigating the future, inventors in search of inspiration – and thanks to their safe-conducts and permits they had gone through the pavilions at their leisure, they had travelled in the coaches that went through the Fair, they had exhausted themselves climbing the empty tower. But their privilege was about to come to an end: the day was approaching when the treasure would be handed over to the masses. For them it was time to leave: drawn by the constant promise of the future, for them the Fair was already beginning to seem like a tired amusement park, a circus they'd already seen, a poor imitation of the modern world.

When I arrived at the Numancia, Dandavi, Caleb Lawson's assistant, warned me, 'They are waiting for you.'

'For me?'

'Today's session cannot start without you.'

'What do they need me for?'

'Since Arzaky isn't here, you have to be. You'll be his eyes and ears.'

'And his tongue as well?'

The Hindu looked at me with his large almond-shaped eyes and adopted a serious but ambiguous tone, it was impossible to tell if he was wise or just vague.

'When the time comes, we all learn to speak, and to be quiet.'

I entered the subterranean parlour. Caleb Lawson had taken Arzaky's place. He seemed happy to be at the centre of the scene, but reluctant, like an understudy who is called unexpectedly after months of waiting and realizes that he's forgotten his lines. Now that the Mermaid was dead and the mystery was still unresolved, the instruments that filled the glass cases seemed like old, useless artefacts. It had been Arzaky's presence that gave meaning to those objects. I looked for Craig's cane, but I only found the label that listed its name and purpose. Wherever the Polish detective was, he had taken the weapon with him.

Caleb Lawson clapped his hands to call order. He wanted to begin, but his voice didn't come out. He coughed, waited for Dandavi's look, and finally spoke above the voices that continued to whisper in the corners.

'We don't know where Viktor Arzaky is, so we'll have to start without him. I want to remind you all that, unless he has a good reason, we should consider his absence a serious breach of our rules.'

'Come on, Lawson,' interjected Magrelli. 'Let's respect Arzaky's grief. Now is not the time to be sticklers about the rules.'

'They say he was seen in a church,' said Novarius timidly.

'And at the tower, looking out over the void, about to jump,' whispered Rojo, the Spanish detective.

'Benito told me that he's been sighted several times,' said Zagala. 'We shouldn't give credence to these rumours.'

'It's likely that he hasn't been in any of those places,' said Castelvetia. 'When great men disappear, instead of not being anywhere, they commence being everywhere at once.'

Caleb Lawson, hearing Arzaky's name mentioned over and over, wanted to change the subject, as if by speaking his name so much they might conjure him up.

'The first speaker on the list is Madorakis.'

The short, stout Greek detective stepped forward.

'This meeting came about as a result of the World's Fair. Arzaky warned us: just as we wanted to display our knowledge with our small exhibition, meetings, and the publication of our thoughts, crime has also decided to display its arts. That is why these three murders happened here and now. And although at first they seemed unrelated, they are obviously part of a series.'

'There were only two murders,' interrupted Lawson.

'The killer wants us to read his signs. We must consider the incineration of the body as the second element in the series. Which is why I say there were three; and there will be another.'

'A fourth?'

'And on Opening Day. There has been one week between each crime, and on that day it will have been a week.'

'And since you seem to know everything, who's the killer?' asked Zagala.

'He is someone who is obsessed with the Twelve Detectives, but especially with Arzaky. The three victims have all been connected to him. His legendary adversary, his victim (Arzaky sent Sorel to the guillotine), and his lover.'

'The private lives of the detectives . . .' began Magrelli.

'Private life ends where crime begins.' Madorakis pointed at me. 'And I would take good care of that boy, since the murderer may use him to complete the series.'

Suddenly everyone was looking at me with a mix of surprise and compassion. It was clear that many of the detectives had scarcely been aware of my existence.

'Why four?' asked Zagala. 'Where did you get the number four from?'

'From *The Four Elements*, of course,' Castelvetia hastened to say.

Madorakis didn't like anyone beating him to the punch. He looked at Castelvetia contemptuously. There couldn't have been two more different detectives: the Greek's crude, threadbare clothes versus the Dutchman's refined affectation.

'Castelvetia is right. It's possible that the killer has set some guidelines randomly. Sorel, whose body was burned, stole a painting entitled *The Four Elements*. And each one of the deaths was linked to one of the elements, Sorel to fire, the young lady to water, and as for Darbon . . .'

'Earth!' shouted Rojo, as if he were Rodrigo de Triana. 'Hitting the ground was what killed him.'

'That's not the only possibility,' said Zagala, dampening Rojo's enthusiasm. 'The killer might consider that what killed him was his falling through the air.'

Voices in favour of one or the other were heard. Finally Madorakis made his booming voice heard above them.

'I lean towards earth, but we don't know how the criminal thinks. Which is why I suggest that on opening day we keep a close watch on anything that has to do with the earth or the air. I was going through the programme for the Fair and I found two displays that might appeal to the killer. One is the dirigible that will fly over the fairgrounds. The other is a large globe at the entrance. The embodiment of the earth.'

'Speaking of earth,' said Zagala, 'I noticed that in the Argentine pavilion they have set up a large glass container filled with dirt that visitors can sink their hands into to test the virtues of the soil in the Pampas and confirm the existence of earthworms.'

'I can't think who would want to do something so

disgusting,' said Castelvetia. He looked at me, as if I, merely by being an Argentine, must be an ecstatic participant in such a filthy act.

Caleb Lawson tried to regain control over the meeting.

'Let's add the Argentine dirt to our suspicions. Now we just need to decide who goes where. And since we've finished talking about murders, let's move on to more important things. Let's talk about Craig.'

THREE

Caleb Lawson hadn't raised his voice when he mentioned Craig, but the name resounded like thunder, like an irretrievable scream. Without knowing why, I took a step back, and I would have taken another if I hadn't bumped into Dandavi, who seemed to have been put there to keep an eye on me.

Now there was complete silence, because everyone wanted to know what Craig could possibly have to do with this matter.

'I don't want what I say to be taken as an attack on Craig, but rather a defence of our occupation. Since forever, since our profession began (which some people like to say was in China, the nebulous origin of all things with mysterious beginnings), every time we say the word "detective" we whisper the other, "assistant", or the word coined by Craig himself, "acolyte". Although we often don't see them, here they are, beside us, silent: our assistants. The strain of logical thought sometimes pushes us towards madness, but our acolytes, with their perseverance, bring us back to reality. There are some who are guides for the others: my faithful Dandavi, for example, or old Tanner, who accompanied Arzaky in his glory days, now sadly over. Even Baldone, although he is not always as discreet as his office requires. With their chatting, often sensible and sometimes trivial, the acolytes remind us what other human beings think, and in contrast, they invite us to change our perspective, to carry out our syllogisms boldly, to astonish.'

The acolytes had imperceptibly moved closer to the centre of the room, amazed at being lauded so profusely.

'Craig, however,' continued the Englishman, 'disagreed with that. He wanted to be different. He wanted to forge a new path, investigate alone, tell his own stories. He wanted to be Christ and the four Evangelists at once. Now we receive news that he has been accused of lying, murder and torture. His final case, which was supposed to have been the culmination of all his wisdom, is a murky matter; unexplainable, which Craig himself has refused to clarify. And if the version in which he actually killed the guilty party is confirmed, we can be sure that his act is a threat to all we believe in. Who would bother following clues if they were authorized to commit torture and summary execution?'

Caleb Lawson left his question floating in the air. I bit my tongue to keep from interrupting. We acolytes were not allowed to speak. Arzaky would have shut him up immediately, but he wasn't there. His absence gave Lawson the authority. Castelvetia followed his words indifferently, looking at his polished nails. The others were too perplexed to respond. Businessmen, criminals, and police chiefs had spread all sorts of rumours about them, but a detective had never been accused of murder by one of his own.

'But perhaps I'm being unfair. Craig deserves someone to defend him, someone who was with him during those dark days. If no one objects, I would like to give the floor to Sigmundo Salvatrio.'

Dandavi pushed me and I stumbled forward. Caleb Lawson approached me.

'Salvatrio, what do you think of the accusations against Craig?'

I remembered the body of Kalidán the magician, with his arms open. In my memory the cloud of flies still buzzed, I feared that the recollection would draw them in to surround me now.

'Craig was my mentor, and I owe everything to him. He would never do something like that.'

'You didn't, at any time, think that not having an assistant could cause him to get lost in the method, lose his mind?'

'It is true that Craig worked for many years without an assistant. But some time ago he established an academy devoted to investigation. We students said that he had created it just so he could groom the finest of us to become his assistant . . .'

'Or a detective.'

'He didn't say anything about detectives or assistants. We just wanted to believe it could happen.'

'And who was chosen to be his assistant?'

'No one. The finest of us was murdered. Everyone knows that.'

'Weren't you the best?'

'No.'

'Then how did you end up here?'

'Because I was loyal to the end. Because I stayed with Craig when all the others abandoned him.'

My words raised a murmur of approval. While all the detectives were well known in their field, they had been through many difficult moments: press scandals, unsolvable murders, traps set by criminals. An assistant's faithfulness was never more valued than when a detective had been discredited.

'And you came here as a messenger.'

'Yes. To bring the cane.'

'Isn't it possible that Craig's message was more complex than just bringing an artefact? Isn't it possible that the infection that has taken over Craig's mind has spread to you?'

'What infection?'

'The attraction to crime. The temptation to cross the line. We're all tempted sometimes.'

'I'm drawn to investigation. Ever since I was a boy, when I read the adventures that you detectives starred in and dreamt of doing the same one day.'

'But boys grow up. And when they do, their dreams change, fade, or become sullied.'

'I still long for the same things,' I replied, without knowing for sure if I was lying or telling the truth.

'Acolytes are quiet and stay in the corners, and you, the newest one, are the most invisible of all. Which is why I wanted to get to know you better before asking you this question: did you visit Paloma Leska the night of the crime?'

'Who?' I asked, even though I knew very well who he was talking about.

'The Mermaid. Did you think she was a real mermaid? Her name was Paloma Leska.'

'I won't deny it. I went to return a stolen object.'

'What was that object? And who had stolen it?'

'It was a photograph. And I stole it. I thought it might be useful for the investigation.'

'And you found the body and didn't say anything?'

'The body? No, the Mermaid was alive. She still wore her green costume. I've never seen a woman as alive as she was.'

'And can you prove that you didn't kill her?'

'No! But why would I kill her?'

Caleb Lawson stopped looking at me and addressed his public.

'I want this young man to be suspended immediately and denied entrance to our meetings from now on.'

'He's Arzaky's assistant. Arzaky is the one who should decide that,' said Magrelli.

'Arzaky isn't here, so we'll be the ones who decide. This young man was at the scene of the crime at the moment it was committed. We'll have to inform the chief of police as well . . .'

That jarred me. I wouldn't fare well with Bazeldin, who would do anything to get rid of Arzaky.

'I'm innocent. It would only take Arzaky a second to prove my innocence.'

'But he's not here, and you have no witness to confirm that, when you left, the Mermaid was still alive.'

Not only was my membership in the circle of assistants about to be taken away, but it also looked as though I was headed for jail. I had entered the world I had read about as a child, but my storyline had unexpectedly digressed. I spoke without thinking, 'Yes, I do have a witness.'

'Who?'

Was I slow to speak? It seemed there was an incredibly long silence, but time passes differently in dreams.

'Castelvetia's assistant.'

Castelvetia stood up. I didn't look at him. He came towards me, to shut me up.

'She'll tell you the truth. Greta . . .'

There was a murmur of surprise. Caleb Lawson smiled. His tense body seemed to relax, his public prosecutor stance disappeared. In that moment I understood that I had been tricked, that they didn't care about the accusations against Craig. Lawson was just waiting for that word, the proof that he needed against Castelvetia.

'She. Greta,' repeated Lawson triumphantly.

Castelvetia looked around him. There were no longer any traces of affectation in him. He had abandoned his posture, and his elegant mannerisms had fallen away like a cape descending to the ground. His hands, which had seemed to be mere objects of contemplation, were now claws. His voice had deepened.

'She isn't an assistant in the strict sense of the word. Besides, I was planning to inform the Twelve Detectives about the presence of my collaborator as soon as the problems we are currently dealing with were resolved.'

'Having a woman as your assistant breaks all our rules,' said Caleb Lawson. 'I propose that Castelvetia be suspended. I'll remind you that voting is by simple majority . . .'

Lawson raised his hand. So did Madorakis and Hatter.

'I support the motion,' said Magrelli, 'but only as a precautionary measure.'

There were nine detectives present; only one more vote would ensure his suspension. Rojo hesitated, but eventually raised his hand.

'And now I call for a vote on the precautionary separation of Arzaky, and his assistant as well . . .'

Would the Twelve Detectives have voted against Arzaky? I don't think so. They wouldn't have dared go that far. Before anyone had the chance to make that mistake, his voice was heard.

'What are you doing, Lawson?'

The Englishman jumped.

'Arzaky! Where have you been?'

'I've been in a lot of bad places these past few days, and throughout my life. But this is the worst place of all. In every dive there are rules of conduct; here, it seems that the only norm is humiliation and dishonour.

You wanted your revenge against Castelvetia? Well, now you have it. Why go after my assistant too?'

'Because he didn't have anyone to assist. Besides, he knew Castelvetia's secret and he didn't say anything.'

'He's an assistant, not a stool pigeon.'

'But our code of honour . . .'

'I demand that Salvatrio be cleared of all guilt and charges, and that he continue to help me with this case.'

Lawson had turned pale. He wanted to challenge Arzaky's words, but he couldn't. Yet he didn't want to give up centre stage, so he said to the Pole, 'We have already realized what you've known for some time: that the killer is following a plan based on *The Four Elements*. We have only to decide whether the first murder was earth or air and, based on that . . .'

Arzaky raised his eyebrows, in an exaggerated look of surprise. He had lost weight during his absence, and now all his features were more prominent, as if he was wearing a mask of himself.

'*The Four Elements*? Who told you that had anything to do with the case?'

'That is what you were trying to hide from us.'

'You're missing either earth or air? Then we'll have to keep a close watch on the entire planet, because there's air and earth everywhere.'

I withdrew to the back of the room, ashamed. No one was looking at me any more, because all eyes were fixed on Arzaky. Magrelli had approached to effusively shake his hand and Zagala was waiting his turn. Novarius was consulting the wall clock, as if the only thing he was worried about was how many days, hours, and minutes were left before he could flee these European complications.

I took advantage of the distraction to open one of the cases and take out Darbon's microscope. It was a small Swiss instrument with bronze and steel pieces. When I closed the case's glass door I noticed that there was someone beside me. I feared it was Neska. I was about to give an explanation for my action, when I saw that it was Castelvetia.

'I was afraid. I spoke without thinking,' I told him.

He looked at me so fixedly that I feared he was going to slap me. He spoke condescendingly.

'No one asks for explanations from fools. At least they have that privilege.'

'But I wanted to explain it to Greta . . .'

Castelvetia smiled, as if he had the right to a modicum of revenge.

'You won't see her again. We are leaving Paris tomorrow.'

Castelvetia pushed me out of the way. The first member in the history of the Twelve Detectives to be expelled left the subterranean parlour of the Hotel Numancia with swift steps.

FOUR

I went to the hotel, locked myself in my room and tried in vain to bring my correspondence up to date. I would begin a letter and abandon it; a drop of ink would accidentally fall on the page and I would watch it expand as if it were a small octopus. I consulted a railway timetable to see when the next train left for Amsterdam. If Castelvetia had told me the truth, perhaps I would have a last chance to see Greta.

I put the handkerchief that Bazeldin had used to wipe the Mermaid's face under the microscope. A weak ray of sun shone through the window. It was enough to light the small mirror that in turn lit the glass. A shape was already beginning to form when they knocked on the door. Just in case, I hid the microscope that I had taken without permission.

It was Arzaky. Should I tell him I was sorry about the Mermaid's death? I remembered my mother writing condolence letters, and overflowing with expressions of grief when someone lost a relative. My father, on the other hand, never knew what to say, and he just lowered his head to look at people's shoes, the only subject he really knew well.

'Don't worry about Castelvetia. He's always been arrogant. He beat Caleb Lawson once and he thought he could always best him. The Englishman entrapped you. But the important thing is that you didn't rat on Craig. That story you told was meant for me and no one else.'

'But I betrayed her . . .'

'You didn't only do it out of fear; you were yearning to say her name. Even when everything around you is going to hell, there is no greater pleasure than saying that word. Any excuse is valid to finally say the name of the one you love. Caleb Lawson knew it. But he didn't get you to snitch on Craig, which was what he wanted even more. There is no greater betrayal than an assistant's disloyalty to his detective, his mentor.'

Arzaky looked at me with a strange seriousness. I felt the same way I had when Caleb Lawson was attacking me: that something was pulling me out of the corners and my hiding places and my invisibility, to give great importance to the most insignificant of my words or deeds, and that was not a good thing for me.

'What do I have to do now? The detectives said my life was in danger.'

'Don't give it a second thought. Await my instructions.

This case is almost closed. I might need your services one last time.'

'And then?'

'Then? You'll go back to Buenos Aires, I imagine. With a clean conscience, knowing you've fulfilled your mission. Craig needs you to tell him everything that has happened, that is happening, and that will happen. He sent you here with a cane and a story; soon it will be your turn to tell him another story, when you return his cane.'

Arzaky left and I wanted to go back to my work with the microscope, but there wasn't enough daylight left.

On 5th May the World's Fair opened.

Never before had so much activity been concentrated in a single place. Even from my bed I could hear the noise of the footsteps that were heading to see the numerous treasures and surprises. The crowds bought up all the tickets and wandered happily through the pavilions, without knowing what to see first. They were all overtaken by a similar anxiety – perhaps the most important thing wasn't what was in front of them, but what was around the next corner. And even those who'd been allocated a pass to go up on the tower suspected that the most thrilling part of the Fair was somewhere else, in some tiny, secret place. Only that which we are denied kindles our true desire.

After taking advantage of the morning light, I set off towards the Numancia Hotel, carrying Darbon's microscope wrapped in grey paper and tied with a yellow cord. It was early and the room was empty. I put the microscope back where it belonged and threw the wrapping into a wastepaper basket.

Tamayak was at the hotel's entrance, accompanied by Baldone, Okano and Benito, all wearing their best clothes. For a moment I thought that they were there because they had discovered that something was missing from the glass case.

'I just took the microscope out for a minute to polish it,' I explained.

They looked at each other. They didn't know what I was talking about.

'We saw you come into the hotel. We want you to come with us,' said Benito. 'We're going to the Fair.'

'How are you going to spread out through the fairgrounds?' I asked.

'Novarius is in the dirigible. He won't budge from there.'

'And you aren't going to be with him?' I asked Tamayak.

'No. If the gods had wanted us to fly, they would have given us wings.'

'What about the others?'

'Rojo and Zagala are keeping watch by the globe. Caleb Lawson went to guard the Argentine Pavilion, with Madorakis.'

'Then you guys aren't going . . .'

'We have another mission. They've charged us with walking around the Fair. Looking here and there. To see if we notice anything strange. If Arzaky hasn't told you otherwise, you should come with us.'

I went because I supposed I didn't have any other choice. In our conversations there was a sense that we were saying goodbye: Baldone mentioned that he had found a hat to bring back as a gift for his mother; Okano asked where he could buy a case of absinthe at a good price. We showed our safe-conducts at the entrance. It was so crowded that it was hard to stick together.

There was only an hour left before Castelvetia's train departed for Amsterdam. Sometimes I thought I had managed to evade the assistants but a few steps later my guardians would appear, feigning distraction. In order to put some distance between us, I pretended to be feverishly excited about things. I rushed to the American Pavilion, but the Sioux was there at the door, so still that the visitors admired him, thinking he was part of the display. I turned and searched for the Galerie des Machines, but Baldone appeared by my side, offering me a minty soft drink he had just bought. I saw my opportunity when a Chinese delegation made their way through the crowd. They carried a dragon that swayed and twisted, with hundreds of people inside. The gigantic head leaned one way and then the other. The choreography was perfect, but the dragon hadn't taken the crowd into account and its blind movements crashed again and again into the visitors, knocking them down. The enthusiasm for the Fair's inauguration was such that people were laughing with delight even as they got bruised and trampled. I couldn't hope for a better chance: I went below the dragon's scales and shared the darkness with my Chinese companions. I walked blindly, like the rest. I felt a deep sadness for the people inside that dragon; they were in a world of wonders but condemned to see nothing. Hidden in the bowels of the dragon, I escaped my four guardians.

FIVE

The trains purred in the north station. I ran towards platform four, from where, according to the schedule, Castelvetia's train should be leaving. I hurried through the cars, bumping into passengers who were stowing their luggage and into guards who were giving instructions and briefly enjoying the power bestowed upon them by their grey uniforms. I found Greta and Castelvetia in the third carriage. All the passengers seemed nervous about the departure, except for them, as if they were railway staff whose job was to provide an image of tranquillity for the other passengers. They sat together, without touching, both serious, as if they were strangers. She was by the window, looking out at a group of grey pigeons pecking at some breadcrumbs.

I went towards them and almost bumped into Castelvetia, who had, just at that moment, got up to get a book out of the case he had stored on the luggage rack. When he saw me, the Dutchman sighed, obviously annoyed.

'What? Were you planning on coming with us?'

I had run quite far, and now that it was time to speak I needed to catch my breath. Castelvetia looked with puzzlement at the catalogue of gestures I used to replace the words I couldn't get out. Greta looked at me seriously with her large grey eyes.

'Only one thing could excuse your betrayal,' said Castelvetia. 'Only one thing. That what Lawson said was true.'

'Lawson said a lot of things.'

'You know what I'm referring to. Craig's crime.'

I didn't respond. I let my fatigue overcome me, as an excuse to remain quiet.

Castelvetia's index finger jammed into my chest.

'It's your fault I'm no longer part of the Twelve Detectives . . .'

'I know. And that's why I've come to apologize.'

'No, you came to say goodbye. Besides, I don't want an apology. I want the truth.'

I lowered my gaze, unable to look him in the eye. Then I realized that Castelvetia thought that my reply would be in the negative, and he was anxiously waiting for me to defend Craig's good name.

'Say it: Craig didn't torture the killer. Say it: Craig didn't kill him.'

I couldn't say anything, and my silence spoke for me. The Dutchman took a watch out of his pocket and measured the length of my silence.

'More than thirty seconds. Now I know what you aren't saying.'

The Dutchman was pale. He came close to whisper in my ear, as if he had suspicions about the passengers around us.

'My expulsion doesn't matter; the Twelve Detectives are finished.'

Castelvetia touched Greta's shoulder. She had been looking out of the window.

'Greta, dear, you can talk to the young man.'

'He betrayed us,' she said, without taking her eyes off the windowpane, refusing to look at me.

'We no longer have any grudge against him, because they have kicked us out of something that no longer exists. That erases the offence.'

That upset Greta, and she stood up, annoyed. Without saying a word, she made her way through the last travellers that were arriving. I went down first and tried to offer my hand to help her with the iron steps, but she refused to take it. I managed to brush her fingers, which were ice cold.

'I knew I shouldn't say your name, but for a moment I was happy to hear it come out of my mouth. Then I realized what I had done.'

Greta now addressed me with formal aloofness, instead of the familiar way she used to.

'Now you can say the name as many times as you wish. As a secret, it was powerful. Once the magic word has been spoken, it loses all value.'

'The magic hasn't lost its power.'

She looked at me for a few seconds. She was a woman, at the end of it all, and she was flattered by my insistence, by my dishevelment, by my foolishly running all the way here.

'Shouldn't you be working? They are expecting the fourth murder to happen today.'

'All the detectives are at their posts, keeping watch over any possible versions of air and earth.'

She pointed towards one of the train's windows. Castelvetia was reading a book with yellow covers, decorated with interwoven roses: a romance novel.

'Castelvetia mocks their preparations. He says that they are all wrong, that it's not about air or earth.'

'Castelvetia knows as much as the others do. At least they are at their posts. He's leaving.'

'He's leaving because they threw him out. He's leaving because he has no other choice. Can you imagine what the press in Amsterdam is going to say about his expulsion?'

'Castelvetia could stay anyway. Investigate on his own. If he knows so much, he should stay, solve the mystery and then negotiate his readmittance.'

'You should trust that Arzaky will be the one to solve the enigma. An assistant must maintain his faith even in the lowest moments.'

'I'm no more than a ghost to him. He doesn't tell me what to do. I don't know what he's thinking. Since Paloma's death . . .'

I said her real name to create some distance from the green costume, from the body in the water, from Nerval's damp verses: I said her name as a way not to say anything. Greta stared as if I had uttered an unexpected blasphemy.

'Who?'

'Paloma Leska. The Mermaid.'

'I didn't know her name was Paloma.'

I was young; my pride thought for me. I wondered if she was jealous that I had used her real name instead of her stage name. Was I going to receive, in that station amidst the steam and smell of engine oil, the gift of her jealousy? The train roared. The last passengers rushed to get on board with their luggage, and they pushed their suitcases as best they could. A guard shouted, another insistently rang a bronze bell. I looked at her again, and I knew it wasn't jealousy. She was trembling. Both of us, almost at the same time, understood. We looked at each other for the last time.

'Weren't you talking about magic words? My name isn't the magic word. Doesn't "*paloma*" mean "dove"? This is the moment you were waiting for when you met Craig, this is the moment that justifies your delays and betrayals. This is the moment that justifies you now saying goodbye to me, Sigmundo Salvatrio. Quickly. Quickly.'

Greta pushed me, and that was her farewell. She took the stairs a few at a time, when the train had already begun to move. I waited for it to completely disappear, as if I didn't have the strength to leave. Some pigeons had gathered to eat the stale bread an old woman dressed in rags threw to them. When I walked past them they flew off towards the tall glass heights.

SIX

There are people who need to be still in order to think, but I work better walking or even running. I knew where I was going, but I didn't know why. Against the opinion of Craig and the other detectives, I didn't think an enigma was a painting by Arcimboldo, or an Aladdin's blackboard, or a sphinx or a blank page. It was what it had been since my childhood: a jigsaw puzzle. My father would come home with a large box wrapped in blue silk paper. By the window, I would tear off the paper, throw the pieces to the ground and revel in that wonderful chaos that was waiting for me to put it in order and to find, in the many shapes, the image. Now I had the big pieces in front of me: Darbon's body, fallen from the tower; Sorel's corpse, first executed by guillotine and then burnt; and, the only one that pained me, the Mermaid's lifeless silhouette. There were other, smaller pieces: the black oil that had initiated

Darbon's plunge from the tower, the witnesses' statements, the fire, the obscure quotes on the walls of Grialet's book of a house. I had read Nerval's verses, which I couldn't get out of my head, but it was those other words that were important, the ones that said:

> *The day will come when God will be a meeting between an old man, a decapitated man and a dove . . .*

The answer was written on Grialet's wall, in full view of everyone. Now I knew for certain that the detectives, spread out through the Fair in search of Earth or Air, were looking in vain: it wasn't a series of four, it was a series of three. It wasn't about the four elements, the four roots that the Greeks saw behind everything, but in the Trinity. The old man was Darbon; the decapitated man, Sorel; the dove, Paloma . . .

I arrived at Grialet's house breathless. I climbed the marble staircase and was about to knock when Desmorins, the priest, opened the door. He was also agitated and sweating, as if his path to me had been a symmetrical race.

'You have to stop Arzaky,' he said.

'Where is he?'

'Upstairs. He thinks that Grialet is the killer. I'm going to get the police.'

Before he could leave or I could enter, the shot rang out, reverberating off the walls. It sounded more like a pistol than a revolver or carbine. There was something in the sound itself that was irreparable, as if it were a bomb going off. A shot can miss its mark: an explosion always has consequences for someone. I went up the stairs, not as quickly as the scene demanded, nor as slowly as my tiredness called for. As I walked I was escorted by the words on the walls, which I didn't read.

Arzaky was standing in a room that the morning hadn't quite made up its mind to illuminate. He held Craig's cane, still smoking, in his hand. It looked less like a firearm than some powerful mythological figure's staff. On the floor, seated, with his back against the writing that filled the wall, was Grialet. The shot had entered his neck and torn his carotid artery. For a few seconds, Grialet held a hand over the wound, which was black with gunpowder, but then, out of weakness or resignation, he gave up. He wanted to say something, but couldn't. His legs shook two or three times, and then he was still.

Then Arzaky did something unexpected: he crossed himself. In the name of the Father, the Son and the Holy Ghost; in the name of the Old Man, the Decapitated Man, and the Dove. He stared at me, as if struggling to remember who I was. Then he said, 'Grialet was the murderer. I'll give the details tonight.'

Arzaky held the cane out to me. At first I didn't dare touch it. I had brought it as a relic, and now it was a murder weapon. The cane felt hot.

'Put it back in the glass case. Now it can take its rightful place.'

SEVEN

Arzaky had promised to state the case that very night, but the detectives and assistants waited in vain for him. At first they thought he had run off again, but I arrived in time to tell them that the chief of police had taken him in for questioning about Grialet's death. Bazeldin's long interrogations, which lasted until dawn, were famous. The police chief maintained that the morning's clarity, after a night filled with conflict, stimulated confessions. The detectives' meeting was postponed until seven the next evening.

On 7th May, the detectives arrived punctually. No one wanted to miss Arzaky's explanation. Grimas, the editor of *Traces*, was also there. The only one missing was Arzaky, who arrived two hours late. He made his way through the detectives and assistants without any greeting or apology. His long beard was flecked with white and he looked as if he hadn't eaten in days. He had that mix of energy and weakness that comes with a fever. Around him, was a halo of silence and anticipation. The only one who seemed to have no interest in Arzaky was Neska, who stood by the door like a conference attendee who fears he will be bored and can't quite make up his mind about taking a seat. I could barely contain my nerves, thinking of the words that would be spoken that night; my fingers clenched around the handkerchief I had in my pocket.

The detectives talked about the Fair: even though it had just opened, it already seemed dated, countless visitors had worn it out with their footsteps. Arzaky called for silence, but it wasn't necessary, because everyone had already grown quiet.

'In April of 1888 Renato Craig visited Paris. He stayed at this hotel, as he always did, and we spent our time together taking long walks and talking about crime. It was then that we came up with the idea (I don't know if he thought of it first or I did, or if, as I prefer to remember, it came to both of us at once) to gather the Twelve Detectives together for the World's Fair. We got the Committee to invite us. We were thinking of sharing our knowledge, our scientific advances, discussing theory relating to our craft. We wanted to rest, for a month or two, from murders and suspects, from evidence and witnesses. Wouldn't you like to live in a world without crime?' No one responded. 'Of course not!'

Arzaky's joke only raised a few smiles. Nobody was in the mood for humour.

'But as the Fair grew, filled out and consolidated itself,

we began a rapid process of decomposition. Craig is absent, ill and maligned. Darbon has been murdered and Castelvetia expelled. I cannot restore the harmony we've lost, but at least I can solve the mystery that has been keeping us up at night. I can say that the deaths of Darbon and the Mermaid and the incineration of Sorel's body followed a pattern.'

Something interrupted Arzaky. There was an argument going on in the doorway. Baldone was trying to stop a short, stocky man from resolutely making his way towards Arzaky.

'What is going on over there?' asked Arzaky.

'I am Father Desmorins. You killed my friend Grialet. I want to know why.'

'This is a meeting of the Twelve Detectives. No one outside the order can be present,' interjected Caleb Lawson.

The priest was adamant, but Baldone started to drag him out of the room. All Okano had to do was press two fingers on his right collarbone and the cleric gave in. 'I'll be waiting for you outside, Arzaky!' he managed to shout. 'The street will be your confessional!'

'Let him stay in the room,' said Arzaky to Baldone and Okano. 'Have him sit and not say a word. If he opens his mouth, even once, send him packing.'

The priest sat down, near the door. Behind him was Arthur Neska. Arzaky continued:

'My work has merely been a continuation of the investigation Darbon began and which led to his death. The World's Fair authorities assigned him to make inquiries regarding threats to the tower's builders. They were small attacks of minor consequence, and the clues led Darbon to the caves where Paris's occultists hide. The old detective encountered various sects fighting among themselves: clandestine churches, Necromantists, Martinists, Rosicrucians. But his suspicions centred on a group that shared an interest in music and literature. They didn't have an official name, but Darbon called them the crypto-Catholics. This group had decided that it made no sense to continue seeing the Church of Rome as an adversary, because the only true enemy was positivism. The crypto-Catholics consider themselves heirs to the secret teachings of Christ.

'There were several members of this group: Father Desmorins, whom you've just met and who was defrocked by the Jesuits; the young writer Vilando; and Isel, the millionaire. I also know of a Russian woman, and of a Belgian former officer who pretended to be Egyptian, but they weren't in Paris at the time the events occurred. As Darbon was investigating the attacks, he came into closer contact with the group. And I believe it was Darbon's persistence that inspired Grialet, the leader, to come up with the idea of challenging all the detectives, and at the same time challenging the World's Fair and the tower. Each of the incidents made a point. Grialet thought up a crime that would show that not everything can be explained. He carried this out in order to remind us that we must leave room for that which is secret. It is likely that he has struck before; I myself investigated the Case of the Fulfilled Prophecy, whose author was a poisoner named Prodac. In that instance, I suspected that Grialet had incited the killer, but I couldn't prove it.'

Father Desmorins had tried to stand up and say something, but Baldone pushed him back into his chair. Arzaky was looking at the floor, as if he didn't know how to continue.

'Grialet moved into a house that had belonged to a printer and bookseller and he devoted himself to a new obsession: he wrote all kinds of quotes on the walls, so words would always be present. Perhaps he was trying to create the sensation of living inside a book. That house is a compendium of knowledge and superstition. It is filled with wisdom but also with the triviality typical of occult enthusiasts, that comes from yearning to know the final meaning of all things. While Grialet was away on a trip, I took the opportunity to go into his house and read everything he had written on the walls, but I didn't find anything to link them to Darbon's death. Yet the key to unravel the mystery was there. The key was written on the wall from the very beginning, but I didn't see it until it was too late.

'The crimes appeared to be completely unrelated: our old Darbon, a burned corpse, a mermaid. The only connection between them was that all three had something to do with me. Grialet had chosen for one of his walls an inspired phrase by Eliphas Levi, an occultist whose works Napoleon tried to ban, and with good reason. The phrase postulated God as the union of an old man, a decapitated man and a dove: the Father, the

Son and the Holy Ghost. Darbon, Sorel and the Mermaid were the three elements of this message.'

Zagala, who had spent the entire opening day under the blazing sun, waiting for the fourth crime, seemed peeved. 'What about *The Four Elements*? That was a false lead?'

'Grialet led us to believe that the connection was *The Four Elements*. There weren't four elements, but three: the three baptismal elements. The first: the oil of the catechumen, like that which the wrestlers in ancient times used to slip away from their opponents, and which symbolizes the ability of the person being baptized to reject evil. The second, illuminating flame, and the third, purifying water. Darbon died bathed in oil, like the ancient wrestlers who greased their bodies so their adversaries couldn't grab hold of them. Sorel's body was burned; the Mermaid, who was first knocked unconscious, drowned.

'After the Mermaid's death I thought about giving it all up. Overwhelmed by grief, I withdrew to think. I drank so I could think, and then so I could stop thinking. In those moments of delirium and drunkenness, when the world seemed to be coming apart, splitting into images and phrases that no one could put back together, my fickle memory showed me the words that explained everything. I went to find Grialet; I tried to take him out of the house but he resisted. I had Craig's cane in my hands, as a way to keep my old friend with me. I'll admit I didn't really know how to use it and in the middle of our struggle it went off. You already know the rest of the story.'

Arzaky went to one side of the room and Caleb Lawson took centre stage. He was about to say something, but one of the detectives started clapping, I think it was Magrelli, and some of the assistants joined in. Soon everyone was applauding Arzaky's words. Even Madorakis was clapping. Lawson had no choice but to do the same, but his applause was so weak that his palms barely touched. Then he said, 'Many of you have already packed your bags to return to your respective cities. Thefts and murders await you. This is our farewell evening. Before we close the meeting and go to dinner, does anyone have anything else to say?'

No one wanted anyone to speak. The assistants, at the back of the room, were already looking towards the exit. It was time for dinner and endless toasts and promises of another gathering, which would never happen. Only a wet blanket would dare to say something now. Then I raised my right hand. And since it had been tightly clutching the handkerchief in my pocket, I raised the handkerchief too. I heard some laughter; it looked as if I was waving goodbye from a boat.

'I just want to give my version of the events.'

EIGHT

Caleb Lawson looked at me with annoyance.

'You need authorization to speak. And I don't feel like giving it to you. We already know what you're going to say: he's innocent, he's free of all guilt and responsibility, and so on, and etcetera.'

Arzaky had collapsed into a chair, and he looked at me strangely. I avoided his eyes and said, 'I'm going to talk to someone. If it isn't you, it'll be the press.'

I had spoken loudly, and those who were already at the stairs now headed back into the room.

'Could you possibly have something new to add to what Arzaky said?' asked Magrelli. 'Something we haven't heard? Or will this be a conference on your vast experience in the world of crime?'

'I want to explain the truth as I see it.'

'Go ahead and talk already,' said Madorakis. 'But

keep it short. If we let one assistant prattle on, soon they'll all want to do the same.'

'Even Tamayak,' said Caleb Lawson.

Everyone looked at Arzaky. His opinion was the only one that mattered.

'I don't know what secrets my assistant is keeping, and his speaking without asking my permission is completely out of line. But what does it matter? I was about to fire him anyway.'

Everyone responded with forced laughter. My intervention, when everything had already been wrapped up, was the detectives' worst fear realized. Each time a case was closed, after laying out the solution rationally and convincingly, they always dreaded the appearance of something (an object, a witness, a detail that didn't fit) that could spoil the whole conclusion.

It was difficult for me to speak above the whispering.

'I arrived in Paris with two things for Arzaky: Craig's cane and a message. That message was a story which I won't tell here. Arzaky was generous enough to take me on as his assistant, especially considering that I was a novice and could hardly be expected to replace Tanner, one of the most respected of the acolytes. It was an honour for me to occupy his post. Which is why now, as I speak, I feel that I am betraying Arzaky, and Craig and the Twelve Detectives. However, I must. I wasn't affected by Darbon's death, I had barely met him. And I could care less if all the corpses in Paris were burned. But the Mermaid's death is something

I can't bear, and which I'll never forget as long as I live.

'I felt that I wasn't getting anywhere with this case. When I saw the truth it came to me in one momentous flash. So I don't think I owe the solution to my skill, but merely to luck. To bad luck, I should say, because I would rather continue blindly. It happened this way: Arzaky knew, because of something I unwittingly conveyed to him, that this, your world, was crumbling and that soon there would be no trace left of the Twelve Detectives. He thought up a plan that would restore the world's trust in the detectives and their methods and at the same time get rid of his enemies. He killed Darbon, his competitor, and he killed the Mermaid, who had been his lover but had been unfaithful to him with Grialet. In solving the crimes, he would also do away with Grialet. And, at the same time, he would ensure his own glory by solving a crime in front of all the other detectives. His feat would not be forgotten. It was like founding the Twelve Detectives all over again.'

Lawson, who had been wanting to take Arzaky's place at the core of the Twelve, was now poised to defend him.

'No one is ever going to forget what you just said either. Get him out of this room!'

'No!' shouted Madorakis. 'Let him continue. Someone is speaking to us through him.'

The whispering had stopped. Now they definitely wanted to hear what I had to say.

'In this room several models of the perfect enigma were

presented. Castelvetia spoke of jigsaw puzzles, and I'm inclined to believe that common image best fits the spirit of the enigma. Magrelli spoke of Arcimboldo's paintings, which abruptly change depending on the perspective of the viewer. Madorakis set forth the image of the sphinx, who questions us as we question it. And Hatter offered Aladdin's blackboard, the toy that holds a trace of the words etched deepest even when everything has been erased, just as our memory holds on to distant facts. But there was also another theory proposed . . .'

'By Sakawa,' recalled Rojo.

'Sakawa, the detective from Tokyo, spoke of a blank page. And Arzaky agreed with him. The enigma, the best enigma, is a blank page. He who reads it, he who deciphers it, is the true architect of the crime. Arzaky had his perfect enigma.'

Everyone waited for Arzaky to speak. Seated, but no longer slumped, and looking as if he were preparing to leap all over me, Arzaky smiled.

'Throw him out!' shouted Magrelli, his voice cracking with emotion. Other voices chimed in to banish me. But Arzaky stood up to calm everyone down.

'We'll take for granted that all this is a figment of your youthful imagination. But, by any chance, did that imagination of yours lead you to fabricate some evidence?'

I spoke without looking at Arzaky.

'I'm the son of a shoemaker. My father gave me a cream that leaves boots shinier than any other polish; it's water resistant. I shined Arzaky's boots myself.'

I showed the handkerchief that had been kissed by the Mermaid's dead lips.

'When Arzaky went to see the Mermaid, she knew that he was going to kill her. She threw herself at his feet, she begged him, she kissed his boots. And she did it on purpose, because she knew that the mark would be left on her lips. That kiss sealed Arzaky's fate. That is the evidence. I studied the substance under Darbon's microscope.'

I held up the handkerchief with the kiss left by the Mermaid's lifeless lips.

Magrelli slapped Arzaky's back.

'Come on, Viktor. Is this monologue from your disciple another one of your jokes? Are we supposed to applaud him as well? Deny it once and for all, and get him out of this room! We have a lot of things to discuss before we leave.'

Arzaky approached me. It was perhaps the most important moment of my life, but if I had a choice I'd rather have been in bed with a pillow over my head. And everyone else would have preferred that too. Now, I thought, is when Arzaky will raise an accusing finger. Here comes the moment where the new guy, the upstart, is unmasked. The boldness they pretended to tolerate will no longer be forgiven.

But Arzaky's silence continued. It lasted for a few minutes, and during that time the faces that were red with rage grew pale, and there were no more angry gestures. Everyone was stock still and silent, like students awaiting an exam. Magrelli looked as if he was about to cry.

Finally, Arzaky spoke. 'I don't expect any kind of pardon. Now I'll leave, and you'll never hear from me again. The boy is right, he saw the truth, and he was the first one to see it, because he was close to Craig, because he was a witness to Craig's downfall. We are lost; we have been for a while. We try in vain to apply our method to an increasingly chaotic world; we need organized criminals in order for our theories to bear fruit, but all we find is endless, unruly evil. Did Darbon solve the railway crimes? Did I? Did Magrelli put a stop to the priest murders in Florence? Did Caleb Lawson catch Jack the Ripper? We have some minor achievements, but they can't compete with the big cases. Sometimes even the police are more adept than we are. We needed a case that had symmetry, a case that would restore faith in the method. I realized that we could no longer count on the murderers for that. I crossed the line, as many of you have wanted to do. I am the bastard child of a priest, which is why I wasn't baptized. I chose my own baptism with the oil of the catechumen, with fire and water . . .'

'But the Mermaid . . . how could you?' I asked. 'She was so lovely . . .'

'And you think that beauty is an obstacle to murder? Beauty is murder's great inspiration, even more than money.'

Arzaky turned his eyes away from me and towards the detectives and the assistants. They were all motionless, except one, who was rushing up the stairs to leave the hotel. It was Arthur Neska.

'All I ask is fifteen minutes before you report me to Bazeldin. I know where to hide. I'll leave, and you'll never hear from me again.'

No one said yes, but no one objected either. Detectives and assistants stepped aside so he could leave. Arzaky began to climb the stairs with long strides. But he wasn't in any hurry; he looked as if he had all the time in the world.

I wanted to follow him, but Magrelli stopped me.

'Leave him alone. You've done enough damage already.'

I tried to escape his grasp, but the Roman, with the help of Baldone, pushed me against one of the glass display cases. The door swung open from the impact. Someone had forced the lock. I turned my attention from Magrelli to focus instead on an empty shelf. Before I had time to remember which object had been stolen, the Eye of Rome said, 'Novarius's Remington.'

The Italian released me. I ran after Arzaky.

NINE

I left the hotel, looking this way and that. The moon shone with a yellow light, promising rain the next day. I began to run through an alley and I heard laboured breathing ahead of me. It was Desmorins, who was also pursuing Arzaky.

'I want to hear his confession,' he told me.

I ran in one direction and then another, with no idea which way I should go. I was about to abandon the search when I heard a bang. It was a single shot, but it was enough. Guided by the noise, I turned the corner. Arzaky lay on the ground, lit by the moonlight. The killer had dropped Novarius's pistol.

I knelt down beside the fallen giant.

'I'm going to get help,' I promised without conviction as the lake of blood around me grew.

I would have liked to have gone for a doctor, just to

get away from Arzaky's death throes. But the Polish detective held me there.

'It's too late. Neska knows how to get the job done.'

'It's my fault, I should have spoken in private . . .'

'No, it was my mistake. Craig sent me a detective, not an assistant. I didn't realize in time. You did the right thing by telling the truth.'

'The truth? I didn't tell the truth.'

'You didn't?'

'No. And neither did you. I don't believe you committed those crimes to take revenge on Darbon, or for glory and recognition, or to save the Twelve Detectives. It was for love. The only one you wanted to kill was the Mermaid, because she betrayed you. You had found out that she and Grialet were still seeing each other. But you had to find a way to hide that crime, the only one that mattered. If they caught you, you could say you had done it for the Twelve Detectives. You didn't care about being branded a killer, but you didn't want the name Arzaky to be remembered for the worst of all crimes: the crime of passion.'

Arzaky tried to smile.

'Well done. But that will be a secret between you and me, Detective.'

'Detective? I'm not even an assistant.'

'From now on you are. I invoke the fourth clause: If a detective were to use his knowledge to commit a crime and his assistant were to discover it . . .'

Soon Desmorins showed up, breathless. The detectives' footsteps were heard close behind.

'I'm going to anoint you with the holy oils.'

Desmorins opened his cassock and took a small bottle of holy water from his belt. Magrelli had arrived and was with us too.

'He's not a real priest,' I said.

'What does that matter now,' said Arzaky. 'In this light, no one is what they appear. But let's pretend that he's a priest, that I'm a detective, and that you are my loyal assistant.'

The priest took a deep breath and said, '*In nomine Patris et Filii et Spiritus Sancti . . .*'

TEN

Arzaky had told the truth, the fourth clause – the one the Japanese detective had burned in that garden – allowed an assistant who discovered that a detective was also a murderer to become a member of the Twelve. I assumed that the detectives had made that rule thinking it would never be invoked. They were so despondent over what Arzaky had done that they believed making me a member of the group would atone for the sin of having strayed from the path.

I returned to Buenos Aires two months later. My family found me a changed man.

'Getting you to talk is like pulling teeth,' said my mother.

My father had already figured out that I wouldn't want to keep working in the shoe shop, and he was training my younger brother in the business.

It took me three weeks to do what I had to do: visit

Craig, return his cane, and tell him the story of Arzaky's downfall. He listened to me for hours, he asked for details, he insisted I go over parts of the story that I didn't think were important. By that point they had quit bothering him about the Case of the Magician, which had been shelved. But he had stayed firm in his decision to give up detective work. I asked to rent out the ground floor of his house and he agreed. I set up my office there. I inherited Craig's former clients, and from then on, every time I went to solve a theft or a murder, they relentlessly praised my mentor's skills, comparing mine unfavourably to his.

When Craig died, I have to confess I felt relieved, as if the doors of the world were opening for me, as if the secret had been a burden on me that no longer carried any weight. I still work in the ground floor of that house, and I make sure Mrs Craig is never out of sugar or green tins of British tea. In the mornings, Angela, the cook, makes French toast and yerba maté tea for me, while she gives her always inauspicious report on the weather conditions. Then I go out following some lead or en route to a crime scene, to see the man who hung himself in the basement, the poisoned hotel guest, the girl drowned in the garden fountain.

In my study, in a glass case, I have Craig's cane. Sometimes, when I'm working late into the night, I take out the cane and polish its lion's head handle as I imagine how it would feel to cross the line, to taste evil's trace. The game only lasts a few seconds. Almost immediately

I close the glass case and return to my thoughts. I still don't have an assistant. Will I take one on some day? The footsteps of Mrs Craig, pacing in her insomnia, echo above my head.